PRAISE FOR THE QUINN SERIES

"Brilliant and heart pounding"

JEFFERY DEAVER, *NEW YORK TIMES*
BESTSELLING AUTHOR

"Addictive."

JAMES ROLLINS, *NEW YORK TIMES*
BESTSELLING AUTHOR

"Unputdownable."

TESS GERRITSEN, *NEW YORK TIMES*
BESTSELLING AUTHOR

"The best elements of Lee Child, John le Carré, and Robert Ludlum."

SHELDON SIEGEL, *NEW YORK TIMES*
BESTSELLING AUTHOR

"Quinn is one part James Bond, one part Jason Bourne."

NASHVILLE BOOK WORM

"Welcome addition to the political thriller game."

PUBLISHERS WEEKLY

THE TAKEN

THE TAKEN

A JONATHAN QUINN NOVEL

BRETT BATTLES

To my friend JoAnn, for giving me a ride on a very bad morning

1

The road to the secret base had been built so that no vehicle could arrive unseen. Though the area was forested, all trees and brush within a hundred meters of the road had been removed, creating a clear corridor not even a wayward rat could sneak through.

The approaching vehicle was not wayward. Nor was it unexpected.

As was standard procedure, the moment the sedan was detected, the base went on high alert. Soldiers took positions in the armored bunkers that lined both sides of the road in front of the base's gate, their rifles poking through slits in a pattern that created a kill box few vehicles could survive. In the very unlikely case that anyone escaped their vehicle and tried to make a run for it, four sharpshooters covered the area from towers just beyond the fence.

The sergeant in charge at the guardhouse continually reported the sedan's progress to the acting duty officer in the base control center. The duty officer then informed Captain Bebchuk.

When the vehicle was within a kilometer of the gate, Bebchuk walked down the hall and knocked on his boss's door.

"Come."

The captain entered and saluted. "It's time, sir."

Colonel Stepan Annenkov sighed as he stood. Directorate Eleven's main base was state of the art, and there was always some high-ranking sycophant wanting a tour of the place.

The man approaching the base at that moment was General Churkin. Ostensibly. Though a member of Russian Army leadership, the general had no official assignment and almost never participated in Defense Ministry affairs. His true power came from being one of the Russian president's most trusted advisors.

Annenkov had no idea why Churkin wanted a tour of Directorate Eleven's headquarters. The president himself had already been there and would have surely told Churkin what he'd seen.

Annenkov checked his uniform in the mirror and donned his hat.

"All right, Captain. Lead the way."

General Churkin's sedan stopped at the guardhouse only long enough for the sergeant in charge to verify the identities of the occupants. Searching the sedan was unnecessary. Sensors under the road had scanned for explosives as the car approached, and a state-of-the-art imaging system, embedded in the walls of the kill-box bunkers, had taken 3D scans that revealed nothing hidden.

The gate was ordered open and the sedan traveled onward.

Annenkov and Bebchuk were standing outside the entrance to the base's main structure when the vehicle arrived. Bebchuk hurried to the back passenger door, opened it, and saluted. After General Churkin climbed out, Bebchuk glanced inside, as if expecting someone to follow, before he shut the door.

Interesting, Annenkov thought. It appeared the general had come alone. Annenkov had never known a Russian with as much status as Churkin had to travel anywhere without at least a handful of aides.

The colonel snapped off a salute. "General Churkin, welcome to Directorate Eleven."

Churkin returned the salute. "You are in the middle of nowhere, Colonel. I do not know how you don't go crazy here."

A quick, perfunctory smile alit on Annenkov's face, but he said nothing.

"This way, General," Bebchuk said. He led Churkin and the colonel inside.

From the exterior, the building looked like an unremarkable one-story warehouse. This was merely a façade for prying spy satellites. Inside, a long hallway led to a central lobby lined on one side by four elevator doors. There were no other entrances or exits.

"We usually start the tour with the training rooms," Bebchuk said. "Unless there is something specific you'd like to see first."

"I think there's been a misunderstanding," the general said. "I'm not here for a tour." He turned to Annenkov. "Is there someplace we can talk privately?"

Annenkov walked to the bar in his office. "Something to drink, General? I have vodka, whiskey, tequila, beer, wine."

"What kind of whiskey?"

"Lagavulin."

Churkin smiled broadly. "That would be perfect."

The colonel was not a drinker himself, but in deference to members of the Russian bureaucracy who were, he kept a well-stocked liquor cabinet. So that Churkin would not feel like he was drinking alone, Annenkov poured two glasses and carried them to the sitting area where the general waited.

Churkin took a test sip, then closed his eyes and smiled. "I could leave right now and this trip would be worth the inconvenience. You wouldn't happen to have a bottle of this I can take home with me, would you?"

If that was all it would take to get the general to leave, Annenkov would be happy to give him a case. "I believe that can be arranged."

Churkin smiled again, took another sip, and set the glass on the table. "I'm very impressed, Colonel. In Directorate Eleven's short existence, you've already accomplished quite a lot. I am particularly pleased with your handling of the Bordin matter."

Annenkov kept his face impassive. Alexander Bordin had been a Russian oligarch who'd made his fortune in oil and natural gas. He also had once been a close friend of the Russian president. But Bordin had been greedy. Well, greedier than most. He had forgotten the foundational rule of survival in the new Russia: don't skimp on the payoffs. More specifically, to the man at the top.

Six weeks earlier, Bordin had suffered a massive heart attack, and despite the heroic efforts of emergency personnel, he had not survived. Odd for a man who had recently undergone a thorough medical examination in the UK, in which doctors had found nothing to prevent him from living at least another thirty years.

As far as Annenkov knew, Directorate Eleven's hand in ushering Bordin into the afterlife was known to only three people outside of his organization, and none was Churkin. Undoubtedly, the general had heard the news directly from the president himself.

"I take it you are not here only to sample the whiskey."

Churkin leaned back, an amused grin on his lips. "If only that were the case."

"What is it we can do for you?"

"For me? Nothing. I am merely a messenger."

There was no need for him to mention the person he was a messenger for.

Annenkov tilted his head. "We are at your service."

2

NINE MONTHS AGO · NEW YORK CITY, NEW YORK

Dimitri Melnikov felt every rattle and bump as the cleaning cart he rode in was wheeled out of his twenty-fourth-floor apartment, down the hall, and into the elevator. He had a brief respite from the banging and bruising as the car descended, before he was bouncing around like a pinball again.

The next time the cart came to stop, he heard the door of a vehicle open.

"On three," someone said. "One. Two. Three."

Melnikov's stomach lurched as the cart rose into the air. A second later, the metal wheels below Melnikov bashed against a metal surface, then the cart rolled about a meter. When it halted, he heard four loud clicks, followed by a voice saying, "Cart secured."

An engine rumbled to life and the vehicle started moving.

After a knock on the side of the cart, its door swung open, and the agent named Janet smiled in at Melnikov. "Still alive in there?"

"Surprisingly, yes. It *is* a bit cramped in here, though. Would it be all right if I can come out?"

"Sorry, Mr. Melnikov. Better if you stay in there until we reach the rendezvous point. But I can leave the door open so you can get some air."

"You have no reason to be sorry. You did save my life."

More accurately, his life had been saved by Janet, a man named Steve, and their boss, a guy who went by the name of Quinn. Maybe others, too. Check that—there was definitely at least one other. Melnikov could see the back of the head of a man sitting in the front passenger seat and was pretty sure that was Quinn. Steve was sitting on the van's floor next to Janet, so an unknown fourth person was driving.

Quinn's team had just foiled an assassination attempt on Melnikov in his very own apartment.

Up until a few days ago, Melnikov would not have imagined he'd ever be the target of a hit. He'd been barely a teen in Moscow when his talent for playing chess had first garnered him attention. By the age of nineteen, he was a grand master, playing tournaments around the world. While he still played the occasional charity event, he'd retired from competitive chess at the age of thirty-four. By then, he'd become disillusioned with the political situation in his home country and immigrated to the States.

For a while, he lived a quiet life, ignoring the problems in Russia. But then two of his friends, both journalists, had died within a month of each other, in eerily similar "accidental" falls from high windows. In the wake of their deaths, he could no longer allow himself to ignore the corruption or the hard turn toward authoritarianism the Russian government had taken. So he began speaking out—in opinion pieces for newspapers, on cable news shows, at conferences on world security and human rights.

He knew his actions would not be received well by those in power, but he thought he'd only be seen as a minor nuisance and would otherwise be ignored. That belief vanished four days earlier, when a high-ranking official in US Intelligence had visited him and informed him the government had creditable intel indicating an assassin had been hired to take out Melnikov. The official had offered to relocate him to somewhere the US government could protect him. And then the man had said, "But there is another option, *if* you'd be willing to help us out."

"Help how?"

The official had laid out a plan where they would make the assassin believe he had an unimpeded path to Melnikov. US operatives would then capture the hit man in the act so they could learn who had hired him.

"You, of course, will never be in any danger," the man had told Melnikov. "We only need you to be seen entering the building and not leaving on the day the assassin plans to take you out. As soon as you're inside, you will be escorted to a safe location elsewhere in the building until the operation is over. The assassin will never be in the same room as you."

Melnikov had never been one to turn away from a fight. Besides, to immediately go into hiding when he'd been calling for others to stand up against the Russian regime would be hypocritical. So of course he'd said yes.

The first part of the mission had gone exactly as planned and the assassin had been subdued. The second part, giving the assassin's client the impression the hit had been successful, was what they were in the process of doing now. The team in the van was on the way to meet with a team from the FBI that would stash Melnikov away for several weeks, giving US Intelligence enough time to identify and neutralize as many of those involved in the conspiracy as possible.

"Five minutes," Quinn called from up front. "Mr. Melnikov, I think it's okay for you to get out now."

"You heard the man," Janet said.

She and Steve helped Melnikov out of the cart and to a spot against the wall, where he rolled his neck side to side and arched his back, triggering a series of cartilage pops up and down his spine.

"I bet that felt good," Steve said.

"You have no idea," Melnikov replied. He nodded at the tiny

space he'd been crammed into. "I have new respect for contortionists now."

Janet tapped her shoulder against his good-naturedly. "Maybe that could be your next career."

Before Melnikov could response, Quinn said, "Bump."

The van rocked as it drove through the opening of a parking garage. Melnikov didn't know all the details of the plan, but he'd been told the handoff to the FBI would occur somewhere out of the public eye. A garage would fit that bill.

They took a curving ramp down a couple of levels before the ride leveled out.

"There they are," Quinn said.

Melnikov looked toward the front, but from his angle all he could see was the roof of the garage.

When the van finally stopped, Quinn said, "Everyone hold," then opened his door and climbed out.

For the next minutes, the only thing Melnikov heard was a conversation too distant to understand.

When it stopped, footsteps approached the van and the side door opened.

Quinn leaned in and said to Melnikov, "This is your stop."

"Thank you," Melnikov whispered to Janet and Steve, then climbed out.

The only other vehicle in the entire level was a black Suburban with tinted windows, parked a half dozen meters away. Beside it stood four men in dark suits, their gazes sweeping the garage.

"Don't forget this."

Melnikov turned back to the van. The man who must have been driving was in the doorway, holding out the bag containing the items Melnikov had wanted to take with him.

"Thanks," Melnikov said as he took it. He turned to Quinn and started to hold out his hand but stopped himself. "Sorry, habit." The pandemic had curtailed most forms of casual contact. "Thank you. I appreciate you and your friends keeping me from dying today."

"Our pleasure. But you know they're going to keep coming after you."

"That's the problem with poking the beast. Maybe if I stopped, they'd forget about me, but…" He shrugged. "I don't think I can do that."

"Good luck."

"Thank you."

One of the suited men took a step from the Suburban. "Mr. Melnikov, I'm Special Agent Landry. If you'll come with me, we'll get you out of here."

Melnikov nodded and walked toward the vehicle that would take him to the next stop on his playing-dead tour.

Landry led Melnikov around the front of the vehicle to the other side. As soon as they were out of sight of the others, the agent clamped a hand around Melnikov's bicep and yanked him toward a door in the wall.

"Hurry," Landry whispered.

Melnikov assumed this was part of the plan and followed.

Behind them, one of the agents at the SUV yelled, "Landry, where are you going?"

Without answering, Landry jerked the door open and pulled Melnikov into a stairwell. Once inside, the agent shoved Melnikov toward a big metal box sitting next to the stairs. "Get in!"

"What? What is—"

"Get *in!*"

Landry pushed him so hard, Melnikov stumbled into the box. Landry climbed in after him and pulled on a panel that would close them inside. The hatch was still a few centimeters shy of shut when a thunderous noise, louder than anything Melnikov had ever heard, enveloped them. At the same time, the entire building seemed to shudder, sending Landry tumbling hard into Melnikov.

All around them, rapid fire bangs reverberated against the outside of the box, from what Melnikov guessed were falling pieces of metal and concrete.

Melnikov was sure the whole building was about to collapse on them and finish the job the assassin had set out to do, so he could hardly believe both he and Landry were still in one piece when the pounding finally stopped.

The agent turned on a flashlight and shoved on the hatch. It didn't budge.

Cursing, he put his shoulder into it. Slowly, the panel moved outward.

"What the hell was that?" Melnikov asked.

Ignoring him, Landry continued to push until the hatch opened wide enough for him to squeeze through. He glanced at Melnikov, said, "Stay here," and moved out of sight.

Melnikov caught glimpses of the stairwell as the agent's flashlight beam bounced around the space, or rather, glimpses of what *had* been the stairwell, because all he could see now were twisted pieces of metal and broken chunks of concrete. And dust. Everywhere dust.

In the calm, Melnikov's mind finally began working again. Landry had shoved Melnikov into the box *before* the explosion happened. Which meant the agent had known it was coming. Which, in turn, meant it hadn't been an accident.

Melnikov's breath caught in his throat and his eyes widened.

The other agents.

Quinn and his team.

None of them had been running for shelter. They were dead. They had to be. Right?

And if all that were true…

Oh, shit.

Landry hadn't saved his life as part of the FBI's plan. He had saved Melnikov's life because—

The flashlight beam shot into his eyes. "Out. Now."

Leaving the box was suddenly the last thing the Russian expat wanted to do.

Landry leaned down and pointed a gun at Melnikov's head. "I said *now.*"

Melnikov crawled out of the box.

"You keep doing what I tell you and you'll live through this. You don't, and you're just another victim of the explosion."

"Who are you?"

"I already told you."

"No. You're not FBI."

"Oh, I very much am. Or I was until a few minutes ago."

"The FBI would not do something like this."

"True. But my new employers are a little more open to unconventional methods. Now, come on. We don't have a lot of time."

"What new employers?"

"No more questions. Follow me."

Landry walked over a pile of broken concrete to where the bottom of the stairs lay in a twisted heap. Hanging above the mess was a harness connected to a rope that rose into the dust and darkness above.

"Your choice," the former FBI agent said. "Get into the harness or die here."

Melnikov donned the harness.

3

The first mission for General Churkin had been a test of how far Directorate Eleven could reach. By any measure, it had been a success.

Directorate sources had leaked information about a plan to assassinate Dmitri Melnikov. The attempted hit had been a ruse from the beginning. Not that the assassin was aware of that. If he had somehow been able to kill the dissident, that would have been unfortunate though not unwelcome. The real goal had been to capture Melnikov and bring him home to Russia.

Upon the mission's completion, General Churkin had paid Annenkov another visit and passed on both his and the president's sincerest thanks and congratulations. He also informed Annenkov that a list of additional targets would be forthcoming.

After several months of not hearing from the general, Annenkov had begun to think the promised list had been forgotten and Churkin had moved his attention to other things.

He was wrong.

Two months earlier, a package had arrived containing the names and gathered intel on each of the new targets the general wanted rounded up. It took Annenkov and his people until just the day before to complete the planning for the missions.

On the afternoon of December 24, Annenkov drove to Moscow to meet with Churkin in the private dining room of an exclusive club five blocks from the Kremlin.

"There he is," Churkin said when Annenkov arrived.

"Good evening, General."

The general poured Annenkov a glass of wine, topped off his own, and said, "Have you brought me good news?"

"I realize your friend is anxious to get started, but…"

Churkin's voice took on an edge as he said, "But what?"

"There have been some delays in finishing our new holding facility, and it won't be ready for another four weeks."

Directorate Eleven's holding facility was a variation on the design of the directorate's headquarters. But due to the harsh weather conditions of the facility's remote location, construction had taken longer than anticipated. Thankfully, the end was in sight.

"So? How is that my friend's problem?"

Annenkov's reason was a sound one. The more times prisoners had to be moved, the more chances for problems occurring. But from the way the general was eyeing him, he knew Churkin wouldn't care.

Annenkov took a breath and flashed another smile. "You're right. It is not. My apologies."

Churkin picked up his glass and leaned back in his chair, as if the last few moments had not occurred. "Tell me, then, when will you begin?"

As much as Annenkov had been hoping the delay would be granted, he had come prepared if it was not. "One week from today," he said.

Churkin raised his glass. "To the success I'm sure you will achieve."

Annenkov did not fail to hear the implied *or else*.

4

A drian Rapace read through the introduction one more time.

He liked it but didn't love it. One of the transitions wasn't working, despite his rewriting it four times already.

He glanced at Uri Sobolevsky, his friend and the subject of the introduction. Uri was propped against the plane's closed window, sound asleep. Between the two men sat Uri's wife, Anya, still wide awake and watching a movie on Uri's tablet.

Rapace had been on enough trips with them to know Anya wouldn't relax until they reached their destination. As Uri always said, "Anya was born a worrier"

Rapace focused back on his laptop.

In four days, he would be introducing Uri as the keynote speaker at the international journalism conference. Uri's work exposing corruption in the highest levels of the Russian government had earned him both international recognition and exile from his homeland. The latter hadn't stopped Uri from what he considered his mission, and he continued collecting information that he used to call out Russian officials on their destructive behavior. Just three weeks prior, one of Uri's articles had appeared on the front page of *The Times* of London, exposing a history of graft by a general named Churkin, a man who—surprise, surprise—was a close ally of the Russian president.

One could argue a general of the Russian Army deserves a dacha outside of Moscow. General Churkin has seven.

This line had apparently resonated with the Russian people, who, in theory, wouldn't have been able to see the article at all. But of course copies had circulated. Four days after the article had come out, protesters gathered outside the Kremlin, chanting how nice it must be to have a vacation mansion for every day of the week. Uri had been particularly tickled by that.

Maybe that anecdote was the answer to Rapace's transition problem.

As the journalist lowered his fingers to his keyboard, Anya grabbed his arm. "Why are we turning?"

"Turning?"

"Can't you feel it?"

He hadn't been paying attention, but now realized the plane was banking to the right.

"Maybe the pilot's trying to get around bad weather."

She turned on the screen mounted to the back of the chair in front of her, and hit a series of buttons until the map of the plane's progress appeared.

The color drained from her face. "Oh, god. No. No, no, no, no."

According to the display, they were more than halfway to Helsinki and, until a few minutes before, had been on a course that would have exited Belarus airspace and entered Lithuania's in another few minutes. But their path had taken a ninety-degree turn straight toward Minsk, the capital of Belarus. One of Russia's closest allies.

This was no weather-related diversion.

Anya shook her husband's shoulder. "Uri, wake up. Wake up."

When he stirred, she pushed the flight attendant call button.

Uri stretched and frowned. "What are you so excited about?"

Anya pointed at the monitor.

He leaned forward to get a better look and swore under his breath.

Anya pushed the call button again, then craned her head to look back and forth down the aisle. "Where are they?"

Rapace was about to unbuckle his belt and go looking for an attendant when a voice came over the plane's intercom.

"Ladies and gentlemen, this is Captain Dasinger from the flight deck. Looks like we have a minor issue with the aircraft. Nothing serious, but it would be best to get it checked, so we will be making an unscheduled stop in Minsk and will soon be starting our descent. Once we get everything sorted, we'll be back on our way again. I'll update you with any new information as soon as I have it."

The intercom clicked off.

A buzz of voices filled the cabin as passengers processed the captain's message.

"Vilnius is closer," Anya whispered. "If there really was anything wrong with the plane, we would land there."

She was right. The Lithuanian capital was right across the border, and if they needed to get on the ground in a hurry, that should have been their destination.

Someone seated a few rows ahead of them said, "Hey, there's another plane out there."

Uri lifted the shade covering their window and he and Anya looked out. Rapace unbuckled his belt so he could, too.

No more than a hundred meters beyond the wing's tip glowed the lights of a fighter jet keeping pace with them.

A flight attendant stopped in the aisle next to Rapace. "Please put your seat belt back on, sir."

"We can't land in Minsk," he told her.

"Sir, please."

"We know there's nothing wrong with the plane. They're going to take my friend off. You can't let them do that."

There was something in her eyes. Concern? Guilt? Whatever it was, she knew the truth.

"You can't let them take him," Rapace said. "They will *kill* him."

Her jaw clenched, and he was sure she was about to repeat her order but she whispered, "They said they'd shoot us down if we don't land."

He stared at her, his mouth agape.

At a normal volume, she said, "Now, please. Buckle your belt."

Rapace did as she asked.

"Give me that," Uri said.

Anya handed her husband the tablet computer and he began tapping the surface. Tears streamed down Anya's cheeks as she watched her husband work, gripping the armrest between them.

As for Rapace, what he was feeling could only be called shock. He and Anya had talked about the possibility of trouble on the flight. They had even considered booking the trip through London Heathrow to avoid flying over Russian allies, but when they'd brought up the possibility to Uri, he'd laughed. "We'll be flying on New Year's Eve. Everyone will be too busy celebrating to worry about a minor journalist like me."

Both Rapace and Anya argued he'd made more enemies than he realized, but Uri would have none of it and had insisted they take the direct flight that night. They should have ignored him and changed their plans.

Uri turned off the tablet and held it out to Rapace. "I've changed the password to your birthday. There are two stories on there that are ready to go, and another that just needs a couple items verified. You'll have access to my cloud account, too. As soon as you can, get everything off there. There are things stored on it that might aid in figuring out who my sources are. No names, though. You'll find those on a thumb drive in a safety deposit box in Marseille. The info for that is on the tablet, too."

"Won't I need a key?"

Uri looked at Anya.

"Are you sure?" she asked.

He nodded.

She removed the watch she always wore. Rapace had asked about it once and been told it had been her grandmother's. It was silver, with a metal braided band and a timepiece that curved around her arm, creating an oblong clock face. She turned the watch over and touched something on the back that popped open the cover. Underneath was a small storage space, within which lay a key. She removed it and gave it to Rapace.

"The bank's not just going to let me in," Rapace said to Uri. "I'm not you."

"You'll find a way."

"But what if they take me off the plane with you?" Rapace asked.

"You're a French citizen. They wouldn't dare."

Rapace reluctantly slipped the key into his pocket, hoping Uri was right, then immediately chastised himself for being so selfish. His friend was about to be thrown in jail, quite possibly to die there, and here Rapace was worrying about his own safety.

He put the tablet in his bag and started to stuff it under the seat in front of him.

"No," Uri said, "they might check under your seat." He nodded at the overhead bins on the other side of the aisle. "Over there."

Rapace undid his seat belt and stepped into the aisle.

"Sir!" the flight attendant from before called from farther back. "Please sit down."

Rapace ignored her and opened the bin directly across from his seat, only to find the space already stuffed full with bags.

"Sir," the flight attendant said as she hurried toward him. "You can't be out of your seat right now."

Rapace opened the next bin and tried to stuff his bag into it, but it didn't have enough room, either.

The attendant reached him as he closed the hatch. "Take your seat."

"I need to stow this before we land." He stared hard at her, trying to make her understand he couldn't keep the bag with him.

Her resolve cracked and she glanced back the way she'd come, like she was checking if other crew members were watching them. When she turned to him again, she whispered, "Give it to me."

He handed it to her. "Thank you."

She gave him a barely perceptible nod and said in a louder voice, "Sir, you must sit down."

Not long after Rapace was buckled in again, the plane groaned as the landing gear extended. He desperately tried to think of some way to keep his friend from being taken but kept coming up empty.

Far too soon, the tires hit the runway and the plane decelerated. When it finally stopped moving, they were beside a closed hangar, surrounded by police cars with their emergency lights ablaze.

Anya jumped to her feet and shouted, "Please, everyone, they're coming to take my husband! Please help us!"

Several passengers looked toward her with a mix of confusion and curiosity.

A passenger across the aisle asked, "Why? Who is he?"

"He is a Russian journalist. Our government is not happy with what he writes."

"Russian?" another passenger said. "Are we in Russia?"

"Belarus," Anya said. "They are close allies."

"But the pilot said it was a problem with the plane."

"Yes. And that problem is my husband."

A voice came over the intercom. "Ladies and gentlemen, please remain seated. The captain has indicated we shouldn't be here long."

Something bumped against the plane, then the air pressure changed as the door to the outside opened.

"Please," Anya said. "Please don't let them take him."

A flight attendant appeared at the front of the cabin. "Ma'am, you need to sit down."

Anya ignored her and continued pleading for help.

From the front of the plane, an angry female voice all but yelled, "You can't just come in here like this! What do you think you're—"

A thud cut off her voice, then heavy footsteps moved rapidly through the plane.

A Belarusian soldier entered the cabin and stopped at the head of the aisle on the other side of the compartment from where Rapace sat. When the soldier's eyes fell on Uri, he barked something into the unseen area behind him.

More moving feet, this time traveling through the pantry that separated the cabin from the one in front of it. Four soldiers appeared at the end of the near aisle, each holding a rifle. The passengers sucked in a collective breath and most ducked, as if the foam and plastic seat backs would save them from gunfire.

The soldiers stopped beside Rapace. In heavily accented English, the nearest one said, "Uri Sobolevsky, you come with us."

"He's not going anywhere," Anya said, putting her body between them and her husband.

The soldier ignored her and looked at Rapace. "Out of way."

Rapace grabbed the armrests of his seat. "I will not."

He expected the soldier to threaten him, maybe even point his gun at him. Instead, the man slung his weapon over his shoulder, yanked Rapace out of his seat, and shoved him down the aisle without breaking a sweat.

Rapace's hip hit the armrest of the seat behind him and he fell on the floor. When he tried to get back up, the woman in the seat he'd landed next to put her hand on his shoulder and whispered, "Stay down."

"Leave him alone!" Anya yelled.

Rapace tried to push himself up, but the woman tightened her grip on him. "You can't stop them. They will only hurt you, and that won't help anyone."

Rapace didn't want to listen to her, but what could he really do? Get himself arrested? Maybe even killed?

Reluctantly, he watched from the floor as a soldier pulled Anya into the aisle. He thought the man would throw her on top of him, but he handed her off to one of his colleagues, who manhandled her out of the cabin.

From Rapace's position, he could just make out the top of Uri's head.

"This is an illegal abduction and an illegal diversion of a commercial aircraft," Uri yelled. "You have no right to take me anywhere. This is an illegal—"

The soldier punched him in the face and hauled him into the aisle, where he passed Uri on to the other soldiers. While they escorted Uri away, the first soldier leaned into the row and grabbed everything in and around Uri's, Anya's, and Rapace's seats. When he finished, he opened the bin above Rapace's seat and started pulling out bags.

"That's mine," the man across the aisle said.

Before he could reach for it, the soldier said, "Prove it."

The man opened his carry-on, pulled out a bottle of pills, and pointed at the label. "See? That's my name."

"That means nothing."

The passenger yanked his passport out of a pocket to prove the names were the same. The soldier pushed the carry-on into the man's lap and pulled out another. After a woman claimed it and provided proof, the soldier removed the last bag.

"That belongs to me," Rapace said.

The man eyed him and passed the carry-on to one of his comrades. He said something Rapace couldn't understand, and the soldier with the bag started walking toward the exit.

"Hey!" Rapace said. "That's my bag!"

"I do not see any bag," the first soldier said.

The woman pressed a finger against Rapace's arm, and Rapace forced himself to bite off what he'd been about to say.

The soldier checked all the bins in the vicinity, including the ones in which Rapace had originally tried to hide the bag with Uri's tablet. When the man was satisfied that nothing belonging to Uri and Anya remained in the cabin, he and the other soldiers left.

The woman who'd been holding Rapace helped him to his feet. "I'm sorry but they would have taken you, too."

He nodded grimly. "You're right. Thank you."

He turned toward his seat and realized at least half the passengers were pointing phones at him. Some must have recorded everything. Before tonight, he'd have thought video of what had just happened would have been enough to make the soldiers back down. But the abduction had been so blatant, so public, that the Belarusian government and its Russian puppet master obviously didn't care who knew. Rapace's only hope was that the videos would prevent his friends from being killed.

"You all saw what happened," he said loudly enough for everyone to hear. "The man and the woman who were just kidnapped are Uri and Anya Sobolevsky. Uri's articles about Russian corruption have been published in *The Times* in London, *The New York Times*, *Le Monde*, and many other news sources. They were taken because the Russian government fears the truth. Please. Tell everyone what you saw here. Share your videos everywhere you can. Let the world know what happened tonight."

As he slumped into his chair, the captain's voice came over the intercom. "Ladies and gentlemen, we apologize for the delay. We have been given clearance to resume our trip and should be back in the air shortly. For now, please remain in your seats and keep your seat belts fastened."

Rapace barely noticed the plane taking off again.

Several minutes later, a voice said, "Sir?"

He blinked and looked over. The flight attendant from before was kneeling next to his seat.

"I-I'm sorry," she said.

She held out his bag and he took it without responding. He returned his gaze to the floor, wondering when he would wake up from this nightmare.

. . .

JANUARY 9, 10:04 AM
LONDON, UNITED KINGDOM

Filip Krutov led Willie, his French bulldog, along the path beside the Serpentine, the small lake in Hyde Park. With his busy schedule, he seldom had time to walk his dog himself, but he made an effort to squeeze in thirty minutes every Sunday for a tour around the park.

It was a brisk morning and a thick layer of dark, heavy clouds was moving in over the city. Snow was in the forecast for that evening, but Krutov suspected the storm would start long before the sun went down.

Five meters in front of him walked two of his ever-present bodyguards, with another pair equidistant behind him. Such was the life of a billionaire in the twenty-first century. Someone was always mad at him for something and, more often than not, unafraid to let him know it. Be it the fans of the Championship League football club he owned, a rival business owner angry over some perceived slight, or his former friend back in Russia who hadn't liked Krutov calling him out on his authoritarian antics.

A frigid gust of wind rippled the Serpentine, making Krutov adjust the scarf around his neck. He pulled a treat from his pocket and gave it to Willie. "Maybe it's time we head back, yes?"

The dog gobbled down the snack, then looked at him with huge adoring eyes and a wagging tail, in an attempt to score another morsel.

"Home," Krutov said loudly enough for his bodyguards to hear.

They followed the same path they always did and weaved around other people out braving the cold. When they reached the street, Krutov barely noticed the three tourist vans parked at the curb as they were a common sight, their passengers milling about on the sidewalk.

Krutov's lead bodyguards angled their route to avoid the vans' passengers, but Willie had other ideas. He darted toward the small crowd, yanking at the leash.

One of the tourists—a beautiful woman with a friendly smile —crouched down and held out a hand toward the dog.

"Willie, no!" Krutov said, but it was as if he no longer existed as far as the dog was concerned.

"He's so cute," the woman said. "May I pet him?"

Dark hair, pale skin, piercing green eyes—if Krutov had a type, and he most certainly did, she was it. Which was why he couldn't stop himself from saying, "Of course," and moving close enough for Willie to reach her.

"I just *love* French bulldogs," she said. "What's her name?"

"*His* name is Willie."

"Oops. Sorry." Her smile turned sheepish. "I like his name, though."

She rubbed Willie's head, but he seemed more interested in her other hand.

"Smart dog," she said with a laugh.

She opened her fingers and showed Krutov the remains of a cookie.

That's why Willie was so eager to come over, Krutov thought.

"Is it all right if I give him this?" she asked. "There's no chocolate."

"That's a kind offer, but he's on a strict diet." Willie wasn't, but Krutov knew never to let strangers, no matter how attractive, feed his dog.

She pocketed the cookie. "Sorry, Willie." She scratched his chest and he wiggled his whole body, loving every minute of it. "How old is he?"

"Two."

"Still a puppy."

"He certainly acts like it."

Krutov had been so focused on the woman that he hadn't noticed the other tourists gathering around them, until one bumped into his shoulder. Krutov had just enough time to wonder where his bodyguards were when something sharp pricked his arm.

"Sorry," said the person who'd run into him.

Krutov looked quickly around for his security team but couldn't see anything through the throng of tourists. To the woman he said, "We need to be going."

She squeezed Willie's cheeks and stood up. "Thanks for letting me meet him." She held out a hand. "I'm Sonya."

He reached out to shake, but before he could clasp her palm, he was hit by a wave of vertigo.

She grabbed his arms, steadying him. "Are you okay?"

He closed his eyes and opened them again, but that only made things worse. "I...I don't know."

"You should sit. There's a spot right over here."

As she led him across the sidewalk, another surge of dizziness washed over him, forcing him to squeeze his eyes shut again.

"Here we go," the woman said. "You'll need to step up."

"What?"

She put a hand on the back of his leg and guided it upward until his foot settled on a flat surface. Only it couldn't have been *her* hand because both of hers were still on his arms. She pulled him forward and helped him onto a surprisingly comfortable park bench.

Where were his guards? They should have come to him by now. They should have—

With a start, he realized his hands were empty.

He tried to call his dog's name but all that came out was an indecipherable croak.

A hand pressed down on his shoulders, holding him in place. "Shhh, just rest." It sounded like the woman's voice but he wasn't sure. "We'll get you some..."

Whatever else was said faded away with the rest of his world into a cloud of nothing.

JANUARY 14, 8:17 PM
CHICAGO, ILLINOIS

"...do more harm. It is my belief, and the belief of those I work with at the Council for Truth and Understanding, that through our continued efforts and with the help of people like you, we will live to see the day when the reign of tyranny finally ends."

The packed banquet room burst into applause.

Dr. Andrei Barsukov acknowledged the response with a single nod and returned to his seat at the head table. This night was not about him. It was about lifting the veil on what he referred to as the third coming of the tsars.

The first had been the original tsars whose reign ended abruptly with the abdication of Nicholas II during the revolution in 1917. The second, the communist party leaders who were the eventual winners of the war. For a brief time, after the collapse of the Soviet Union in the late 1980s, there had been hope that a true democracy, with officials accountable to the people, would emerge. But that dream had been crushed by a president who now ruled by tyranny and corruption, hence the third coming of the tsars.

Barsukov had been a prominent physicist when Gorbachev resigned as general secretary, ending the communist's reign. The scientist had stayed in Russia, believing for many years longer than he should have in a brighter future. He'd even been cautiously optimistic that the cunning former KGB official who'd seized control of the government would steer the country in the right direction. That mistake had nearly cost him his life, and he'd been able to flee to the west only with the help of a Russian expat whose contacts had sneaked Barsukov out of the country.

In the years since, he and several other self-exiled Russians had formed the Council for Truth and Understanding. Its purpose was to shed light on what was happening in their homeland, in hopes of creating the cracks needed to set their fellow citizens free. Speaking at events such as tonight's opening banquet for a

conference on human rights was one of Barsukov's main responsi-
bilities.

"Inspiring as ever, Alexei," Robert Handler said. He was a
longtime friend of Barsukov's and the man who had invited him
to speak.

They made small talk as the wait staff descended on the room,
distributing dessert. Barsukov was halfway through his when a
young man in a suit walked up behind him.

"Pardon me, Mr. Barsukov," the man whispered. "But I have a
message for you."

He passed a sealed envelope to the scientist and left.

"Secret admirer?" Handler asked.

"One can hope."

Inside the envelope was a single sheet of paper that read:

Mr. Barsukov—

Thank you for talking to us this evening. I wholeheartedly
agree it is imperative that the public doesn't confuse the Russian
government with the Russian people. To help you spread your
message, tomorrow I will be donating $500,000 to your orga-
nization.

The signature at the bottom was impossible to read. He
considered asking if Handler recognized the scrawl, but he'd
know the answer if the money arrived. He'd received enough
notes in the past with empty promises of large donations that he
never counted on a pledge until it was in the bank.

He slipped it into his pocket and promptly forgot about it.

Several minutes later, as he was polishing off his raspberry
cheesecake, his stomach started cramping. He tried to ignore it,
but it only grew stronger.

"Excuse me," he said to Handler. "Do you know where the
bathrooms are?"

Handler pointed at a door on the right. "Go through there and
take a left. You'll find them halfway down the hall."

"Thank you."

Barsukov was well past the age of being embarrassed by something like an unsettled stomach, but he wanted the takeaway from tonight to be his call for action, not that he'd come down with diarrhea, so he tried not to look like he was in a hurry as he rose and walked out of the room.

The hallway was mercifully empty and he reached the men's room unseen, then made a beeline for one of the stalls. After he finished and washed up, he reentered the hallway and found himself suddenly in the middle of a group of men.

"Excuse me," he said as he tried to find a path through them.

But instead of moving out of his way, two of the men grabbed his arms, while a third poked something into the base of his neck.

He tried to shout but his lips wouldn't move. Nor, he soon realized, would his legs or arms.

The two who had grabbed him propped him up between them, and the others packed in close. Then, as a group, they headed down the hall.

5

"Sixteen for Control."

"Go for Control."

"We have vehicles in sight. Half a kilometer west."

"Copy, Sixteen. Verify and report back."

"Copy."

When the radio behind them went silent, Orlando raised an eyebrow and said, "It's your turn."

"Yeah, I know," Jonathan Quinn said.

"Then what's the holdup?"

The holdup was he couldn't decide if he should break hearts now or play it sneaky and go for all the points. He had almost the perfect hand for a run. *Almost.*

The radio speaker crackled again. "Sixteen for Control."

"Go for Control," another voice said.

"Verified, verified. Target in third vehicle. Rear seat, passenger side."

"Copy, Sixteen. Target verified. Third vehicle, rear seat, passenger side. Control for Triton."

"Go for Triton."

"Target verified. You are a go. ETA to your position, eighteen minutes."

"Copy, Control."

Why not? Quinn thought, deciding to go for it. He flipped the eight of clubs onto the table.

"Triton for Callisto."

Nate tossed down the five of clubs and picked up the radio. "Go for Callisto."

"Looks like we're on. Should be ready for you in approximately forty-five."

Jar set the seven of clubs on top of the deuce Orlando had led with.

"Copy, Triton," Nate said. "We're ready and waiting."

"I believe that's yours," Orlando said to Quinn, nodding her chin at the cards on the table.

The delivery van they were sitting in rocked with a sudden gust of wind, bringing with it a not-so-subtle reminder of how cold it was outside.

Quinn scooped up the cards, set them facedown in front of him, and tossed the nine of diamonds onto the table.

As planned, he took that trick and then let Orlando get the one after that. The only cards he had left now were either hearts or the queen of spades—all point cards. If Orlando led with clubs or diamonds, he'd abandon his plan and dump as many points as possible on the others. But if she led with spades or hearts...

Orlando set down the four of spades.

Bingo.

"Crap," he said, acting like he'd been caught in a trap, and reluctantly laid down the queen of spades.

"Well, well," Nate said. "Things just got real."

No one played anything higher and Quinn took the hand. He was halfway home and in control. His only potential hang-up was that the ten of hearts was still out there. He just needed to tease it out. He began playing his hearts, taking the next few tricks, but the ten did not appear. He was down to the king of hearts, the ace, and the nine.

He set down the king, sure this was the round that would

force the ten out. After Nate threw in the jack of spades, Orlando carefully chose a card and laid it down. It was the ten of diamonds. Which meant they'd both run out of hearts.

"Crap," he mumbled. This time it was not an act.

"Sorry, honey," Orlando said. "I think you're a card short."

Jar stared at him, her usual neutral expression verging on bored.

He had counted on the two hearts not in his hand that hadn't been played yet to be split between two players. No matter how he played his final two cards, he would come up short of running the hand. He laid down the ace and Jar the four, while Orlando and Nate threw out trash cards, giving Quinn the trick.

"Son of a bitch," he said and threw down the nine of hearts.

After Nate followed with a seven of clubs and Orlando with the four of spades, Jar set down the ten of hearts, winning the final trick and leaving Quinn two points short of his attempted run.

"Well played," he said.

"I cannot say the same for you," Jar said.

"Ouch!" Nate said.

"It's true, is it not?"

"Well, yeah, but you don't want to hurt Quinn's feelings. He gets very touchy about losing."

Orlando gathered up the cards and started shuffling them. "Another hand?"

"I think we should probably get ready," Quinn said.

Nate put a hand next to his mouth and stage whispered to Jar, "See what I mean?"

"She was smart enough to block me," Quinn said. "*You* were just along for the ride."

"I'm not too proud to ride her coattails."

The radio burst back to life. "Seventeen for Control."

"Go for Control."

"Vehicles pulling into the parking area now."

"Copy, Seventeen. Control for Triton."

"Go for Triton."

"Did you copy that?"

"Vehicles pulling into the parking area—copy. We are in position and waiting."

"Copy, Triton."

Orlando switched on the trio of video monitors mounted to the inside wall of the van. The center screen filled with the feed from a camera Nate had hidden outside the resort's entrance. On it, four Mercedes-Maybach sedans pulled to a stop in front of the main building. A beat later, a woman exited the lead vehicle and strode into the hotel. Everyone else remained in the cars.

When the woman returned, she was in the company of a man in a suit and four bellhops pushing luggage carts. The trunks of the four sedans popped open and a bellhop went to each. The woman approached the rear passenger door of the third car in line, the suited man stopping a couple of meters behind her.

The camera angle allowed Quinn and his team to see the car's window lower but not who was inside. The woman spoke a few words through the opening. When she stepped back, the doors of all four Maybachs swung open.

In total, there were seven guests including the woman, all there to attend an invitation-only conference bringing together representatives of some of the deadliest neo-fascist organizations in the world. Intelligence reports indicated 123 attendees. Most were wanted by law enforcement agencies of one country or another.

The attendee of interest to Quinn's client was Morgan Edwards, the man who had just exited the Maybach the woman had arrived in.

Edwards was the founder and head of a group that went by the name One. In Edwards's own secretly recorded words, One was the unseen power behind the only cause that mattered—the fight to keep the white race in its rightful place at the top of society. The grandson of a famous Wall Street money manager, he'd inherited over half a billion dollars upon the old man's death.

With this wealth, One quietly financed groups and operations that were in sync with its cause, happy to let its beneficiaries take the limelight.

Edwards had made a costly mistake, however. Not in the amount of money spent, which in this particular case had been minimal, but with the target chosen by a local chapter of the Marshals of Truth, an organization Edwards funded.

Said target was a church in a modest neighborhood in Columbia, South Carolina, that ministered to a primarily African American congregation. One of the church elders had served as head juror on a trial that had convicted Wayne Polk, a member of the local chapter of the Marshals of Truth.

The Marshals had not been pleased and retaliated by breaking the church's windows, spray-painting graffiti on its walls, and slashing tires of cars parked in its lot.

As vile as those actions had been, the big mistake came a week later, when the Marshals decided to burn the church to the ground. To accomplish this, they snuck a crude bomb into the building. Unfortunately, someone screwed up when setting the timer. Instead of going off at three a.m., when the place would have been deserted, the bomb had exploded at three p.m. on a Wednesday afternoon.

Though there had been no church service at that time, a planning meeting for the upcoming Christmas pageant had been underway in one of the community rooms in the basement, and a young couple had been waiting in the anteroom of the pastor's office to discuss their upcoming wedding.

Thanks to a cinder-block wall and the proximity to an emergency exit, all but one person in the meeting had been able to get out alive. The couple waiting for the pastor had not been so lucky, as the bomb had gone off less than fifteen feet below them.

The bride-to-be had been the grandniece of the senior US senator from Virginia. Calls were made and a meeting was set up where the senator made it clear he wanted everyone responsible for the heinous act to be brought to justice.

Every member of the Columbia branch of the Marshals for Truth was arrested in coordinated raids on Christmas Eve. During the interrogations that followed, Morgan Edwards's involvement as the group's primary funder came to light.

Edwards was not someone the powers that be wanted to bring to trial. With his bankroll, he could drag court proceedings out for years, during which time he could continue sowing evil. He would also likely sneak out of the country to somewhere that did not have an extradition treaty with the US.

Another meeting was held, which no elected officials attended, where it was decided a different form of justice was needed. Intelligence was gathered, plans were drawn up, and a nineteen-agent-strong tactical force was dispatched to this resort in Germany to deal with the issue, a tactical force that included Quinn's small team of cleaners.

Now, as soon as Edwards and his entourage entered the building, Orlando switched the camera covering the lobby to the center screen. The seven new arrivals were met by three members of the hotel staff, who, after a quick greeting, escorted them to the elevators.

"My money's on car number three," Nate said.

"It will be number two," Jar said.

"Ten euros?"

"Make it twenty."

"Oooh. All right, twenty, then." Nate glanced at Quinn and Orlando. "Either of you want to get in on this?"

"Pass," Quinn said. He'd already been burned by Jar once in the last ten minutes.

"I never bet against Jar," Orlando said.

"She can't be right all the time," Nate countered.

As if on cue, the door to elevator car number two opened.

"Twenty euros, please," Jar said, holding out her hand.

On the monitor everyone stepped into the car, except for Edwards, the woman who first entered the hotel, and one of the hotel employees. The door closed.

"Hold on," Nate said.

The door to car three opened, and the trio who'd remained behind entered.

"Ha! I was right," Nate said.

Jar stared at him. "The bet was for which car would arrive first."

"I never said that."

"If you meant for the bet to be which car Edwards would take, you needed to be specific. You were not."

"She's right," Orlando said. "Give her the money."

"Seriously? At the most, it's a draw." Nate looked at Quinn. "Back me up on this."

Quinn snorted. "I am *not* getting involved."

"Twenty," Jar repeated, her hand hovering in front of Nate.

Nate begrudgingly pulled a twenty out of his pocket and slapped it into her palm. "Happy?"

"Don't I look it?"

"How would I know? You look the same all the time."

Orlando switched the feed to a camera in elevator car three.

One thing that always bugged Quinn about spy movies was they tended to either rush through or completely skip the amount of prep work that went into operations such as this. His team had spent the last three days getting ready, and the tactical team had been in the area for over a week.

Quinn and his colleagues were responsible for cleanup after tactical dealt with the target. Though few in the secret world would acknowledge it, a cleaner's job was quite possibly the most dangerous of all the specialties. Cleaners ran the highest risk of getting caught, if not by associates of the recently deceased, then by the untimely arrival of civilians or local authorities responding to a call for assistance. It was never good to be caught with a corpse in your possession. There were plenty of stories about other cleaners to whom that had happened and others who had been caught due to less than thorough prep work. The best result from such a mistake would be prison, and the most likely a bullet to the head.

Needless to say, Quinn's team was always thorough.

On the monitor, the elevator stopped at the top floor. The hotel rep led Edwards and his companion down the hallway to the suite at the northeast corner.

As they stepped inside, Orlando switched to a camera the team had put in the living room area, and Quinn picked up the radio mic. "Callisto for Triton."

"Go for Triton."

"Target's in the roost."

"Copy, Callisto. Target's in the roost."

The double-doored hotel service entrance opened and a familiar guard peeked out. "Back again?"

"Hopefully for the last time," Quinn replied in flawless German.

The guard pushed the doors open all the way and moved to the side. "You know where the elevator is."

Quinn entered, pulling a metal cart upon which sat a large box. Nate followed, pushing the other end.

The guard eyed their cargo. "You're going to have to replace it after all?"

"Unfortunately."

"I don't envy you. It's cold up there."

"Happy to trade jobs if you want."

"Uh, no, thanks."

This was the third day in a row Quinn and Nate had visited the hotel via the service door. Like the two previous times, they were wearing coveralls identifying them as employees of the local heating and air conditioning company that had a maintenance contract with the resort. As planned, the multiple visits had allowed the guards to become familiar with them, making their return today unremarkable.

Quinn and Nate entered the service elevator and Quinn pushed the button for the roof, where the HVAC equipment was located. When they arrived at the top, they propped the doors open for the amount of time it would take to move the cart off, and then let them close without getting off. They descended one stop to the sixth floor and exited into a modest-sized room, hidden from the public behind a locked and unmarked door.

Quinn activated his comm mic. "This is Callisto. We're in position."

His words were acknowledged with a single click.

On his phone, he brought up the feed from the living room of Edwards's suite. Three members of the tactical team were already inside, each dressed head to toe in black and carrying a dart gun.

Quinn switched to the bedroom camera.

The woman was sitting at a vanity, putting on makeup. Edwards was nowhere to be seen, but the light was on in the master bathroom. Quinn brought up that camera and could see little due to fog on the lens, but he could hear the shower running.

He flicked back to the bedroom cam in time to see the door creep open and the first of the tactical team slip in. The first sign the woman gave of realizing something was wrong came when a tranquilizer dart pierced her thigh, when she let out a brief yelp of surprise before falling unconscious.

The operative caught her before she tumbled to the floor. He touched his comm and three clicks came over the radio, prompting two more members of the tactical team to enter the room. One helped the first agent lay the woman on the bed, while the other approached the bathroom door and peek inside.

"Who the hell are you?"

The operative backpedaled as Edwards charged out of the bathroom. The agent pulled the dart gun's trigger but his shot went wide. Edwards lunged at him, getting one hand on the op's shoulder and the other on the barrel of the gun. Before Edwards could twist it away, another dart burst from the barrel. This time, the target was too close to miss.

Edwards stumbled backward, yanked out the dart that had pierced his stomach, and charged the agent again.

Unlike the sedative the woman had received, the drug now coursing through Edwards's veins took longer to take effect.

But only by seconds.

Edwards was a step away from the operative when the first convulsion rocked him sideways into the wall. He tried to push away, but fell to his knees before collapsing onto the floor.

Many different drugs could have been used to kill him. Some would have done so painlessly. Some would have come with only mild discomfort. The one now coursing through Edwards's bloodstream had been chosen specifically to make him wish he were dead long before he took his last breath.

Quinn was not a fan of it. A quick and efficient death, no matter how heinous the acts committed by the target, should always be the preferred method. But no one had asked him.

Edwards spent every single second of the next seven minutes writhing in pain, until his body finally had enough and his heart stopped beating.

The agent who had delivered the justice clicked on his comm. "Triton for Callisto."

Quinn activated his mic. "Go for Callisto."

"Come on down."

Quinn and Nate dealt with the woman first.

The sedative she'd received would keep her under for only two hours tops. The timing wasn't a problem; Quinn and Nate would be long gone by then. The issue was one of remembering. Or, more precisely, not remembering.

To correct that problem, Nate retrieved a black case from their clean kit, pulled out a syringe, loaded it with a dose from the vial marked with a black dot, and administered the shot between the woman's toes, where the entry point would likely heal before it could be noticed. When she woke, she would be unable to recall anything that had happened in the last few hours.

While Nate took care of her, Quinn removed a sheaf of paper containing five notes from the kit. Each note had been written by an expert forger in Edwards's handwriting and provided the same basic information. The differences between them were only in how the information was presented, giving Quinn options depending on how the assassination had gone down.

He selected the note designed to be found by someone Edwards was sharing the room with and set it on the living room coffee table.

Henrik Neymar called. He's in the area for a few hours. Going downstairs for a private talk. Be back soon. Hope you were able to sleep off the migraine.

E.

Neymar was a Germany-based alt-right strategist but not one of the scheduled conference attendees. He really was in the area so the meeting would seem legitimate. Or he *had* been in the area, up until thirty minutes ago when he'd been captured by a different team. At this point, he should be on his way to a black ops site in eastern Europe, where, after every bit of information had been squeezed out of him, he'd be escorted to the cell in which he'd spend the rest of his life.

When the woman finally woke, she would read the note and, with any luck, wait an additional hour or so before raising an alarm. By then Edwards's body, Quinn's team, and everyone else involved in the man's termination would be long gone, and any search for him would come up empty.

But at this moment, Quinn and Nate still had a bit of work to do. After all, cleaning was all about the details.

Nate dealt with drying surfaces in the bathroom, to remove any evidence of Edwards having taken a shower. As for Quinn, he used a recording of the tactical team's operation as a reference to wipe down every surface the operatives had touched, even though they had all been wearing gloves. You could never be too cautious. He then retrieved a powerful but near-silent handheld vacuum from their kit and sucked up any stray hairs and dead skin cells.

When he and Nate had finished these tasks, they put Edwards in the box that supposedly held a new air circulation unit, placed their kit on top of him, and sealed the box closed with a strip of tape.

After taking a final look around, they pushed the cart out of the room and back to the service elevator.

6

Nate backed the delivery van up to a walkway that led to the docks of the marina, then he and Quinn exited the van.

Waiting for them on the sidewalk was Johan Werner, their contact and captain of the luxury yacht *The Seven Goddesses*.

Johan smiled. "Right on time."

"You know Quinn," Nate said. "He hates being late for anything."

"Good to see you, Johan," Quinn said.

Johan shook both men's hands.

"Are you ready for us?" Quinn asked.

"All set."

Nate extended the van's built-in ramp and opened the doors. Jar and Orlando stood inside, behind the cart on which sat the box containing Edwards's body. Nate undid the brakes holding the cart in place and pulled the cart onto the ramp. Orlando guided it from the other end and Jar followed, carrying her and Nate's bags.

When the cart reached the ground, Nate took Orlando's place at the back and she moved over to where Quinn waited.

"Text me when it's done," Quinn said.

"Will do," Nate said. "Safe flight." He nodded to Johan. "Lead on."

The German headed toward the docks, and Nate and Jar followed with the cart.

Disposing bodies at sea was not a new thing for the team. If done correctly, it was the most reliable way to guarantee a package would never be found again. This was imperative, especially with Edwards being a high-profile target. To accomplish this goal, Nate, Jar, and the corpse of the late CEO of One would be taking a voyage aboard *The Seven Goddesses*.

The ship would sail with minimal crew. As far as any of them save Johan would know, this was a late-night romantic cruise for friends of the owner. Once the *Seven Goddesses* was two hours out, Nate and Jar would strap weights around Edwards's body and dump it into the sea. They would then return to the marina in plenty of time for their seven a.m. flight home to Los Angeles.

In the van's cab, Orlando placed a call on her mobile and activated the speaker.

After one ring, the familiar voice of Hanna Bharara said, "Yes?"

"It's Orlando and Quinn."

"She's waiting for you. One moment."

A few seconds later, Misty Blake came on the line. "How'd it go?"

"As planned," Orlando said. "Final drop-off will occur sometime in the next couple hours."

Misty and Orlando were co-heads of the Office, a small, autonomous organization that provided specialized services to a variety of clients. The Office had coordinated the Edwards mission.

"Good work. I'll let the client know. When do you fly out?"

"Our flight's in the morning," Quinn said.

"Listen, if it wouldn't be too much trouble, I'd like you to reroute to DC."

Quinn and Orlando shared a glance.

"Why?" Orlando asked.

"It's something better discussed in person. When you have flight details, let me know. I'll have someone pick you up at the airport. See you soon."

The line went dead.

Quinn and Orlando stared at the phone.

"Can I assume you have no idea what she wants to talk about, either?" Quinn asked.

"Not a clue."

JANUARY 17, 4:49 PM
VIRGINIA, USA

Hanna stuck her head into the conference room. "It shouldn't be much longer. Can I get you anything else?"

"Coffee?" Quinn asked.

"Me, too," Orlando said.

"I'll be right back," Hanna said and left.

The Office's headquarters were located on a former horse ranch in Virginia, not far from DC. It also served as Misty's residence.

Thanks to the time difference between Germany and Virginia, Quinn and Orlando had arrived at the ranch in the late morning and had hoped to meet with Misty right away and be on a San Francisco-bound plane by lunchtime. But no such luck.

It turned out Misty had spent the previous night in the capital, preparing for meetings that, according to Hanna, would keep her away until late afternoon. With little else to do, Quinn and Orlando had crashed in a guest room until Hanna called to let them know Misty was on her way.

"You don't think she's going to send us right back out, do you?" Quinn asked.

His team had just finished two back-to-back missions. When

he was younger, he'd enjoyed being kept busy, but these days he found himself longing for time at home with Orlando and the kids and Mr. and Mrs. Vo, Garrett and Claire's surrogate grandparents.

Orlando glared at him, eyes narrowed.

"Right, right, you have no idea, either," he said. "But correct me if I'm wrong, aren't you the co-head of this organization?"

This time her glare was more planet-destroying death ray than annoyed.

"Sorry," he said. "What was I thinking?"

"I was wondering the same thing."

He was saved from digging himself a deeper hole by the return of Hanna with a tray holding several cups and a steaming carafe of coffee. She placed everything on the table and poured each of them a cup.

"Can I get you anything else?" she asked.

"I think we're good," Orlando said. "Thanks."

"I'm just down the hall if you change your mind," Hanna said and left.

Less than a minute later, the door opened again and Misty entered.

Quinn had expected to be meeting with just her, but she arrived with a pair of men and a woman, each wearing a dark business suit. Quinn didn't recognize either man, but the woman he'd met before and he was not happy to see her again.

"Sorry for the wait," Misty said briskly, then motioned to the older of the two men. "This is Deputy Director Pierce from the FBI." She gestured at the bald man. "And this is Director of Operations Suarez from the CIA." She looked at the woman. "And this is—"

"Special Agent Thomas," Quinn finished for her, forcing a smile. "Where's your partner, Agent?"

Quinn and Daeng had endured a ridiculous and completely unnecessary interrogation at the hands of Thomas and her partner, Special Agent Wilkins, the previous spring, in the aftermath of a bombing in New York City that had put an abrupt end to the mission they'd been on.

"Mr. Quinn," the woman said, leaving it at that.

To Pierce and Suarez, Misty said, "Jonathan Quinn and Orlando."

Both men nodded.

"Please, sit," Misty said.

The others took seats.

When no one seemed interested in starting the conversation, Quinn said, "And we're here because...?" Orlando slipped her hand onto his thigh and gave him a gentle squeeze. "Sorry. I meant how can we help you?"

"What do you know about Uri Sobolevsky?" Suarez asked.

"Who?"

"Isn't he that journalist?" Orlando said. "The one taken off that plane a few weeks ago?"

Quinn still didn't recognize the name but he remembered the incident.

"He is," Suarez said.

"What about him?" Quinn asked.

"How about Filip Krutov?"

"I've definitely never heard that name before."

"Ditto," Orlando said.

"Andrei Barsukov?"

Quinn shrugged, but Orlando thought for a moment and said, "He's a scientist or something like that, isn't he?"

"As I told you," Misty said to Suarez and Pierce, "they have nothing to do with any of it."

"We all know that's not completely true," Thomas said.

"Does someone want to tell us what you're talking about?" Quinn asked.

"Here's a name they'll both know," Thomas said. "Dimitri Melnikov."

Up until this point, Quinn had been only annoyed. Now he was angry.

He and his team had been brought in to thwart the assassin sent to take out Melnikov and then fake Melnikov's death. Those two parts of the mission had gone off without a hitch. The problem came when Quinn, Daeng, and two other operatives had taken Melnikov to the location where they handed him off to the FBI. Moments after, a bomb had exploded, partially collapsing the underground garage they were in. It had left Quinn's team injured and trapped, and the FBI agents and Melnikov dead.

Quinn and his people had come under immediate suspicion, and been suspended from taking work from any organization associated with US Intelligence. In other words, any official work at all.

Three months passed before it was decided they likely had not played a role in the bombing and their work prohibition had been lifted. Though the reinstatement had occurred seven months ago, the whole experience still irritated Quinn.

With a barely controlled voice, he said, "What is this? Why are we here?"

Thomas looked skeptical, as if she believed he should already know the answer to his own question.

Deputy Director Pierce spoke for the first time. "We have reason to believe Mr. Melnikov is alive."

Quinn laughed. "And some people believe the moon landings were faked, but that doesn't make it true." He took a breath. "The garage collapsed *directly* on the spot where Melnikov and your agents were. No way any of them could have survived that."

"Except that no trace of his DNA was found."

Quinn stared at him for a moment, then shook his head. "No way. Someone must have messed up."

"I thought the same," Pierce said. "Which is why I had the lab recheck everything multiple times. But the results were the same. None of the remains we found belonged to him."

The room fell silent.

"Only Melnikov? Or are there others missing?" Orlando asked.

Thomas shifted uncomfortably in her seat.

"As much as it pains me to say this," Pierce replied, "one of our agents is also unaccounted for."

"One of your *agents*?" Quinn asked. "Wait, wait, wait. Are you saying this agent took Melnikov?"

"Whoa!" Thomas snapped. "No one said that. We have no idea what happened."

"Was there any way they could have gotten out of there?"

Thomas looked like it took every ounce of her will to say, "There was a...stairwell."

"Still intact?" Orlando asked, incredulous.

"Damaged, but someone with the right equipment could have climbed out," Pierce said.

"Where was this stairwell?" Quinn asked.

"Directly behind where our vehicle was parked."

"Then how did it not cave in on itself?"

"The force of the blast was angled away from the stairwell, in a way that would minimize damage to it. Someone could have climbed up the shaft if they had help from above."

"Even if the blast was angled away," Orlando said, "anyone that close would have been injured, at the very least."

Pierce nodded. "True. Except for the fact we found a reinforced blast box in the stairwell." A blast box was a portable bomb shelter, a kind of last resort for people working in dangerous areas.

Quinn snorted. "You've got to be kidding me." He cocked his head. "If you're still thinking we had something to do with it—"

"No," the deputy director said. "We are convinced you did not."

The look on Thomas's face told Quinn that the *we* Pierce used did not include her.

"The other names you mentioned," Orlando said, "what do they have to do with Melnikov?"

Suarez said, "As you have already noted, Sobolevsky was the journalist removed from a plane in Belarus. His wife, Anya, was also taken. Krutov is a Russian oligarch who ran out of favor with the Russian president and has been living in London for the last several years. A little over a week after Sobolevsky was kidnapped, Krutov was abducted while taking a walk in Hyde Park. Barsukov is a physicist and founding member of the Council for Truth and Understanding. One of the organization's main objectives is to expose the lies and deceptions of the Russian government. Three days ago, Barsukov gave a speech at a banquet in Chicago. After dinner, he went to the bathroom and never came back."

Orlando cocked her head. "The Russians are kidnapping expat dissidents?"

"Yes."

"Okay, admittedly, that's pretty messed up," Quinn said. "But I don't see what this has to do with us."

"We made a promise to Dimitri Melnikov that we would protect him," Pierce said. "And we need you to help us keep it."

"Excuse me?"

"We'd like you to find Melnikov and bring him back. If you can free any of the others, that would be a bonus. But Melnikov is the priority."

Quinn stared at him, confused. "He's been gone nearly a year. Chances are he's dead. Hell, they probably all are."

Pierce tilted his head at Suarez and said, "Our friends at the CIA have reason to believe otherwise."

"Seriously?"

"Seriously," Suarez said.

Quinn said nothing, waiting for more.

Suarez said, "I can't go into the details at this point, other than to say we have information indicating several of those rounded up were still alive as of two days ago. Melnikov included."

"Okay," Quinn said, "let's assume you're right, and the Russian government is rounding up people who hurt their dear leader's feelings. My team and I are cleaners. We don't do rescues."

Pierce opened his phone and read aloud from the screen. "Mila

Voss. A school bus full of children in California. Thomas Brunner. Keiko Hirahara." His gaze flicked to Quinn. "Your own children. That doesn't sound to me like the history of a group who doesn't do rescues. Shall I go on?"

Through clenched teeth, Quinn said, "That won't be necessary." No one besides himself and his friends should have known about Mila Voss, let alone what had happened to his and Orlando's kids.

He'd heard enough, and opened his mouth to say they were leaving, but Orlando tightened her hand on his thigh and said, "Do you know where they're being held?"

"In Russia," Suarez said.

"Russia's a big place," she said.

"We know where they've been, but not where they are now. That's part of what we need you to find out."

Thomas had been looking more and more agitated as the conversation progressed. No longer able to hold herself back, she said, "I would think you'd be jumping all over this to make up for your mistake."

"*Our* mistake?" Quinn said. Orlando's fingers clamped down harder but he was beyond noticing. "*We* didn't make a mistake. *We* stopped the assassination. *We* snuck Melnikov and the assassin out of the building. And *we* delivered them both to your people at the designated drop-offs, per the plan *you* drew up. Our part of the mission went off perfectly."

Before she could respond, Pierce said, "There's no need for finger pointing. By anyone."

Her nostrils flared a few times before she finally mumbled, "Sorry, sir."

"Oh, no," Quinn said, "we're not going to brush this under the table. If it's the FBI's position that we were even one percent responsible for what happened in New York, then this conversation is over. You already made us pay for something we had nothing to do with by preventing us from working for nearly four months."

"Like you really didn't do any work during those four months," Thomas said.

"Agent Thomas," Pierce said. "Enough."

She looked away, chastened but still pissed.

The deputy director returned his attention to Quinn and Orlando. "Your suspension served its purpose. It allowed us time to conduct a thorough investigation and determine that you and your team were not involved." He shot a look at Thomas. "In *any* way."

Thomas still didn't look like she agreed, but she kept quiet.

"It's not a matter of you making up for a mistake you may or may not have committed," Pierce went on.

"Did not commit," Quinn said.

"Sorry, did not commit," the deputy director corrected. "We're coming to you because you and your colleagues have a broad base of skills and experience well suited to the task at hand. You have also met Melnikov, which we're sure will help when you find him."

"Unless he also thinks we were in on it," Orlando said, tilting her head toward Thomas.

Pierce said nothing.

"Why are *you* involved in this?" Quinn asked Suarez.

"What do you mean?" Suarez asked.

"Going after Melnikov." Quinn looked at Pierce. "I mean, I guess I could understand the FBI being embarrassed and wanting to do something to rectify the situation. But what's the CIA's angle? Because I have a hard time believing you're jumping in and mounting an operation because your bureau buddies goofed up and need to set things right.'"

"Technically, neither agency is mounting an operation."

"Right," Quinn scoffed. "This one is off the books."

"As far off as you can imagine."

"The planning and execution will be entirely up to you," Pierce said.

"I'm guessing, if things go wrong, you'll both play the deny-ing-involvement card?" Quinn said.

Both men answered with their silence.

"Typical. But you still haven't explained why the CIA is involved." Quinn paused. "Sorry, I meant *not* involved. There is no way the rescue isn't covering up some other purpose."

"What purpose would that be exactly?"

"I have no idea. That's why I asked."

Suarez studied Quinn for a moment, then said, "You're right. There is another motivation. By removing so many prominent voices, Russia is trying to create a void where there has been grow-ing, boisterous dissent. The result is that we're already seeing an increase in troubling rhetoric and cyberattacks aimed at us and our allies. We predict we will also see more military maneuvers against former members of the Soviet Union, like what's happened in Ukraine, and further tightening of social controls on their own citi-zens. None of these things are in the interest of the rest of the world."

"In other words, you want to take the Russian government down a peg or two."

"Not the way I'd phrase it, but essentially yes. And we need your help to do it."

Quinn crossed his arms. He didn't have an opinion one way or the other about giving the Russians a black eye, but if Melnikov was truly alive, Quinn couldn't deny the desire to help free him. Not due to guilt, per se. More like finishing a job.

"When do you need our answer?" he asked.

"We were hoping we could get it now."

"Too bad. The end of day tomorrow or it's an automatic no."

"What if you're one day too late to save them?" Thomas asked. "Will you worm out of responsibility for that, too?"

Quinn locked eyes with her. "You're free to find someone else and send them tonight. That choice is on you."

Pierce gave Suarez a nod before Suarez said, "Tomorrow is acceptable. I'm sure you already realize this, but if you choose to undertake the mission, details are to be kept on a need-to-know basis. And the list of those who need to know should be very short."

"We know the drill."

"Then we look forward to hearing from you."

~

"Well?" Misty asked, after she returned from escorting Suarez, Pierce, and Thomas to their cars.

"You could have given us a heads-up about what we were walking into," Quinn said.

"You're in a cranky mood."

"I don't like being ambushed. And I don't like being accused of things we didn't do, especially after we've already been cleared."

"We'll do it," Orlando said.

Quinn whipped around so fast, he was lucky he didn't pull a muscle. "Wait. We haven't even—"

"We'll do it. You know we will."

"I was thinking we'd talk about it first."

She placed a hand over his. "I know you were. And that's sweet. But would we really have said no?"

Just because the answer to that was no didn't mean he had to like it. "Fine. But we don't tell them until tomorrow evening."

"Tomorrow morning."

Even as he narrowed his eyes, he knew this wasn't a fight he'd win. "All right, all right. Tomorrow morning."

7

W hen Misty had called Deputy Director Pierce to tell him Quinn and his team were in, she'd also relayed how they wanted to proceed. Pierce had been more than happy to approve their request and arranged for a Learjet to Asheville Regional Airport. He also said he'd have someone pick them up when they arrived.

What he hadn't mentioned was the person would be Special Agent Thomas.

"This is getting off to a great start," Quinn mumbled as he and Orlando walked from the plane to the gray Chevy Suburban where the agent stood waiting.

"Play nice," Orlando whispered.

"I will if she will."

Orlando rolled her eyes. "Then just don't say anything."

"I won't if she won't."

"Oh, for God's sake," Orlando groaned, then plastered a smile on her face and raised her voice. "Good morning, Agent Thomas."

Thomas opened the rear passenger door, hints of displeasure slipping through her otherwise neutral expression. "Welcome to North Carolina."

Orlando climbed in and scooted to the other side so Quinn could enter.

Once he was inside and the door was closed, he mumbled, "This is going to be so much fun."

Orlando looked at him with the kind of glare she gave their son, Garrett, when he said something stupid.

"I get it," he said. "Play nice."

Thomas climbed into the driver's seat and started the engine. "It'll take us about forty minutes." She handed a folder to Orlando. "This should keep you busy until then."

Orlando held the file for Quinn to see.

The label on the tab read:

ROMAN DUROV

AKA JOHANNES BRAUN, AKA HANS JESPER, AKA THE FOX

"The Fox?" Quinn said.

Orlando shrugged, opened the folder, and slid out a packet of documents, several dozen pages thick. Clipped to the front of the top document was a photo of the assassin who had been hired to kill Melnikov. In the picture, Durov had a cut lip and a bruised temple, neither of which had been there when Quinn last saw him.

The page directly under the photo was a fact sheet. Durov had been born in St. Petersburg thirty-four or thirty-five years ago—his birth year had not been confirmed. He had started his career in a small crime syndicate in his hometown, where he gained a reputation for being good at the discreet elimination of targets. This led to him being loaned out to other organizations, and eventually to his venturing out on his own.

Evidence pointed to him being involved in assassinations in Berlin, Istanbul, Pretoria, Delhi, Hong Kong, Tokyo, Toronto, and dozens of other locations around the world. From all available evidence, his attempt on Dmitri Melnikov had been the first time he worked in the States.

Other documents in the stack went into more detail about the various missions he'd undertaken, ending with several pages dedicated to the Melnikov incident.

The last handful of sheets were transcripts of interviews the FBI had so far conducted with Durov. Though there had been over forty sessions since the man had been locked away, the transcript for each took up no more than two sheets, thanks to Durov's lack of cooperation. About the only things he'd willingly given up were how much he'd been paid for the Melnikov job and how it had been routed to him.

Federal investigators had used that information to backtrack the money transfer to a bank in Luxembourg then to a shipping company in Italy, a manufacturer in Bulgaria, and finally to a communications company in Belarus. Past that point, the trail ran cold.

Orlando closed the folder and offered it to Quinn, but he shook his head. He'd seen all he needed to.

He was sure this trip would turn out to be a waste of time. If the assassin hadn't given anything to the FBI in the last ten months, it seemed unlikely he'd decide to talk to the people who'd captured him and handed him over to the feds.

Quinn had said as much to Orlando when she suggested this trip last night, so there was no need to remind her of his misgivings. She was busy with something on her phone, anyway, and admitting they were on a fool's errand in front of Thomas was not something he was interested in doing.

Soon, they were in the forested mountains outside Asheville. The sky, which had been partly sunny when they landed, was now covered by gray clouds, and as they turned off the highway, the first drops of rain hit the windshield.

As they neared the forty-minute mark of their journey, Thomas turned the Suburban onto a freshly paved road, with lane markers looking as if they'd been painted that morning. Two hundred yards in, the road split around a guardhouse. Running into the woods on both sides were parallel four-meter-high fences topped with razor wire.

A man in uniform exited the guardhouse as Thomas pulled up.

She rolled down her window. "Special Agent Nicole Thomas." She nodded back at Quinn and Orlando. "Special Agents Burke and Kwan." She handed three IDs to the guard.

"Wait here." The man disappeared into the building.

Thomas caught Quinn's eyes in the rearview mirror. "When we get inside, follow my lead and don't say anything unless asked a direct question."

"Yes, ma'am," Quinn said.

She scowled but said nothing more.

When the guard returned, he handed the IDs back to her. "Thank you, Agent. You know where you're going?"

"I do."

He took a step back and motioned to someone in the guardhouse. A moment later, the gate rolled out of the way.

The road beyond twisted and turned through the wilderness before stopping at another gate. On the other side of the gate was a tunnel into a hillside.

Thomas showed the IDs again and the guard waved them through. The brightly lit tunnel extended into the mountain for about a hundred meters, and ended at a large, half-filled parking area. Three doors lined the back wall. Thomas parked near the door in a spot marked VISITORS ENTRANCE.

She unbuckled her seat belt and looked into the backseat. "Remember, not a word. There are some people who would not be happy knowing that…"

Quinn raised an eyebrow. "Go on. I'd love to hear how you were going to finish that sentence."

Orlando put a hand on his arm and said to Thomas, "We understand."

A guard station was just beyond the visitor door. After they cleared it, they rode an electric cart to a room Thomas called the waiting area. There was no check-in desk, no phone to let anyone know they were there, only a dozen unoccupied plastic chairs.

Since Thomas remained standing, Quinn and Orlando did the same.

The heavy-looking door at the other end of the room opened a few minutes later, and a woman in the same style of uniform as the others they'd seen asked them to follow her.

She took them to a room with white walls and a concrete floor. In the center was a metal table. On one side lay a set of handcuffs connected to chains that were welded to the table's surface. Four chairs were around the table, one on the side with the cuffs and three on the other.

They sat, Quinn and Thomas at either end and Orlando in the middle.

When the door opened again, two guards entered and looked around. One of them nodded to someone outside. Durov came through next, chains connecting the cuffs around his ankles to those around his wrists. Following him in was another guard. Two more guards stopped in the doorway, blocking the exit.

Durov was guided to the chair, where he sat without having to be told and held out his hands. A guard attached the cuffs connected to the table around his wrists without removing the ones he was already wearing.

"We'll be right outside," the guard said to Thomas, then he and his colleagues left.

Durov looked at Thomas and Orlando first. When his gaze landed on Quinn, his eyes narrowed. "I know you."

"You do," Quinn said. "We met in Dimitri Melnikov's office."

The man squinted at Quinn for a few more seconds and smiled. "You were son of bitch pretending to be him."

"I was." The trap they'd set for Durov had occurred in the office of Melnikov's apartment, where Quinn had waited at the desk, wearing clothes and makeup that made him look like the former chess champion from behind.

Durov shook his head and laughed. "That was good. I was not expecting."

"That was the plan."

"And you come to pay me visit. Am honored."

"Don't get too excited. We have a few questions."

Durov smiled broadly. "I, too, have questions."

"Like?"

"How long before do you know I am coming?"

Thomas put a hand on the table. "Mr. Durov—"

"Please, can call me Roman. I not know you are friends with this man. If you had told me, we would not have been so formal before." He looked at Quinn. "The man who bring down the famous Fox. I bow to you, sir." Durov dipped his head.

"How long did we know?" Quinn said. "I don't remember exactly. Three days, I think. Though we knew something was going to happen for at least a week." He glanced at Orlando. "Right?"

"Yes to both," she said.

"One of your colleagues?" Durov asked, his gaze flicking from Quinn to Orlando and back.

Quinn nodded.

"Three days." Durov sounded like he could hardly believe it. "I only know for four myself. Was it me? Something I do?"

"No," Orlando said. "Our information came from other sources."

Durov leaned back, looking relieved. "Not my fault. I cannot tell you how happy this makes me. Is any way you can let my employers know this?"

Quinn had to brace himself from not sharing a look with Orlando. It could *not* be this easy. "Happily. Just tell us who to call."

Time seemed to freeze for a second, and then Durov laughed and wagged a finger at Quinn. "You are very good, my friend. Very good. But am sorry, the Fox cannot divulge such information. If you do not already have this, you must find from different source."

"Any you'd like to suggest?" Quinn asked.

Another laugh and finger wag, but Durov said no more.

When Thomas scoffed, Durov laughed again. "She is jealous. When she come before, I say maybe five words to her." He glanced at her. "Or was it six?"

She did not reply.

Durov gave her a conciliatory smile and waved a hand at Quinn and Orlando. "Is only professional courtesy. They work out in the—how you say it?—the wild, like me. Not behind desk like you. We are colleagues in a way."

"Um, not colleagues," Quinn said.

"This is why I say *in a way*. I say correct, yes?"

The corner of Quinn's mouth crooked upward. "In a way."

Durov's smile threatened to split his face in two. "Oh, nice, my friend. I must remember this."

"This is a waste of time," Thomas said. "Can you ask your questions so he can refuse to answer and we can go?"

"May I?" Orlando asked, her phone in her hand.

"Be my guest," Quinn said.

"Mr. Durov—"

"Roman," the assassin said.

"Right. Tell us, Roman, does this house look familiar?" She turned her phone for him to see the screen.

Quinn and Thomas leaned forward so they could also see. On it was a photo of an aged house in the countryside. It looked more European than American.

Quinn shifted his gaze to Durov and saw that all traces of humor had disappeared from the prisoner's face.

"I'll take that for a yes," Orlando said, then swiped a finger across the screen.

The photo of the house was replaced by one of an older woman standing in front of the same house.

"I'm guessing it's safe to assume you recognize her, too?"

"How?" he whispered, clearly knowing the woman.

"Is that important?" Orlando asked.

"Yes."

"Too bad. You're in prison, Mr. Durov. I'm sorry, *Roman*. You answer questions, not ask them. First question: do you want there to be even a small chance you'll see your mother again or not?"

Durov tensed, his gaze flicking between Orlando and her phone. Finally he said, "What do you want to know?"

"Everything."

"If I cooperate, you promise she will be left alone?"

"You have my word...as a colleague."

He closed his eyes, let out a long sigh, and started talking.

As soon as they were back in the Suburban, Thomas spun around in her seat. "How in the hell did you get those pictures?"

"Contacts," Orlando said.

"What contacts?"

"Ones the US government doesn't have, obviously," Quinn said. He was curious, too, but he could wait until they were alone to find out.

"We need those photos," the agent said.

"No," Orlando said, her tone unchanged.

"We could force you."

"Try it. It won't end the way you think."

"We're supposed to be working together," Thomas said.

"Special Agent Thomas, if our roles were reversed, would you share sources with us?" Quinn asked.

She let out an exasperated breath and didn't respond.

"That's what I thought," he said. "If it's not too much trouble, could we get back to the plane, please? We still have a long day ahead of us."

8

Quinn, Orlando, and Thomas flew north on the Learjet to Joint Base Andrews, where they were met by the sedan that would take Quinn and Orlando to their next flight.

"Thank you for the escort," Orlando said to Thomas once they were all in the car.

Thomas huffed. "You're saying that like I was given a choice."

"Nevertheless, we appreciate it."

They rode across the airport to an Air Force C-40B scheduled to leave for the UK within the hour, and upon which Deputy Director Pierce had secured seats for Quinn and Orlando.

Quinn retrieved his and Orlando's bags from the sedan's trunk while Orlando waited with Thomas near the front of the car. Whatever conversation they'd been having stopped when he joined them. In an attempt to be magnanimous, he held out a hand to the agent. "We'll let you know how things go."

Leaving his hand hanging, Thomas said, "I know you will."

Orlando cleared her throat. "Apparently, Special Agent Thomas will be joining us."

He shot a glance at her, then at Thomas, and back at Orlando. "What do you mean by *joining*?"

"Deputy Director Pierce has requested she be part of our team."

Quinn held her gaze for several seconds before saying to Thomas, "Excuse us for a moment." He motioned for Orlando to follow him and walked far enough away to avoid being overheard. "No one said *anything* about her tagging along."

"The request came through Misty while we were at the prison. She just texted me about it."

"It's a request. We can say no."

"We both know that wouldn't be a good idea."

"Agent Thomas still thinks we're responsible for what happened to Melnikov, for God's sake. She's going to meddle in every decision we need to make."

"She won't. That's what I was talking to her about. I've made it clear that if she comes with us, she'll be the junior member of the team and answers to everyone else."

"You think that'll stop her from countermanding an order or even going rogue?"

"I'm hopeful."

"Hopeful." He scoffed. "I'm telling you right now, this is a bad idea."

"If it doesn't work out, we'll send her back."

"Right. I'm sure she'd go willingly."

"If she doesn't, we'll ghost her."

He looked at the sky for a moment, trying to reel in his anger. "It's going to be pretty damn hard for either the FBI or the CIA to deny their involvement if their agent gets caught."

"True. There may be some things we shouldn't involve her in."

"*Some* things? How about everything?

She gave his arm a gentle squeeze. "It's going to be fine."

He glanced toward Thomas. "This is a bad idea."

"Think of it this way. When we finish the job, she'll report back about how good we are at what we do. Couldn't hurt to have some good PR with the FBI right now."

"Our standing with the FBI should not be an issue. We haven't done anything wrong."

"I know, but things are what they are. And isn't it better to be proactive about improving our reputation than waiting around for others to realize they were wrong?"

He took a deep breath. "If she screws up anything, no matter how small, she's out."

Orlando stretched up and kissed him on the cheek. "See, that wasn't so hard."

When they returned to Thomas, Quinn sucked in his pride and said, "Welcome to the team."

Thomas gave him a flat *thanks* and headed toward the stairs to the C-40B without another word.

After she was out of sight, Quinn said, "We need to contact the others."

"I've already reached out," Orlando replied.

Of course she had. "Tell me again it's going to be fine."

"It's going to be fine."

"Liar."

2:27 PM LOCAL TIME
REDONDO BEACH, CALIFORNIA

"You saw it, didn't you?" Nate asked.

"Of course I saw it," Jar said. Did he expect her to *not* pay attention?

They joined the others in the huddle.

"We're not out of this yet," Clint said. "Defense, everybody. Defense." He clapped his hands twice, and Jar, Nate, Bailey, and J.J. did the same.

They spread out across the sand, Jar taking the setter position in the middle, and Nate the left-side blocker.

Jar had expected Nate to be skeptical when she told him she wanted to learn how to play volleyball. When not wearing shoes, she was a couple inches shy of five feet, and based on what she'd seen, volleyball tended to be a tall person's sport. But Nate hadn't even blinked. He'd rounded up a few people who lived near their Redondo Beach townhouse, and they'd played at one of the sand courts for hours.

Jar had taken to it like she'd played it all her life. Though she'd never be able to spike a ball, she'd proved to be an excellent setter. So much so that after a few weeks, she and Nate had been asked to join several league teams. Instead, she and Nate and some of those who'd taught her to play formed their own team and joined a local league for beginners.

So far, they had won all of the seven matches they'd played.

The game that afternoon was proving to be their toughest test. Jar and Nate had made it back to L.A. with less than twenty-four hours to spare before their afternoon match against the Kealy Street Wanderers. The Wanderers had already taken the first game and were up seven to three in the second. If Jar and her Redondo Grave Diggers teammates didn't want to suffer their first defeat, they needed to get it into gear.

It was Nate who'd suggested the team's name. It was a little too on the nose for Jar's taste, given what she and Nate did for a living, but no one else on the team knew that so she'd limited her annoyance to an eye roll only Nate could see.

The serve streaked over the net and Bailey dug it out just before it hit the ground. Jar maneuvered under it and flicked it in an arc that would drop right next to the net by Nate.

The tell she and Nate had noted had to do with the guy directly across from Nate. He was a cocky ex-jock type, with a name like Bruno or Brutus or Broomhandle. Jar hadn't really cared and hadn't been paying close attention during introductions. He could deliver a pretty good spike and was a decent enough blocker, except for one thing. Right before he went up for a block, he'd foreshadow which direction he'd lean toward with the slight dip of his shoulder.

This time, as Nate jumped up to spike the ball, the guy's right shoulder dipped. Jar clicked her tongue just loudly enough for Nate to hear. The defender dove right as Nate smashed the ball into the sand on the left.

The Diggers scored four straight points in the same manner before the other team switched positions around so that someone else took the now pissed-off defender's place. But it was too late by then. The Wanderers' confidence had been shaken. The Diggers easily won the final two games of the match, fifteen-eight and fifteen-four, keeping their perfect record intact.

Clint beamed and high-fived everyone after the final point. "That's the way we do it!"

He hesitated when he reached Jar.

"It's okay," she said and held up her hand. With few exceptions, physical touch was not something she participated in.

He slapped it. "Well, all right!"

She was tempted to give him the stare of death, but she'd been working on restraining herself when other people acted stupid. Which wasn't easy, because other people acted stupid *all the time*. The tempering-her-reaction rule did not apply to Nate, of course. That would have been too much to ask of her.

From the pile of personal items next to the court, Nate grabbed their windbreakers and tossed Jar's to her. As he donned his, he pulled out his phone. He checked the screen and stilled.

"What?" Jar asked.

He turned his phone so she could see. On it was a message from Orlando.

Air France LAX to Paris 9 pm tonight

Jar checked her phone and saw a similar message.

"Next game's right here, eleven a.m. Saturday morning," Clint said. "The Ocean's Five. I've heard they've got a couple of big guys but aren't that organized."

Jar looked at Nate, eyebrows raised.

He sighed before whispering, "I got it." Putting on his best apologetic smile, he walked over to the others. "Hey, Clint. It looks like Jar and I will be out of town on Saturday."

"Out of town? But you just got back. I thought you said you'd be around for a while."

"I thought we would be." Nate waggled his phone. "But a new job came in and there are some people you can't say no to."

As far as Clint and the rest of the Diggers knew, Nate and Jar worked as prop masters on film shoots. The job was excellent cover for their frequent trips and unpredictable schedule.

"What about the game next Tuesday? You'll be back for that, right?"

"I wouldn't count on it," Jar said.

"How long do you think you'll be gone?"

"Not sure, but I'll let you know as soon as we know."

"Please tell me you'll at least be back in time for the play-offs."

The play-offs were in two weeks.

"Maybe?" Nate's response didn't seem to improve Clint's mood, so Nate clapped him on the back. "I promise we'll do everything we can to be back before then."

"Anyone need a ride to Gunnar's?" Bailey asked.

"You guys are coming, right?" Clint asked Nate.

Nate glanced at Jar. "What do you think?"

Gunnar's Beach Bar and Grill was the teams' post-game hangout. Though Jar and Nate had plenty of time before their flight to join the celebration, Jar stared at him, silently reminding him that as far as she was concerned, any excuse to not hang around large groups was worth making.

"Yeah," he said. "We'll definitely stop by for a bit."

Jar didn't say another word to Nate until they were at LAX that evening, waiting to board their plane to Paris. When he asked if she wanted to pick up any snacks for the flight, she responded, "No."

The next time she spoke to him was after they'd been in the air for an hour. They were flying business class, and each had a private seat that could recline into a bed. She had to get up, cross the aisle, and lean into his space for him to hear her.

"Why?" she asked.

He was watching *Kill Boksoon* on his monitor, headphones on. When he didn't say anything, she tapped him on the shoulder.

He jumped in surprise and yanked off his headphones. "Are you trying to give me a heart attack?"

"I asked you a question."

The bridge of his nose creased. "I'm sorry?"

"I do not accept your apology."

"I didn't...that wasn't...I meant, what did you say?"

"I asked you why."

"Why what?"

She narrowed her eyes into death-ray slits.

His confusion lasted a few more seconds before a light bulb seemed to go off. "Gunnar's, right?"

"Gunnar's."

At the bar after the match, Jar had sat silently on her stool, while the others laughed and told jokes and generally sapped as much energy from her as they could. To Nate's begrudging credit, he made excuses for them to leave after forty-five minutes, but that was forty-five minutes she would have much rather spent in the townhouse, sitting alone in her room.

"You want to know why I said we'd go."

She stared at him, waiting.

"Because it's what you told me to do," he said.

She blinked. She most definitely had *not* told him she wanted to go to the bar. The look she'd given him at the time had been pointedly telling him the exact opposite. And she knew he knew it.

Seeming to read her mind, he said, "I don't mean today. Last month."

"Last month?" Now she was the one confused.

"You told me to help you expand your social boundaries, remember?"

She opened her mouth to refute him and then closed it again.

Dammit.

She had said that. It was part of her plan to improve her tolerance for...people. She broke eye contact, muttered, "I'm sorry," and turned back to her seat.

"Hold on."

She stopped.

"You don't need to say sorry. It's part of the process."

She nodded but didn't look back.

"Jar."

She took a breath and faced him again.

"If something like this happens again, and you *really* don't want to do it, just tell me."

"Okay."

He held out his pinkie and she rolled her eyes.

"Come on," he said.

With a sigh, she wrapped hers around his and they each pulled until their fingers came apart, sealing the deal.

"Can I return to my seat now?" she asked.

"Could I stop you?"

The answer was actually yes, but she wasn't going to tell him that.

When she was finally settled back in her cubicle of solitude, she double-checked that her tablet's advanced security settings were on, then connected to the airplane's Wi-Fi and opened her email. In her inbox was a message from Orlando, containing the mission brief.

Finally.

The only information they'd received before leaving had been their boarding passes and a list of equipment to bring that would pass security checks.

Jar opened the document and didn't even make it past the first sentence before her eyes widened in surprise.

Dmitri Melnikov was alive.

Or at least he had been after the explosion in New York that had almost killed Quinn, Daeng, and the others.

She read quickly through the rest of the brief, then popped out of her seat and returned to Nate.

The movie was still playing but he'd fallen asleep. She shook his shoulder. This garnered a groan but didn't wake him. She leaned next to his ear, pulled out his earbud, and said more loudly than she probably needed to, "Wake up."

He gasped and blinked. "Oh, um…hi again."

"You haven't checked your email."

"I tend not to do that when I'm sleeping."

"Orlando sent the brief."

"That sounds like something I could have checked out after I woke up."

"You are awake."

"I meant later."

Nate was lucky she liked him. Leaning even closer, she whispered, "Melnikov is alive."

It took him a second to process her words. "Wait. Did you say—"

"I did."

"Seriously?"

"You would already know it if you had read the brief." She spun around and returned to her seat.

9:12 AM LOCAL TIME
MELBOURNE, AUSTRALIA

"Again, again!"

Daeng swept Charlie off the ground and placed her at the top of the slide, then held her hand as she rode to the bottom. It was her eighth trip in a row.

At only two and a half years old, she wasn't big enough to

climb the slide's ladder yet, nor had she developed the sense of self-preservation that would have prevented her from leaning too far over the side to see the ground while she slid down, which was why he held her hand until she reached the ground again.

As Alison had said on multiple occasions, "She has a daredevil's heart, which we both know is your fault."

Alison would know, being Charlie's mom and all.

Three years ago, Alison and Daeng had met at a seaside bar on Koh Samui, Thailand. They'd fallen into easy conversation that had lasted deep into the night. When she rose to leave, she took his hand and led him to her room. In the morning, he'd offered to show her the best place for breakfast, and what both of them had initially thought would be only a memorable one-night stand turned into thirteen days of never leaving each other's side.

When she had returned to Australia, Daeng knew he was unlikely to see her again. She had been on holiday, and he'd been on a break between jobs with Quinn. Still, he had secretly hoped to at least hear from her.

A year later, he did. Only instead of a message saying, *Hey, I'm coming back to Thailand. Are you free?* what she wrote was *I should have sent this to you sooner. Surprise. You're a dad.*

The path Daeng's life had taken up to that point had already been filled with more twists and turns than most people experienced in an entire lifetime, but the one fork he'd come to believe he'd never take was the one toward fatherhood. His own father had been all but absent, never more so than after Daeng's mother died when Daeng was eight, and his father had immediately sent him to live with his aunt in California.

Having no intentions of repeating his father's mistakes, he had flown to Australia as soon as he could after getting Alison's message. She had been both surprised and more than a little wary when he showed up at her door, suspecting he would try to kidnap Charlie and take her back to Thailand. She had also made it clear there was no chance of rekindling their relationship. She had a boyfriend she loved and had no intention of leaving him.

Daeng told her he was only there to be a dad and would never think of taking Charlie away. He proved this by finding an apartment close by and, when he wasn't away on a mission, taking care of Charlie while Alison was at work.

He and Alison's then-boyfriend (now fiancé) had even become good friends, and with Charlie, the four had created an unexpected family.

When Charlie flew off the end of the slide now, Daeng grabbed her and lifted her into the air again.

She laughed, pointed across the playground, and said, "Swing!"

He tucked her under his arm and ran her across the playground like she was an airplane, then swooped her upward and plunked her down into the swing set's toddler seat. His phone vibrated in his pocket as he gave her a push.

He pulled it out, thinking it was Alison checking up on them. Instead, he found a text from Orlando.

We have a job that I think you'll want to be on.

He gave Charlie another push before he typed a reply.

?

Two more pushes, and his phone vibrated again.

The grand master is alive.

He stared at the screen. She couldn't mean what he thought she meant. How could Dmitri Melnikov have survived the bombing? Daeng and the others in the van had been lucky to live through it.

But he didn't know any other grand masters. So...

He texted:

DM?

Orlando:

Yes

Daeng:

How?

Orlando:

Will send you the brief if you're in

Daeng:

What kind of job is it?

Orlando:

Rescue

"Push, push!"

Daeng looked up from his phone. Charlie was looking over her shoulder, her swing moving in smaller and smaller arcs.

"Sorry, sweetie." He gave her a push as another text came in from Orlando.

Yes or no?

Though he'd done a few jobs since the team had been reinstated, he'd passed on several to stay with Charlie. But if this did indeed have to do with Dimitri Melnikov, how could he decline?

He tapped the screen and hit the send arrow.

When would I need to leave?

There was a pause of nearly a minute before she responded.

There's a flight that departs today at 1 pm your time. Doable?

Alison wouldn't be home until that evening. But her mom also lived in Melbourne, and she helped out when Daeng was out of the country.

I need to check something first but let's assume I can make it.

Orlando:

I'll book it and send you the info.

He texted her a thumbs-up emoji, which was probably the most dad thing he'd done all morning, then called Alison.

9

DIRECTORATE ELEVEN HEADQUARTERS

The phone on Annenkov's desk buzzed.

The colonel looked at it, annoyed. In order for him to focus on the latest version of the plan for the directorate's upcoming mission, he'd told Bebchuk he was not to be disturbed until he gave the okay.

He stared at the phone, expecting Bebchuk to realize his mistake and hang up, but the buzzing continued.

He snatched up the receiver. "What part of *do not disturb me* do you not understand?"

"My apologies, Colonel, but…"

"But what?"

"Em, General Churkin is on the line. I told him you were tied up but he insisted on being put through."

Annenkov moved the phone away from his ear, closed his eyes, and counted to ten. As much as he'd like to ignore Churkin, doing so would be unwise.

"Colonel?" Bebchuk said.

Annenkov pressed the receiver back to his ear. "Put him through."

The line clicked off and a second phone button began blinking. Annenkov gave himself a second for his anger to cool before he pushed it. "This is Colonel Annenkov."

"Good afternoon, Colonel."

"General Churkin, how nice to hear from you." Normal protocol would have been to engage in meaningless small talk, but the colonel had no time for pleasantries, friend of the president or not. "What can I do for you?"

"Straight to business. I appreciate that. If only more of the people I deal with were as efficient. Do you know how much time I waste talking to idiots, when all that needs to be said could be accomplished in less than a minute?"

"I'm sure the answer is a lot." Annenkov noted, but did not say, that Churkin seemed to be adept at wasting time himself.

"More than you can imagine. I appreciate that you are not one of them." The general paused. "There appears to be a problem with one of the projects you've done for me."

Annenkov was confused. All the missions thus far had gone off flawlessly, and every target now occupied a cell in Directorate Eleven's newly finished holding facility in the far north.

"Which project, General?"

"Sobolevsky."

Annenkov knew every detail of all the directorate's missions by heart, and knew the abduction of Uri and Anya Sobolevsky had gone exactly as planned. "Could you be more specific?"

"The Sobolevskys were traveling with a friend."

"Yes, Adrian Rapace. We were aware of that before the mission started. Per your instructions, we left him on board."

Even if that hadn't been the general's instructions, Annenkov would have insisted on leaving Rapace untouched. Kidnapping foreign nationals was something to be avoided at all costs.

"Yes. And I stand by the decision. The problem now is that Rapace continues to push the Sobolevskys' story to the media. It is a small thing, and honestly not something I'd normally be worried about, but it is annoying my friend. He would be much happier if Rapace was less...vocal."

In other words, the president wanted the reporter silenced.

"I see."

"There are others I could approach to deal with this problem, but…"

"You would rather not involve anyone else."

"You catch on quickly," Churkin said. "Can I assume handling an issue such as this wouldn't be a problem?"

"You can. I will look into it right away. I am a little concerned, though, that terminating Rapace will have the opposite effect on news coverage than your friend desires."

"Ah. I should have been clearer. We don't want him eliminated, for the very reason you just mentioned. We would just like him…discouraged."

"I understand."

"Thank you. I knew I could count on you."

"In all things, General. Now, if there is nothing else, I really must—"

"Can you update me on the status of the Levkin mission?"

"That was what I was working on when you called."

"Has the date been set?"

"Not yet."

"Do you at least have a range in mind?"

"I think it would be—"

"My friend is very anxious for this particular individual to be dealt with."

Annenkov reluctantly brought up the proposed schedule. "If no issues come up, he should be in our hands within the next six days. But we are still working on the details so that's a big if."

"Six days is acceptable. Anything longer is not. I'm counting on you to make it happen."

10

The Air Force flight from Maryland to the UK landed at RAF Mildenhall, where Quinn, Orlando, and Thomas were met by a man who introduced himself as Special Agent Davidson and led them to a waiting sedan.

After the bags were stowed in the trunk, Davidson said, "It'll be a little tight, but I should be able to get you to Heathrow in plenty of time for your flight."

"Change of plans," Quinn said and extended his palm. "Keys, please. We'll take it from here."

"That's not my orders."

"Your orders have changed."

"I-I don't think you can do that."

Quinn glanced at Thomas. "Could you handle this for us, please?"

Forcing a smile, she pulled out her phone.

As she dialed, Quinn said, "And tell them they can cancel those plane tickets. We'll arrange our own transportation from this point." The original plan had been to take a puddle hopper from Heathrow to Paris, but after going through all the info during the flight from Andrews, Quinn and Orlando had decided on a different plan.

Thomas looked as if she wanted to say something, but someone answered her call. She grimaced and walked off to talk out of earshot.

Less than a minute later, the driver's phone rang.

"Davidson," he answered. "Yes, sir...yes, sir...I see...yes, sir, I understand." When he hung up, he fished the car fob out of his pocket and handed it to Quinn. "The car's checked out in my name. Try not to scratch it."

～

The moment they left the airport, Thomas asked, "Where are we going?"

"To visit a friend," Quinn said.

"Friend?"

"Someone who might have information that could help us."

"Hold on. We're supposed to keep this quiet. What if this *friend* starts telling people?"

"Then she wouldn't be much of a friend, would she?" Orlando said. "Don't worry. She's safe."

Thomas didn't look happy but said nothing more.

Traffic slowed as they neared London, the morning rush in full swing. It would take forever if they were to drive all the way to their destination, so with Orlando navigating, Quinn took them to the nearest train station, where they left the car and caught the next train to King's Cross station. There, they rode the Tube into the heart of the city.

By the time they arrived, it was nearly 9:30 a.m. Since the Queen Anne Pub had yet to open for the day, they went into a nearby Pret a Manger, picked up coffees and sandwiches, and took a table near the window.

It took four rings before Annabel Taplin answered Quinn's call. "I almost let you go to voicemail."

"That's not a very nice way to say good morning."

"Good morning. Let me guess—you're in town."

Quinn was sure it wasn't a guess. Annabel was MI6, after all, but he could play along. "Good morning. And as a matter of fact, we are."

"Where are you now?"

"Too early for a pint so we're at the Pret a Manger just down the street."

"Of course you are. Give me ten minutes."

"I think it would be best if we came to you. It's a little too public here."

A pause. "That depends on what you want to talk about."

Her caution was understandable. Annabel worked in a nearby office building for a covert branch of MI6 masquerading as an organization called Wright Bains Security, her title being business consultant. She no doubt thought if he wanted to discuss something her British Intelligence overlords wouldn't approve of, it would be safer for her to do so on neutral ground.

"Relax," he said. "I don't think M will be upset."

"How many times do I have to tell you there is no M?"

"Yeah, but you're a professional liar."

She snorted. "Fine. Come over."

Annabel was waiting for them in the lobby when they entered the building.

She'd changed her hairstyle since Quinn had seen her last. Gone were the dirty-blonde locks that used to fall between her shoulders, replaced by a dark brown pixie cut. But as always, she was impeccably dressed, today sporting a sleek gray business suit and stylish green low-heeled pumps.

She smirked and shook her head as they walked up to her. "Henry forgot to set the coffee machine to start this morning. I should have known it was a sign to call in sick."

"Who's Henry?" Quinn asked.

"My husband."

Quinn quirked an eyebrow. Apparently there had been more changes than just to her hair.

"Congratulations," he said before giving her a hug.

"Wonderful news," Orlando said, doing the same.

"When did this happen?" Quinn asked.

"Last summer."

Quinn glanced at Orlando. "I don't remember receiving an invitation, do you?"

She shook her head. "Nope."

"No one did," Annabel said. "It was just the two of us."

"Is he in the business?"

"Oh, God, no. He's a writer. Horror stories mostly. Ghastly stuff. I can barely finish any of them."

"That bad, huh?"

"He's very good, actually. Scares the hell out of me." Her gaze flicked to Thomas. "Who's your friend?"

"Annabel Taplin, meet FBI Special Agent Nicole Thomas. Agent Thomas, Annabel Taplin." In a faux whisper, he added, "MI6."

Annabel offered her hand. "Nice to meet you."

Thomas took it with obvious reluctance. "You, too." After they shook, she said to Quinn, "Can I speak to you for a moment?"

"Can it wait?"

"No."

He motioned for her to lead the way, and they walked to a quiet corner of the lobby.

"Are you serious right now?" she asked, her voice hushed but her tone sharp as knives. "MI6? That is *not* keeping this operation quiet."

"First off, I was under the impression that the UK was the US's closest ally."

"Who they are to us isn't the issue. We're supposed to stay under the radar. Running straight to MI6 is not doing that."

Quinn chuckled. "Do you think they'll announce what we're doing to the world?"

"Maybe not, but they will ask questions of their contacts at the CIA, and those people know nothing about our mission."

"Because it's off the books."

"Exactly."

"Great. Then there shouldn't be any problem." He started walking back to Annabel and Orlando.

Before he could take more than two steps, Thomas grabbed his arm. "Are you not listening to me? We *can't* tell her anything."

Quinn stared at her hand until she removed it, then locked eyes with her. "Agent Thomas, your superiors chose me and my team to do this because we are good at our jobs. They have also left decisions on how the mission is carried out to Orlando and me."

"Deputy Director Suarez clearly said—"

"Keep the mission on the down-low. I remember. But that doesn't mean avoiding opportunities that could improve our chances of success." He paused, considering her for a moment. "I realize you're having a hard time believing my team and I had nothing to do with the bomb in New York."

Her cheeks reddened. "This has nothing to do with—"

He held up a hand to stop her. "Not entirely, no. But your feelings about what happened are a big part of why you feel it necessary to question my actions."

He gave her time to respond but she held her tongue.

"What you need to understand is that neither I nor any member of my team will do anything to jeopardize the job. That means you should assume if we say there's a source we're going to talk to, we've considered the risks and decided they're acceptable. Annabel's job is to coordinate off-the-book operations for British Intelligence. She knows how to keep a secret, and if I tell her to keep our conversation on the *down-low*, she will."

"You honestly believe that when you tell her where we're headed and what we're doing, she won't share that with her bosses?"

"I do."

Thomas stared at him in disbelief.

"If you're going to continue being a part of this mission, you need to trust me. If you can't do that, you're out."

Several tense seconds passed before she took a step back and shrugged. "Fine. It's your show."

"It is," he said.

He turned and walked back to the others, Thomas following closely.

"Everything all right?" Annabel asked.

Quinn looked at Thomas.

She grimaced and said, "Everything's fine."

"Shall we go up to your office?" Quinn suggested.

"I have someplace quieter in mind."

"Lead on."

The room Annabel escorted them to was in the building's secret third basement. It was what many in the secret world referred to as a black box—a soundproof room, constantly swept for bugs. Inside was a long white oval table surrounded by ten retro-style chairs—orange fabric-covered cushions backed by a white plastic shell. The setup looked like it had come out of a bad 1960s spy movie. Or one with Austin Powers.

"If you say one word about the décor, I will kick you out and not listen to a word you say," Annabel said.

"What if I was going to say it looks nice?" Quinn ventured.

"I wouldn't believe you. It looks horrible. We all know it. It's secondhand from some ministry office."

"It *is* a little on the nose," Orlando said.

"That is dangerously close to throwing-you-out talk."

Orlando mimed zipping her lips closed, and Annabel motioned for everyone to take a seat.

Once they were settled, she said, "So tell me, what's so important that you would rush straight from your flight to see me?"

Thomas looked surprised, but Quinn merely smiled. "You know I always like to pay my respects when I'm in country."

"That is complete bullshit. We both know you've been here at least a dozen times without even sending me a text."

It was probably closer to three dozen but he saw no reason to correct her. He caught Thomas's eye then said to Annabel, "Before I answer your question, we need your assurance that whatever we talk about stays between us. No one else can know, unless I give you the okay."

"Standard operating procedure, then."

Quinn nodded.

"Is it anything my superiors *should* know about?"

"They'll eventually know anyway. But I'm sure you'll agree once you hear us out that it would be best for them to have plausible deniability. For the time being, anyway."

"Will they be upset when they find out?"

Quinn scrunched up the corner of his mouth. "Define *upset*."

"Ready to break off diplomatic relations."

"Absolutely not. They may wish they'd had a heads-up, no more than that. And let's be honest, we all do things our friends wish they'd known about ahead of time."

"I can't argue with that." She leaned back. "And this won't be the first time you've put me in a difficult position, so I agree to your terms. For the *time being*, anyway."

Quinn looked at Thomas. "Satisfied?"

"You're the boss," she said, though her expression was anything but approving.

Quinn laid out the basics of their mission. As he spoke, Annabel's expression appeared almost bored, as if she were listening to someone droning on about Microsoft's latest software update.

When he finished, she stared at him for a moment and then laughed, loud and incredulous. "You've got to be kidding me."

"I am not."

"Wow." She shook her head to herself. "That is some Cold War badass shite."

"If you'd like to join us, you're more than welcome."

"While it sounds like fun, I'd have to tell my boss about where I was going, and you've forbidden me from doing that."

"Excellent point. Next time, then."

"Sure. Next time. So, I assume you didn't just come here to tell me what you are up to. What is it you need?"

"To start, we'd like as much information about Filip Krutov's kidnapping as you have. Also, your latest intel on Russian activities. And we'd appreciate the names and information of any contacts you think could help us."

She raised an eyebrow. "Is that all?"

"There *is* one more thing."

"I would have been disappointed if there wasn't. Go on."

"We've heard rumors that Starfish is operational."

"Starfish? I have no idea what you're talking about."

"You do. And we could use its assistance."

"Now I know you're joking."

"Not joking."

"Do you really think I have the power to magically let you use"—she paused, eyes flicking to Thomas—"Starfish for a mission you'll probably fail at anyway?"

"First off, thank you for your confidence. And second, if we do fail, then we won't need Starfish."

"Whether you fail or not, I would need to make sure it was in position, just in case."

"You can call it a training mission."

"A training mission?" she muttered under her breath and snorted. "You have it all figured out, don't you?"

"Does that mean you'll do it?"

She grimaced, pushed out of her seat, said, "I need a minute," and exited the room.

"She's calling her boss," Thomas said.

"She's not calling her boss," Orlando said.

"That's exactly what she's doing," Thomas countered.

"Why? Because that's what you would do?"

"Of course."

"Annabel is not calling her boss," Quinn said.

"How the hell can you know that?"

"Because she's a friend."

Thomas scoffed but said nothing else.

Nearly five minutes passed before the door opened again and Annabel returned, carrying a pot of tea and four cups on a tray. She placed it on the table and poured them each a cup of tea.

After she retook her seat, she said, "Well, then. This was not the way I expected my day to start, but here we are." She took a sip from her cup. "I'll collect what information I can and send it to you. Give me a couple hours. A list of contacts will take a little more time but I'll do what I can."

"Thank you," Quinn said. "And Starfish?"

She glared at him, sighed, and asked, "How soon do you think you'll need it?"

Quinn, Orlando, and Thomas took the Tube to a safe house near Victoria Station.

The moment the door closed behind them, Thomas said, "So, what's Starfish?"

"Better for you if you don't know," Quinn said, then disappeared into a room at the back.

"Excuse me," she called after him. "That doesn't work for me."

Orlando said, "Let's just say it's even more hush-hush than this mission."

"Then how do you two know about it?"

"That's hush-hush, too."

Thomas rolled her eyes. "Whatever. Where's my room?"

"Upstairs and on the right."

Thomas headed up without another word.

Orlando set up shop at the table in the dining room and checked her email. At the top of her inbox was a message from Annabel.

Something to get you started. More to come.
A.

The included link took Orlando to half a dozen CCTV clips of Filip Krutov's kidnapping in Hyde Park. While several cameras covered the area, the perpetrators had been smart, and everything from the moment the billionaire had been approached by the woman who petted his dog, to when a clearly drugged Krutov was guided into a tour van that quickly drove off, had occurred as far as possible from the cameras. There were additional clips of Krutov's bodyguards being distracted, and then taken out with what postmortem tests revealed was a drug cocktail that had paralyzed them and then stopped their hearts. These events also took place far from CCTV lenses.

Orlando did what she could to enhance the images of the kidnappers, in hopes of creating screen grabs of their faces, but the results were too fuzzy to be of any use.

Right after she sent Annabel an email asking if British Intelligence had been able to follow the van to its final destination, Quinn returned. She let him watch the footage alone while she went to take a shower. By the time she returned, Thomas had joined Quinn and they were both going over the footage.

"This isn't very helpful," Quinn said. "Do they at least know where the van went?"

"I've asked but haven't heard back yet," Orlando said.

Thomas frowned. "So what now? We just wait?"

"Not at all," Orlando said. "I was thinking we should do a little shopping." She glanced at Quinn. "There's that book we wanted to pick up."

"Right," he said. "Great idea."

11

"You know, he was probably lying," Thomas said.

"Maybe." Quinn sipped his coffee, his gaze never leaving the store across the street. A sign above the window read RAVEN'S ROOST BOOKS • RARE, NEW & SECONDHAND.

When Quinn, Orlando, and Thomas arrived thirty minutes earlier, they'd found a handwritten note taped in the bookstore's window informing customers that Raven's Roost would be closed until four p.m. Since then, they had been keeping vigil in a nearby bakery, waiting for the shop to reopen. It was now a quarter after four and the sign was still up.

The reason they'd come here was to follow up on information obtained from the Fox. According to the assassin, the bookshop was where he'd received his instructions to terminate Melnikov. It was a long shot, but tracing how his orders had found their way to the bookstore might lead them to someone who knew where the detainees were being held.

After another couple of minutes passed, Thomas huffed, "This is a waste of—"

"Maybe not," Orlando said. "The man near the corner, heading this way. He fits the description."

Quinn picked the man out and nodded. The guy had a Friar

Tuck-style ring of white hair around his head, and walked with a hunch that made him look smaller than he was.

"Is that a cat?" Thomas said.

Pressed against the man's chest was a bunched-up blanket, and sticking out of the top was what indeed looked like the head of a cat. He stopped when he reached the bookstore's entrance, struggled to pull a key out of his pocket without dropping the cat, and unlocked the latch and went inside. A few moments later, the sign taped to the glass was removed.

Thomas pushed back her chair. "Let's go."

"Patience," Orlando said. "Let him settle in first."

Quinn finished off his coffee and stood. "I think I'll have another. Anyone else?"

The sidewalk in front of the bookshop was blessedly free of waiting customers when Simon Darnell returned from taking Lucinda to the vet. His seventeen-year-old cat was half blind and one hundred percent deaf, and trips to her doctor were becoming almost a weekly event. The vet kept telling him it was a miracle she was still alive, but the old girl had always been stubborn. Simon had no doubt she still had a few years left in her.

He carried her inside and set her on her bed behind the counter, then returned to the front door and pulled down the note he'd posted when he left. After giving Lucinda a few of her favorite fish treats, he set to work on the online orders that had come in.

He loved books. They were his passion. He couldn't imagine doing anything else. But owning a bookstore in this day and age wasn't easy. Internet orders helped, but they still weren't enough to keep his doors open. If it weren't for his side hustle, he would have had to close long ago.

He checked the list of orders, then slipped the first edition of

Kazuo Ishiguro's *Never Let Me Go* into a mailer as the bell over the entrance rang.

A diminutive Asian woman entered and approached the display of classic novels by Jane Austen, Charles Dickens, and the Bronte sisters at the front of the store. Years ago, Simon had created the display to save him from being asked for the gazillionth time, "Do you have *Pride and Prejudice*?"

He figured the woman would find what she wanted there, but to his surprise, she soon moved to the bookcase opposite his counter.

Simon's philosophy was that if a customer needed help, they would ask for it. So he returned to his task and slid a first edition of Tasha Suri's *The Jasmine Throne* in with the Ishiguro.

When the bell rang again, he thought the woman was leaving. But no. A man entered.

The new customer nodded at Simon and, without even glancing at the classics display, headed straight for the bookcases that stretched to the back of the store.

The Raven's Roost was off the beaten path and not exactly easy to find. One customer at this time of day was unusual. Two at the same time? He couldn't remember the last time that had happened.

And yet, as he glanced out the front window, he saw a woman walking toward the door, making Simon think he was about to have a third customer. But she stopped a few meters in front of the door and pulled out her phone.

Oh, well. Two customers were still good.

He sealed the package, placed the preprinted label on top, and checked the next order on the list. Right. *The Storied Life of A.J. Fikry, Young Jane Young,* and *Tomorrow and Tomorrow and Tomorrow.* Someone was clearly a Gabrielle Zevin fan.

He pulled the books off the cart holding his online orders, turned to transfer them to the counter, and jerked in surprise. The woman stood silently on the other side, looking at him.

"Sorry," he said quickly. "I didn't hear you walk up. Ready to check out?"

"I have a question," she said, her accent American.

"Of course. How may I help you?"

"I'm looking for a 1951 Hamish Hamilton edition of *The Catcher in the Rye*. With dust jacket."

Simon froze.

Catcher in the Rye was not an uncommon request. Occasionally, a person would also ask about the first UK edition. But only three people had ever phrased the request the way the woman had, and none of them were actually looking for J. D. Salinger's book.

The woman had just given him one of the code phrases used by the people involved in his side job. The last time he'd heard this particular phrase was nearly a year ago, and it had been his understanding that the drop box associated with it was no longer in use. Even if that weren't true, he had not been notified someone would be coming, nor did he have anything to pass on.

A situation like this had never occurred before, and it took Simon a moment to remember he'd been given instructions on what to do if it did.

"I-I-I'm sorry. I don't have that. Perhaps another shop? I can suggest some to check if you'd like."

He'd been told this would be enough to send the inquirer away. But the woman just smiled and repeated the code.

"I'm sorry. I wish I could help but I can't."

A sound from the bookshelves drew his gaze toward the back. The male customer was standing at the end of an aisle, facing him and the woman. The smile on his face was identical to the woman's.

"I believe she asked you a question," the man said.

Simon glanced toward the front door, thinking it might be a good time to get some fresh air, only to realize that was not an option, either. The woman who'd been looking at her phone earlier now stood directly in front of the door, like a bouncer at a nightclub.

His side job was supposed to be easy. *Had* been easy up until this very moment. Someone would give him one of the code phrases, and he'd answer with something like, "You're in luck. I received a copy this week." The book he gave them would have a message inside. Simon never knew—or even wanted to know— what the messages contained. The recipient would leave and that would be that.

He turned back, glancing first at the man and then the woman, before saying, "I-I-I..." but could think of no words beyond that.

Any one of the three people could beat the crap out of him. Even the small woman in front of him looked like she'd have no trouble crushing his windpipe before he took another breath.

Her smile broadened and she walked to the door, turned the sign to CLOSED, and engaged the lock. "No sense in being interrupted."

Behind Simon, Lucinda meowed.

"She sounds hungry," the man said.

"It's snack time," Simon croaked.

"Then you shouldn't keep her waiting."

Simon nodded and reached a shaky hand toward the treat bag.

"Let me," the woman said. She came around the counter and took the bag from him. After shaking out several nuggets, she laid them on the cat's bed. "What's her name?"

"Lucinda."

She petted her. "You're a pretty one, Lucinda."

"Please don't hurt her."

The woman looked at him in horror. "We would never."

Simon's gaze switched back and forth between her and the man. "Then, em, what about...?"

"We have no plans on hurting you, either," the man said. "But I'm not sure how our friends at MI6 are going to react when they find out about you."

"Me? I haven't done anything wrong."

The woman winced. "I'm pretty sure the British government

won't look kindly on you for passing on messages for the Russians."

"The Russians? What are you talking about? I don't work for the Russians."

"Then who do you think you're doing it for?"

"I...I don't know what you're talking about. I run a bookstore."

"Mr. Darnell, let's not play games, shall we? We know about the messages."

He swallowed hard. "Okay. Yes. There are messages, but I don't know who they're for."

"Spoiler alert," the man said. "It's the Russians."

Simon opened his mouth to protest, but then all his strength left him and he slumped onto his stool.

"Mr. Darnell? Are you okay?"

Deep down, he'd known the Russians had always been a possibility. *No.* He'd gaslighted himself long enough. Not a possibility, a probability.

"Mr. Darnell?"

He blinked and jumped when he realized the woman was hovering right in front of him.

"What do you want?" he asked.

"We want to give you the chance to make things easier for you."

"Easier?"

"I'm not going to sugarcoat it," she said. "You are in serious trouble. But if you help us out, we'll put in a good word for you, and that could be the difference between seeing daylight every day or never seeing it again."

"Wh-wh-wh-what?"

The woman glanced at her friend. "Can you get him some water, or..." To Simon, she said, "Would you like some tea?"

He nodded, more out of habit than as a conscious act.

"Some tea, please," she said.

The man disappeared into the stacks without a word.

The woman smiled. "Here's what's going to happen, Mr. Darnell. You're going to tell us everything about how your operation works. How you receive messages, how you pass them on, who you talk to when you have problems, and how you contact them. Do you think you can do that?"

He tried to swallow, but his mouth had gone bone dry. He nodded.

"Good. You've made the right choice." She gave him an encouraging smile. "Let's start at the beginning."

So Simon did, and held nothing back. He told her how he would receive calls asking about one of twelve different books. Each book was code for a specific drop box, from where he would retrieve a message. He would then put that message in a copy of the book that matched the code and put the book on his hold shelf. Someone would visit the bookstore, usually that same day, and he'd give them the book and never see them again.

"Does the same person call you every time?" she asked.

His throat had gone dry again, and he took a sip of the tea the man had brought him. "Not always. There are…five of them. Maybe six. Two sound similar but not exactly the same."

"Men? Women?"

"Both."

"Accents?"

"None that I've noticed."

"Have you met any of them in person?"

"No. Not that I know of, anyway."

"What happens when you have a problem? Say, a message isn't in the drop box or a courier fails to show up."

"If anything like that happens, there's a number I'm supposed to call and leave a message."

"And after you do, what happens?"

"I don't know. I've never had to call it."

"What's the number?"

He gave it to her.

She locked eyes with him. "If you call them after we leave, we'll know."

"I won't," he said quickly.

She stared at him.

"I swear," he said, meaning it. She hadn't said how they would know, but he had no doubt they would.

"Okay, I believe you." She leaned back. "I need to discuss something with my colleague. If you'll excuse us for a moment..."

"Of course."

The woman and the man walked to the back of the store, out of earshot, and stayed there for several minutes before returning.

When they did, the woman said, "May I have a piece of paper and a pen?"

Simon immediately complied.

"Thank you," she said.

Before writing anything, she removed the top sheet from the pad he'd given her and handed the pad back to him. She then wrote something on the removed sheet, folded it, and gave him both the paper and the pen.

"That's a phone number. If at any time in the next week you're asked to pass on a new message, call us."

"Okay, but, um..."

"Yes?"

"What if it's more than a week?"

Her expression turned into something he could only describe as pity. "My guess is at the end of that time, you'll be a guest of MI6."

Simon momentarily forgot to breathe.

"And just in case you get the idea to run, don't. We have someone monitoring your activities, and if in the unlikely event you give them the slip, my friends and I will find you. In which case, any goodwill you've gained from working with us will be gone. Are we clear?"

"Yes," he croaked, and nodded in case he hadn't been understood.

"Mr. Darnell, sadly, whether you realized it or not, you have been actively working against your country's interests. It is now your duty to do everything you can to rectify the damage. A tip—when MI6 questions you, be as cooperative with them as you've been with me."

"I will, but…"

She cocked her head, waiting.

"What about Lucinda? She needs me."

The woman thought a moment before answering. "I can't promise anything, but I will let those in charge know about her. I have no doubt they will make sure her needs are met. Does that work for you?"

"Thank you."

She nodded. "Remember, call that number if you are contacted."

"I will."

He watched her and her companion walk out before he picked up Lucinda.

"I'm sorry, sweet girl," he whispered, even though she couldn't hear him. "I'm so, so sorry."

12

N ate texted Orlando and Quinn, letting them know he and Jar had arrived at the safe house in Paris.

Within seconds, Orlando called. "How was the flight?"

"Not sure," he said. "I slept through most of it."

"And how is Jar?"

Nate could hear Jar in the kitchen, opening and closing drawers. Knowing every inch of wherever she was staying was a habit she'd developed during her turbulent childhood.

"Jar normal," he said.

"I hope you didn't make plans for this evening."

"Other than grabbing dinner and calling it an early night?"

"That first part's fine. The second, not so much."

Jar's head popped over the edge of the roof, and she fed the rope down to where Nate waited at ground level. Moments before, she had scaled up the side of the building, using makeshift handholds that would not have supported Nate.

The building was in an area of industrial offices and warehouses near the shipping port on the Seine river, north of Paris, and from the outside, it looked as if it had been vacant for at least a year.

Orlando and Quinn had received information from the Fox indicating this was where he'd met up with the people who smuggled him into the US. That had been ten months ago, so the likelihood was low that they'd find anything there to help them locate Melnikov and the others, but they wouldn't know for sure unless they checked the place.

After Nate reached the roof, he pulled up the rope, untied it from the cooling unit Jar had secured it to, and carried it over to where she knelt next to a closed hatch. The hatch's lid sat about five centimeters above the surface but had no obvious way to be removed.

"A crowbar would be nice right about now," he said.

Jar scanned the roof and pointed. "That should work."

He spotted the piece of wood near the edge of the roof. "Oh, so you want me to get it."

"I would not have pointed at it if I was going to get it."

"My apologies," he said, bowing deeply. "I live to serve you."

"If that were true, you would have already retrieved it by now. Stop wasting time."

Nate retrieved the piece of wood and jammed it into the gap at the bottom of the hatch. He pushed down on the other end, and the hatch rose a few centimeters before catching on something.

"Hold it there," Jar said.

She maneuvered her gooseneck camera through the gap and studied the feed on her phone.

"There's a latch but I can free it."

She removed a coil of wire from her pack, bent the end into a loop, and inserted the loop through the gap. After a few tries, she yanked the wire back out, made an adjustment to the loop, and slipped it in again.

Seconds later, there was a metal click. Jar grabbed the edge of the hatch and swung it up and out of the way.

"What do you even need me for?" Nate asked.

She eyed him. "Are you sure you want me to answer that?"

"Probably not," he said, then pulled out his flashlight and shined it through the opening.

The room below was about twice the size of the living room in his townhouse. Whatever the original intent for it, the space was now being used as a graveyard for broken chairs, old desks, and other unidentifiable junk.

They descended into the room via the rope, searched the floor to make sure no threats were present, and took the stairs down to the second floor.

Most of the rooms there looked as unused as the ones above. The one glaring exception was the relatively dust-free room at the end of the hall, where three sets of bunk beds had been stuffed inside. The beds were made up as if ready for guests, and sitting against one wall was a table with six unopened water bottles lined up on it in a neat row. Next to the water was an empty box that had once held energy bars.

The lack of any bags or personal items indicated no one was currently using the space, but just in case, Nate removed his Glock from its holster before they proceeded.

Upon reaching the ground floor, he crept to the open stairwell doorway and listened. The building was silent, but he sensed…*something*. Jar must have, too, because she held as still as he did.

Another thirty seconds passed.

A minute.

Then—

A scrape. Soft and short.

They crept through the doorway into a vast, high-ceilinged room with at least a dozen shadowy hunks of rusty machinery running down the center.

They heard the sound again, this time accompanied by a very human grumble or huff. Jar pointed at the machine nearest where the sounds had come from, and made a gesture conveying the noise had come from the other side of it. Nate acknowledged with a nod, and they quietly sneaked from machine to machine until they reached the one shielding whoever it was.

Jar went left and Nate right. As he neared the back end, the person coughed, low and phlegmy, then spit. Nate peeked around the machine and spotted a woman sitting on the ground about two meters away, her back to him.

The glow of a phone or computer spilled around her like a halo. From the way the light flickered, Nate guessed she was watching a video. He couldn't hear anything, though, so either she was wearing earbuds or the sound was off.

Her shoulder-length hair was gray and matted, and she wore a winter jacket that had been patched up with different types of tape.

At the other end of the machine, he saw Jar step out.

The unknown woman's attention was glued to her screen and she didn't react.

Nate stepped out to match Jar, and purposely dragged a foot across the cement. The scrape wasn't loud but should have been enough for the woman to hear. Still, she didn't move.

Earbuds, then.

Nate held up a hand to get Jar's attention and motioned for her to meet him back at the other end.

"She probably lives here," he whispered once they were together.

Jar nodded. "It's possible she saw something. You should ask her."

"Me? I was thinking you."

"Why?"

"Because she might feel less threatened by you."

"Really?"

She had a point. Jar did not exactly exude warmth.

"Okay, fine," he said. "I'll—"

"Who the hell are you?" a gravelly voice barked in French behind him.

He turned. The woman stood at the corner of the machine,

scowling at them. In her hands was a metal rod, cocked and ready to strike.

"We don't want trouble," Nate said in French.

"Too late!"

She feigned a step toward him.

"There's no need for anyone to get hurt," he said.

"If you don't answer my question, there is."

"Right. Sorry. I'm Nate." He gestured behind him. "She's Jar. And you are?"

"The person who will bash in your head if you don't leave me alone."

"That's kind of a mouthful. Do you have a nickname, perhaps?"

Behind Nate, he heard Jar groan and say, "*Parlez vous anglais?*"

The woman's gaze shifted to her. "A little," she said in English.

Jar stepped next to Nate. "Do not pay attention to him. He thinks he is funny but he is not."

When the woman laughed, Nate sensed she knew more than just a little English.

"May I ask you a question?" Jar said.

A beat passed before the woman said, "*D'accord.*"

Jar pointed up. "Have you seen the people who were staying upstairs?"

"Everyone gone."

"Which means you have seen them," Nate said.

The woman raised the rod a few centimeters. "She say to not listen to you."

"Oh, for God's sake."

"When was the last time someone was there?" Jar asked.

"I do not know. *Peut-être deux jours.* Two days. Three." The woman shrugged.

"Is it common for no one to be there?"

The woman wrinkled her brow in confusion.

Jar batted Nate's arm with the back of her hand. "Ask her."

"You told her not to listen to me."

"Ask her."

He repeated Jar's question in French.

"Sometimes yes, sometimes no." the woman said in English.

"The last people who were here—did they leave anything behind?" Jar asked.

The woman's hand dropped to a rectangular shape in her jacket pocket.

"The mobile phone you were watching the movie on?" Jar said.

The woman turned the pocket away from them and tightened her grip on the rod.

"We'll buy it from you."

"*Non.* It is mine!" She took another step backward and looked on the verge of running away.

"We'll give you two thousand euros," Nate said.

The woman froze. "Two *thousand*?"

"For the phone and anything else that was left behind that you might have," Jar said.

The woman glanced at her pocket, clearly reluctant to give up such a prized possession.

"And a new phone," Jar said. "We will give you the money tonight and bring the phone tomorrow."

The woman's eyes narrowed. "Tomorrow?"

"We promise," Nate said.

The woman put both hands on the club and again looked like she was about to flee.

"*I* promise," Jar said.

She and the woman shared a long look before the woman finally asked, "You get me Netflix, too?"

13

"What do you mean, there's nothing else to report?" Adrian Rapace all but shouted into his phone. "They haven't been seen since they were taken off the plane! Report that."

"We've already published dozens of articles about it," Paul Marchant said. Marchant was a reporter at *Le Parisien*, and the only contact there who still took Rapace's calls.

"You should be publishing something about them every day."

"You know that's impossible."

"If you don't, people will forget, and Uri and Anya will never be freed."

"Adrian, I sympathize with what you're trying to do. What happened to them is horrible."

"Yes, it is."

Marchant continued as if Rapace hadn't interrupted him. "And we will write about them again, but not until there is something new to write about."

"Uri's a reporter just like you and me. What happened to him could happen to either of us. If you went missing, how would you feel if everyone forgot about you?"

"No one's forgetting about—"

"They will if you stop reminding everyone what happened."

"Adrian, please. I'm on your—"

Someone knocked on Rapace's door.

"—side, but we also can't continue to rehash the same thing over and over."

Another knock, louder this time.

Rapace moved the phone away from his mouth. "One moment." Into the phone, he said, "You have to find a way."

Marchant sighed. "I'll do what I can."

Rapace knew it was a brush-off, but it wasn't a no. "They're counting on you, Paul."

"I need to go. I'll talk to you later."

As the line went dead, Rapace's visitor knocked a third time.

Rapace shoved his phone into his pocket and headed to the door. Though it was after eleven p.m., it wasn't unusual for one or more of his friends to drop by to see how they could help with his effort to keep Uri and Anya in the news.

He'd thought keeping their story alive would be easy. Two people physically pulled from an airplane that had been forced to land should have led the news for months. Especially since there were over a dozen videos of the event online.

But the world was a dumpster fire, and it was only a matter of days before some new calamity captured the public's attention.

He reached the door as the person on the other side knocked again.

"Yes?" he said. "Who is it?"

"Police."

Thinking there was news about Uri and Anya, Rapace pulled the door open.

Three men stood in the hallway, each seeming larger than the last.

"Adrian Rapace?" the middle giant said.

"That's me. Is this about the Sobolevskys?"

The speaker answered by knocking Rapace in the chest and sending him flying onto the hardwood floor. Before Rapace could process what was happening, one of the other men yanked him back to his feet.

"You talk too much," the giant said, his accent foreign.

"What? What do you—"

A fist slammed into his face. The only reason Rapace didn't fall again was due to the hand still holding on to him.

He heard crashing noises behind him, but he was too stunned to look for the cause.

"Forget your friends. Understand me?"

Rapace blinked, the dots finally connecting. This was about Uri and Anya.

"I asked if you understand," the giant said before hitting Rapace in the face again.

The blow sent the reporter spinning into his dining table. Before he stopped moving, he was grabbed again and spun around to face his attacker. He could now see the other two, opening cabinets and sweeping everything inside onto the floor.

"You will stop," the monster said. "If you do not, we will come back. And if we come back, we will kill you. Do you understand?"

"Yes," Rapace whispered, his voice weak.

"What?"

"Yes," Rapace repeated. "I understand."

"Good, but in case you forget…"

A fist smashed into his face again, and again, and again.

"I was going to make a sign that said 'Welcome home, sweet cheeks' but in French, of course," Nate said to Daeng. He and Jar had just picked up Daeng at the airport and were driving back into Paris. "Jar wouldn't let me. Buzzkill."

"I did not say no to kill your buzz," Jar said. "I said no because it was unoriginal and not funny."

"I see you two are still getting along just fine," Daeng said.

"Why would we not get along?" Jar asked, seriously.

"Because I know how Nate can be, and I figured you would have gotten sick of him by now."

"Ah. Yes, that makes sense. I have been working on my patience."

"Hey," Nate said, "I'm sitting right here."

"You started it by calling me a buzzkill," Jar said.

"She has a point," Daeng said.

Nate pressed his lips together and focused on the road.

"How is Charlie?" Jar asked Daeng.

Daeng's smile broadened. "Perfect."

"No one is perfect."

"Wait until you're a parent and then tell me that."

"Why would that change anything?"

"You know what?" Daeng said. "You're right. In your case, it probably wouldn't."

"Of course I'm right."

Twenty minutes later, Jar checked at the map on her phone. "Two more blocks and then park."

Once they were stopped, Nate glanced at the buildings lining the other side of the street. "Which one is it?"

Jar pointed at a ten-story building on the corner of the upcoming intersection. She'd studied the blueprints of the building while they were waiting for Daeng, and now silently counted off the floors before picking out the correct window. "His apartment is the one on the seventh floor. The one with the lights on."

"Maybe he's still up," Nate said.

"Or he left them on when he went out," Daeng countered.

"Okay, do we pay him a visit now or get some rest and come back in the morning?" Nate asked.

"I slept most of the way here," Daeng said. "I say we check if he's home."

Jar voiced her opinion by opening her door and climbing out.

"So now, then," Nate said.

This stop was one of the items on the to-do list Orlando had given them. The thought was that Adrian Rapace, the reporter colleague of Uri Sobolevsky and his wife, Anya, might have information that would aid the mission, and it was to his apartment they were heading.

The entrance to the building had a security door and an intercom system, but calling up to Rapace was not necessary. Someone had taped down the door's latch so that it couldn't lock.

"Great security," Daeng said.

"Does anyone else feel uneasy?" Nate asked.

Jar nodded.

They saw no one on their way to the elevator. The car itself was not occupied when they got in, nor did it make any additional stops on the way to the seventh floor.

They walked down to apartment 74 and Nate knocked.

No answer.

"Maybe he did go out," Daeng said.

Nate knocked again, but still nothing.

Jar pressed her ear against the door. She heard something, hushed and raspy. When it repeated, she took a step back. "There is someone inside."

"Could he be asleep?" Nate asked.

"I don't think so. We need to open the door. Now."

Though Nate could be annoying at times, one of the many things Jar liked about him was he always trusted her instincts.

From his wallet, he retrieved a plastic card into which was scored a set of disposable lock picks. He punched them out and made quick work of the lock, then inched the door open far enough to get a peek inside.

"Shit." He shoved the door the rest of the way open.

He rushed into the apartment, with Jar and Daeng right behind him. Lying in the middle of the room was a man, and despite the blood oozing from his mouth and nose, Jar recognized him as Rapace.

Whoever had done this to the reporter had also done a job on his apartment. Bookshelves and cabinets and counters had been swept clean, their contents scattered across the floor. In the kitchen, plates and bowls lay in shattered piles.

Nate checked Rapace's pulse. "Steady but weak."

Jar helped him check the man for injuries. Rapace's nose was broken, and his right eye was swollen shut, possibly indicating an orbital fracture. Jar touched Rapace's belly and he reflexively jerked away.

"He needs a doctor," Nate said.

"That is obvious," she said.

Rapace's good eye opened a few millimeters and closed again.

"Adrian?" Nate said in French. "Can you hear me?"

Rapace's eye opened again. "Who...."

"It's okay. We're here to help."

"Who...are you?"

"Friends."

"I...don't...I don't know...you."

"Not important right now," Jar said in English. "Who did this to you?"

His gaze shifted slowly to her and he said, also in English, "They...wanted to...shut me...up."

"About Uri and Anya?"

"Yes."

"How many were they?" Nate asked.

"Three."

"And *will* you shut up?" Jar asked.

He tried to laugh and ended up coughing. When he regained control of his voice, he said, "They would have to...kill me first."

"They might just do that," Nate said.

Rapace shrugged. "I'm not...going...to stop."

Jar turned to Nate. "It would be safer to send him someplace private."

"Agreed."

There were medical institutions used by the general public, and then there were facilities that catered to those who worked in areas hidden from the rest of society. Places where treatments for wounds that would normally be reported to the police could be taken care of with no questions asked. Places where no one could find you.

Nate placed a call. Fifteen minutes later, a private ambulance arrived and Rapace was discreetly removed from the building.

Jar, Nate, and Daeng spent an additional quarter hour searching the room for anything that might assist them, and then made their way to the safe house.

14

Orlando punched a code into the pad next to the apartment building's entrance and pulled open the door.

"Hold up," Thomas said. "Whose place is this?"

"No idea," Quinn said.

The agent looked at him, confused. "How can you not know?"

"It's a safe house," Orlando said. "Like the place we stayed at in London. Who owns it doesn't matter."

Thomas snorted a laugh. "So, what—you're saying these places are everywhere?"

Orlando shrugged and she and Quinn entered the building without answering.

Hurrying after them, Thomas said, "Wait. Are these kinds of places everywhere?"

"What does it matter if they are?" Quinn asked.

"What about the States? Are there any there?"

"Again, what does it matter?"

"Because if there are, my bosses need to know."

"Trust me," Orlando said, "your bosses already know."

That stopped Thomas. "Do they know where they're located?"

"If they did," Quinn said, "these places wouldn't be safe houses, would they?"

They all headed up to the third floor and down the hall.

"How is an apartment *safe*?" Thomas asked. "You've got people living next door, above you, and below."

"How do you know that?" Orlando asked as she opened the door.

"Are you kidding me? Because there are apartments on three sides."

"Astute observation, Agent Thomas," Quinn said. "Go ahead and knock on the doors and see if anyone answers."

"Are...are you saying they're all empty?"

"Wouldn't be very safe if they weren't, would it?"

They found apartment 35 at the end of the hall. Orlando consulted her phone, put the correct code in the digital lock, and they entered.

"It took you three minutes longer than projected," Jar said.

She was sitting in the living room, working on her computer. There was no sign of Nate or Daeng.

Quinn smirked. "Good to see you, too."

Jar glanced at Thomas. "Who is she?"

"Who am *I*?" Thomas said. "Who are you?"

"Jar, this is Special Agent Nicole Thomas," Orlando said. "She will be joining us. Agent Thomas, this is Jar."

"Jar," Thomas said. "Like a...jar?"

"Is that a problem?" Jar asked.

Thomas ignored her and said to Quinn and Orlando, "She's just a kid."

"I am not a kid," Jar said matter-of-factly. "I am old enough to drink in your country."

"Oh, well, that makes me feel a lot better."

"Jar is an extremely competent and effective member of our team," Quinn said.

"If you say so."

"I do say so."

"Not only is she an excellent field agent," Orlando said, "she's smarter than all of us. You would be wise not to underestimate her."

Thomas stared at them for a few seconds, then turned back to Jar and said in a not-quite-conciliatory tone, "My apologies for calling you a child."

"Your mistake is understandable. I am small. An apology is unnecessary."

Thomas whispered to Orlando, "Does she always talk like that?"

"What is wrong with the way I talk?" Jar said.

"I probably should have mentioned that her hearing is also exceptional," Orlando said.

Thomas forced a laugh. "Right. Sorry again. And, um, nothing's wrong with the way you talk. You're just a little more direct than most people."

"I have noticed that, too," Jar said, and turned her attention back to her laptop.

"Where are Nate and Daeng?" Quinn asked.

"Sleeping."

"Still?"

"We did not arrive here until four a.m."

"Four? Did something happen?"

"Yes."

Quinn waited for more, but Jar seemed to have finished, so he said, "Could you elaborate?"

Jar raised her fingers off her keyboard, turned to Quinn, and in succinct Jar-like fashion, told them about the visit to the warehouse, picking up Daeng, and the subsequent events at Rapace's apartment.

"How is Rapace doing?" Orlando asked.

"I talked to his doctor twenty minutes ago. He has several injuries and will take some time to heal, but his life is not in danger."

A door opened somewhere deeper in the apartment, and a moment later Nate wandered into the living room.

"Morning," he said, then nodded at Thomas. "Who's this?"

"Special Agent Thomas," Jar said. "She thought I was a child."

"Hey, I already apologized for that," Thomas said.

Nate walked toward the kitchen. "Nice to meet you. Anyone else need coffee before I run out?"

"Where are you going?" Quinn asked.

"Promised someone a new phone."

Another door opened and Daeng entered the room. When he saw Thomas, he stopped in his tracks. "I remember you."

"Agent Thomas is working with us on this one," Quinn said.

"Is that so?" Daeng considered it and shrugged. "Welcome to the dark side."

"What's that supposed to mean?" Thomas asked.

"Even I can figure out that reference," Jar said.

Thomas looked at Jar, then Daeng, Nate, Orlando, and finally Quinn. She shook her head, sighed, and raised her bag. "Where can I put this?"

8:34 AM LOCAL TIME
LONDON

Simon Darnell glanced at the clock on his nightstand. It was already half eight. He should have been up an hour ago. But instead of getting out of bed, he pulled his comforter over his head and groaned.

Snippets of yesterday's encounter at his shop flashed in his mind.

You are in serious trouble.

My guess is at the end of that time, you'll be a guest of MI6.

He let out another groan. Life as he knew it was over.

Raven's Roost. Lucinda sleeping behind the counter while he helped customers. The weekly teas with Mrs. Abbott from the antique shop two stores down. All of that, days from disappearing.

Why had he ever agreed to be a conduit in the first place?

He should have let his bookshop go out of business. That would have been better than the shame and guilt he now felt. Not to mention the fact he'd likely be spending the rest of his life in prison. But oh, no, he'd chosen to take the cash and willful ignorance and the strings that came with them.

He was a fool. No, more than a fool. He was a—

His mobile rang.

His fingers tightened around the comforter, holding it over him as if the caller might reach through the line and rip it away.

Go away. Go away. Go away.

Finally, the ringing ceased. He waited a beat, relaxed his grip, and started to take a deep breath. Before he could blow it out, another call came in.

"Please!" he yelled. "Go away! Leave me alone!"

After five rings, the call went to voicemail and the room quieted again. Simon waited, expecting the caller to make a third attempt. But when a whole minute passed without that happening, he pulled the covers from his head.

The best way to make sure his mobile remained silent would be to turn it off. He grabbed it, intending to do just that.

It rang again.

"Oh, God," he said as he nearly dropped it.

The caller ID read UNKNOWN. That was the same ID that always appeared when he received calls from the people who used him to pass messages. He wanted to let the call go to voicemail again but knew he couldn't. He had made a promise to the woman. And if helping her made his future even slightly less horrible, he had to keep that promise.

Finger shaking, he touched ACCEPT. "Hello?"

"Did I wake you, Mr. Darnell?"

Simon's stomach clenched. As he feared, it was the Russians. The man on the other end was Simon's least favorite contact. Every word the man spoke dripped with condescending disinterest, like Simon was wasting the man's time.

"No. I'm awake."

"Then why did I have to call three times?"

"I'm sorry. I-I-I was in the shower."

"Shouldn't you be on your way to your store already?"

"I'm not feeling well." It wasn't a lie.

"But you *will* be going in."

"Oh, uh, yes. I'm just moving a little slow this morning."

"I suggest you pick up the pace. I have a friend who is looking for a book."

And there they were, the words Simon had known were coming. "Of course. And the title?"

"*Cat's Cradle* by Kurt Vonnegut, Jr. A first edition."

"I'm sure I can locate one. How soon does your friend need it?"

"It's a rush, I'm afraid. Eleven a.m."

Darnell blinked. "Eleven?"

"Is that a problem?"

"I-I don't…I mean, it's not a problem. I'll get right—"

The line went dead.

Darnell threw the comforter back and swung his legs off the bed. There would be no staying home today. The *Cat's Cradle* drop box was all the way over in Hammersmith, and if he was going to stop by Raven's Roost on the way and make it to the drop box by eleven, he needed to get moving.

But there was one thing he needed to do before anything else.

9:38 AM LOCAL TIME
PARIS

"It's mostly coded messages like this one," Jar said.

Quinn, Orlando, and Daeng were crowded behind her, looking at her computer screen. On it was a message retrieved from the phone Jar and Nate had bought from the homeless woman. It read:

Harvard carries twenty, seen on lamppost. Will send former
flowers.

"I hope I'm not the only one who thinks that doesn't make any
sense," Daeng said.

"You are not," Jar said.

"Is there anything on the phone that will decode it?" Quinn
asked.

"There is not," Jar said.

"Would it help to run it through an analyzer?" The team had
access to programs that could analyze messages and often figure
out what kind of code was being used.

"That was the first thing I did. The code could not be
determined."

"Is there anything on the phone that *can* help us?"

"Yes," Jar said and clicked open another file. The document
consisted of two columns of multi-digit numbers.

"More code?" Daeng asked.

"No." She clicked a tab at the bottom of the document and
another page appeared. It was similar to the first page, but now
each string of numbers contained a decimal point near the start.

"GPS locations," Orlando said.

Jar nodded.

"To where?" Quinn asked.

Jar brought up a world map, upon which several red dots
glowed. She pointed to the one hovering over New York City.
"This is the first location on the list." She pointed at the dot over
Athens, Greece. "Second." She pointed at the one above London.
"Third." Her finger moved to Chicago. "Fourth." With her finger
still hovering over the last stop, she said, "Dr. Andrei Barsukov."
She moved back to London. "Filip Krutov." And Athens. "Uri and
Anya Sobolevsky."

"I thought the Sobolevskys were taken in Minsk," Daeng said.

"They were," Jar said. "But their flight originated in Athens.
And that is where they had been living."

Quinn reached over Jar's shoulder and pointed at the New York dot. "Dimitri Melnikov."

"Correct."

"How many locations are there?" Orlando asked.

"Seventeen."

"Then if this list is what you're suggesting," Quinn said, "there are at least thirteen additional targets who either have already been taken or will be."

"From my analysis—"

"What list?" Thomas said as she walked into the room.

Orlando brought her up to speed.

"There are—how many did you say?" Thomas asked Quinn. "Thirteen others?"

He nodded.

"Do we know who they are?"

"The list is only locations. No names. Right, Jar?"

"Yes."

"Then I don't see how this helps us," Thomas said. "We're supposed to be finding out where Melnikov is *now*, not speculating about other targets. If we succeed at getting him out, the Russians will have no choice but to let go of whoever they have and stop the kidnappings."

"No choice?" Orlando said. "Have you ever dealt with the Russians?"

"The list may not be useful right now, but it could be in the future," Quinn said. "So I'm not ready to discount it out of hand."

"Quinn is wrong," Jar said. "And you, Agent Thomas, are shortsighted."

In unison, Quinn and Thomas said, "I am?"

"Yes." She looked at Quinn. "If you had let me finish, you would know the list is useful now. As I was about to say when Agent Thomas joined us, my analysis indicates that none of the additional targets have been taken yet."

"And how exactly do you know that?" Thomas asked.

Jar picked up the leatherbound notebook next to her computer. "I found this at Adrian Rapace's apartment last night." She opened it to a page marked by a strap. The page was filled with writing in French. "He uses this journal to record anything he thinks might have something to do with Uri and Anya's kidnapping. On this page, he makes the connection between their abduction and those of Barsukov and Krutov. He has yet to suspect Melnikov is also a victim. Most likely this is because he thinks Melnikov is dead."

"Since when do you read French?" Quinn asked.

"I have been learning. Also, in the interest of time, I may have used a translation app."

Jar turned to another page, marked this time by a slip of paper. On it was a list of names.

"These are people Rapace thinks the Russians might target in the future."

"How many?" Quinn asked.

Jar looked at him, eyebrow cocked. "Thirteen."

"Really? Huh. Do you know—"

Jar held up a hand. "If you will let me finish."

"Sorry."

After a couple of clicks on her track pad, the red dots representing GPS locations disappeared from the map and thirteen yellow dots appeared.

"Based on the most up-to-date information I could find, the new markers are where the people on Rapace's list live." She clicked another button, and the yellow markers were joined by the seventeen red ones. Every yellow marker had a corresponding red marker. The only markers unpaired were the four red ones representing those already taken—Melnikov, the Sobolevskys, Krutov, and Barsukov.

"Good work, Jar," Orlando said.

"Could be coincidences," Thomas said. "Correlation does not mean causation, right?"

Jar zoomed in on a pair of dots over Florence, Italy, until only a single city block filled the screen. The dots glowed from the exact same spot within the outline of a building.

"That doesn't look like a coincidence to me," Quinn said.

"Fine," Thomas said. "Maybe that one's right. It doesn't mean the others—"

"The other twelve are like this one," Jar said. "Rapace is a trained investigative reporter. He knows what he's doing."

"Okay. But I stand by what I said earlier. I don't see how this helps us."

"And I stand by what I said. You are being shortsighted."

Thomas forced a smile. "Perhaps you can enlighten me."

"Is it not obvious?" Jar looked at her and then the others. When no one spoke up, she sighed. "Isn't our priority to find out where the detainees have been taken?"

"It is," Quinn said.

Jar waited. When no one spoke again, she rolled her eyes and motioned at her screen. "These people are on the to-be-kidnapped list. When the next one is abducted, where do you think they will likely be taken?"

"Oh, crap," Orlando said. "To where Melnikov and the others are being held. If we can get to them before they are kidnapped, bug them, then when one is abducted, we can track where they go."

"Like I said. It is obvious."

"What do you mean track them?" Thomas asked. "Put a bug in their shoe?"

"A bug in a shoe will be easily found," Jar said. "The best location would be subcutaneous."

"You want to plant trackers under the skin of thirteen people?"

"I did not say that." Jar clicked her track pad and a list of the thirteen potential abductees replaced the map. "This is the order of who I believe will most likely be taken next. To be safe, I think we should bug the first four."

"And you determine the order how?" Thomas asked

"By considering many factors, such as accessibility, how large of an annoyance they have been to the Russian government, what they—"

Quinn put a hand on Jar's shoulder, stopping her. "Agent Thomas, Jar is not one to speculate easily. When she does, I can guarantee she has done her homework."

"Let's pretend that she's right. Do you—"

"There is nothing to pretend," Jar said. "I am right."

Thomas took a breath. "Do you honestly believe anyone on that list will volunteer to be taken, let alone bugged?"

"We will not know until we ask them," Jar said.

"I can tell you right now, the only thing they'll be interested in will be finding someplace to hide."

"I'm not sure I agree with that," Quinn said. "These people have been speaking out against their government for years. When we explain why we need their help, there's a decent chance at least one of them will say yes."

"A chance, sure," Thomas said. "But a decent one?" She shook her head.

The front door opened and Nate walked in.

"Was she there?" Jar asked him.

"Oh, yeah," Nate said. "And she wasn't happy. She swore that we promised to give her all the streaming networks for free, not just Netflix."

"What did you tell her?"

"That we'd look into it."

"I'll take care of it," Jar said.

Orlando's phone vibrated on the table.

She glanced at the screen. "Everyone quiet." She raised the phone to her ear. "Yes?....That's right....When did this happen?....What was said?....As best you can remember....All right. Don't do anything until you hear from me....Yes, I understand the time constraints. I'll call you back in a few minutes." She hung up and looked at the others. "Everyone grab your stuff. We need to go."

"Go where?" Quinn said.

"That was Mr. Darnell. He just received a request for one of his special books. It's being delivered today."

"You heard Orlando," Quinn said. "We leave in five."

15

LONDON

Thanks to the one-hour time difference between France and the UK and the use of a private jet, the team made it to London by ten a.m. local time. Forty-five minutes later, they were on the grounds of Waltham Abbey in north London, where the Kurt Vonnegut drop box was located.

Orlando had not told Darnell they would be there to witness the pickup, as it would be better for him to remain focused on the task at hand than thinking about who might be watching him. Since Darnell had never met Nate, Daeng, or Jar, the three took positions that might be seen by him.

According to Darnell, the *Cat's Cradle* drop box was located at a wooden bench in the walled garden—specifically, in a hollowed-out nook on the underside. Nate was currently sitting on said bench, reading a newspaper, while Daeng and Jar were following Darnell as he walked toward the garden from the taxi drop-off on the other side of the grounds.

Quinn was ensconced on a garden path ten meters from the bench, hidden from view by a tangle of leafless bushes. Orlando and Thomas were in similar positions near the garden entrance.

"Fifty meters away," Daeng said over the comm.

"Copy," Quinn whispered.

He eyed the bald man loitering near several hibernating rose-bushes. A few minutes before Darnell's cab arrived, Quinn had spotted the loiterer and had a feeling the man was a watcher for the Russians. Quinn had kept tabs on him since. Given that the man was now staring toward the approaching Darnell, Quinn considered his suspicion confirmed.

"Entering rose garden," Daeng said.

"Copy," Quinn replied.

At the bench, Nate tucked his newspaper under his arm, stood, and started down the path to the garden entrance. He passed Darnell and continued on his way to his next task.

Quinn watched Darnell arrive at the bench and sit down. After resting for about a minute, the bookseller reached under the bench, removed the message from the nook, and slid it into his jacket pocket. He sat there for another two minutes doing nothing. According to what he'd told Orlando, this was what the Russians had instructed him to do each time he retrieved a message.

As soon as he rose and began walking back the way he'd come, Quinn said, "He's leaving."

Just before he reached the garden exit, Jar said, "We see him." She and Daeng had repositioned to the midway point between the garden and the street at the other end of the grounds.

An automated voice came over the comm. "Heading to the train station." This was from Nate, who had walked straight to the street to catch a cab to the train station. He was using a text-to-speech app to avoid the cabbie overhearing him. It did not prevent Nate from being Nate, however, as the voice came on again and said, "I sound like a TV robot."

"Cut the chatter," Quinn said.

"Yes, Commander. Beep. I hear and obey. Beep."

"How do you people ever get anything done?" Thomas asked.

"I said, cut the chatter."

Quinn's attention was now focused on the watcher, who was following Darnell via a different path, eyes locked on the bookseller's back.

"The leech is still on him," Quinn said.

"Copy," Jar and Orlando replied, one after the other.

Quinn scanned the area, making sure no additional operatives were present, then began following the watcher. When he reached Orlando and Thomas's position, they joined him.

It took Darnell five minutes to reach the street. As he approached one of the waiting cabs, the watcher stopped, so Quinn, Orlando, and Thomas did the same. Darnell climbed into the taxi and it departed. The moment it was out of sight, the watcher headed leisurely down a path that led to a different street, the man's mission clearly completed.

Because of lucky breaks with traffic lights and the promise of a generous tip, the cabbie dropped Nate off at the Waltham Cross train station ten minutes before Darnell arrived.

This gave Nate plenty of time to scope out the passengers for any additional watchers. No one set off any of his internal alarms.

When Darnell showed up, he looked as if he might jump out of his own skin at the slightest provocation. Jar and Daeng walked onto the platform next, and a minute later Quinn's voice came over the comm. "Just arrived. How are things looking?"

"No sign of trouble," Nate reported.

"Good. Continue as planned."

The train arrived right on schedule. Daeng and Jar boarded the same car Darnell did, while the rest of the team members divided themselves between the remaining cars and moved through the train, alert for potential problems, as it headed into the city.

At Tottenham Hale station, they switched to the Tube, made two line changes, and finally exited at a station six blocks from the bookstore. When they reached ground level, Orlando sent Darnell a text.

Find a café and have a coffee. In 15 minutes, head to the store.

Nate, Quinn, Orlando, and Thomas continued to Raven's Roost, while Jar and Daeng remained behind to keep an eye on the bookseller. Once they were sure the area around the bookshop was free of any watchers, they let themselves into the store and made sure it was also free of trouble.

Right on time, Daeng's voice came over the comm. "He's on the way."

"Copy," Quinn said.

Darnell entered the bookstore six minutes later, and froze at the sight of Quinn, Orlando, Nate, and Thomas standing near the counter, waiting for him.

"Good to see you again, Mr. Darnell," Orlando said.

"Yes, em...hello."

At the sound of the door opening behind him, Darnell whirled around and stared wide-eyed at Jar and Daeng as they entered.

"Relax," Orlando said. "They're with us."

Jar locked the door.

"Do you have the message?" Orlando asked.

"I...yes," he answered.

"May we see it?"

He chewed the inside of his cheek. "Em..."

"It *is* why you called us, remember?" Orlando said. "Or have you decided not to cooperate? If so, I need to call MI6." She pulled out her phone.

"No," he said quickly. "That's not necessary. Of course you can see it." He shoved his hand into his jacket pocket and pulled out a brown square, but didn't hand it over. "The thing is...the messages...they're always sealed. I-I was told to never open them."

Orlando held out her hand. He hesitated another second, then reluctantly put the square in her palm.

She flipped it around and looked at each side. "What if it opened accidentally? What were you supposed to do then?"

"I was told that would never happen."

"Has it?"

"No."

She handed the message to Quinn, and he and Nate examined it. The square was about the width of a US quarter, half a centimeter thick, and made from some kind of plastic. Nate had seen something similar once before, on a mission that—surprise, surprise—involved Russian intelligence. He knew if the container was not opened in the correct way, a chemical reaction would dissolve the message inside before it could be removed.

"Was anything different about the pickup this time?" Orlando asked.

Darnell shook his head.

"Good. Now, Mr. Darnell, if you wouldn't mind, may we use your storeroom for a few minutes?"

"My storeroom?"

"Or we could take the message with us."

A new wave of terror flashed in his eyes. "Please, by all means, use my storeroom. No need to take it anywhere."

Nate felt kind of sorry for the guy. Darnell clearly had no idea whom he should be more scared of: them or his Russian handlers.

The correct answer was both.

Orlando, Quinn, and Jar retreated to the storeroom. After a beat, Thomas followed them.

Darnell looked at Nate and Daeng. "You're not all going?"

"Nah," Nate said. "They don't need our help. Besides, my friend and I are both looking for something to read."

Darnell's brow creased. "What?"

"This *is* a bookstore, isn't it?"

"Oh, em, it is."

"Great. Perhaps you can point me in the direction of a good fantasy."

From behind the counter, Lucinda meowed.

"I think your cat's hungry," Daeng said.

∼

This was the first time Jar had seen a package like this. She held it up to the light, wondering if it was translucent. It was not.

"May I tap on it?"

"Sure," Orlando said. She was rummaging through her back-pack, looking for something. "But only on the top or bottom, not the edges."

Jar tapped a fingertip against the square. The smooth plastic covering didn't bend from her touch. Holding the square close, she turned it around, looking for a seam. When she finally saw it, she nodded in appreciation. It was so thin she almost missed it. The container was truly a work of art.

"You've opened these before?" she asked as she set it on the storeroom table.

"Once," Quinn said.

"Twice, actually," Orlando said.

Quinn looked at her, surprised. "Twice?"

"Something I helped Misty with." Orlando attached a scanner wand to her phone and waved it over the square. "This isn't the best way to do this, but it's all we have to work with."

On her phone's screen was a grainy black and white image, similar to a sonagram. Jar could clearly make out the shape of a folded piece of paper inside the square but nothing else.

Orlando ran the wand along the edges, then went back and forth along one side before saying, "There it is."

On her screen was a tiny, almond-shaped dark spot near the midpoint of an edge.

Orlando exchanged her phone for two magnets, each the diameter of a dime. She placed one on either side of the dark spot, then scooted the magnets along the edges. Before she reached a corner of the square, it opened like a book.

Orlando glanced at Jar. "You use the magnets anywhere else and it's poof, no more message."

"Thank you," Jar said. She loved learning from Orlando. She always explained things clearly and directly.

Using tweezers, Orlando extracted the paper inside. She

checked it for foreign substances before she unfolded it, still with only the tweezers to avoid leaving any fingerprints.

The message was in English.

Vassily Levkin
Málaga
Extract team in place in 36 hours
Contact Bravo

"That's one of the names on the list, isn't it?" Thomas said.

"Yes," Jar said. "He is number three."

"I think he just moved up to number one," Thomas said.

Jar noticed Quinn frowning at the paper. "Is there something wrong?"

He didn't seem to hear her, but before she could ask again, Orlando said, "Quinn knows him. And I've met him once. We had a mutual friend."

Thomas looked at Quinn. "This guy's your friend?"

"Acquaintance," Quinn said.

"Do you think he will let us bug him?" Jar asked.

"I guess we'll find out, won't we?"

The team split up again.

While Quinn, Orlando, Jar, and Thomas headed to Spain on the private jet, Nate and Daeng remained in London, to see who showed up at Raven's Roost to pick up the message and follow the person when they left. They took hidden positions at either end of the block and waited.

At 6:37 p.m., a man in his late thirties, wearing a black peacoat and gloves, exited a cab and entered the shop.

Nate switched on the feed from the camera they'd put inside the bookstore in time to catch the man walk up to the counter and say, "I'm looking for a first edition of *Cat's Cradle* by Kurt Vonnegut."

"I believe I have one in back," Darnell said, sounding a little too nervous for Nate's liking. "One moment."

"It's Felix," Nate said over the comm, using the codename for the message receiver.

"Copy," Daeng responded.

Darnell walked toward the storeroom in back and moved out of frame. When he returned, he had the book with him.

"It's my last copy."

"Whatever. I'll take it."

Darnell handed it to the man and the man handed him an envelope. Per the bookseller, this was how he was paid.

"Would you like a bag?"

"Sure. Why not?"

A half minute later, Felix exited the shop, bag in hand, and headed left down the sidewalk.

"Coming your way," Nate said into his comm. "I'll catch up with you as soon as I can."

"Copy."

Nate scanned the street for anyone who might be working with Felix. When he was satisfied the man had come alone, he returned to the shop.

Darnell looked drained when Nate walked in.

"You all right?" Nate asked.

"I'm just glad that's over with."

"You did well. Thank you."

Darnell nodded in acknowledgement but said nothing.

"We'll be leaving that where it is," Nate said, gesturing at the micro camera hidden on a shelf behind the counter. "So stay on your best behavior."

"When...when will they come for me?"

"I don't know," Nate said. "Until they do, continue your normal routine."

The truth was, Quinn and Orlando had not informed Annabel

of the bookseller's situation yet. That would occur right after Nate texted them that the message had been picked up.

Looking more defeated than ever, Darnell mumbled, "Okay."

"Look at it this way. If the Russians were the ones who shut you down, you'd probably be dead now. Your countrymen aren't that cruel. They'll just lock you up for life."

Given the way the remaining blood drained from Darnell's face, Nate realized perhaps that hadn't been the right thing to say.

16

The first time Quinn met Vassily Levkin had been the year before Nate became Quinn's apprentice, back in the dark days when he and Orlando had not been talking to each other.

Quinn had been on a job in Barcelona with his late friend Julien.

"Dinner?" Julien asked. "My treat."

It had been a long day, and Quinn wanted nothing more than to return to his hotel room and sleep. But resisting the large gregarious Frenchman was not a simple task, and it didn't take much prodding before Quinn relented.

The restaurant Julien took him to turned out to be owned by Vassily. As soon as the Russian expat spotted them, he strode across the dining room and wrapped Julien in a bear hug. With both men being tall and wide, it was quite the sight.

When they parted, Julien motioned toward Quinn. "This is the man I told you about."

Quinn tensed. Why would Julien talk to this man about him? Before he could say as much, Vassily engulfed him in a hug. Thankfully, it didn't last as long as the one with Julien.

As he stepped back, Vassily said, "You are most welcome. As they say, any friend of my friend is also my friend."

"Um...thanks?" Quinn shot a questioning look at Julien, but Julien didn't meet his gaze.

Vassily escorted them to a secluded table on the deck overlooking the Mediterranean and took the chair next to Quinn. "If you will allow me, I will order for you." Not waiting for Julien and Quinn's assent, he called a waiter over and rattled off several items. When Vassily finished, he said to Quinn, "So, I understand you are here on business."

Quinn gave him a tight-lipped smile but said nothing.

"Right, right. I am sorry. I forget." He gestured at Julien. "If you are like him, business for you is hush-hush, *da*?" He laughed, then leaned in and whispered, "Not to worry. I understand." He pointed a thumb at his chest. "Former KGB."

"Is that so?" Quinn glanced at Julien again, but the Frenchman still wouldn't look at him.

"Da," Vassily said. "But was a long time ago, so do not hold against me." He laughed.

"And now you're a restaurateur."

"I love this word. Restaurateur. Sounds important."

The small talk continued through dinner, and it wasn't until *tarta de queso* had arrived for dessert that Quinn learned Vassily's business interests were not limited to the food industry. It turned out the Russian also provided services—both legitimate and not so much—to Russian citizens living abroad.

After that bomb dropped, Julien jumped in with, "Vassily has something he could use our help with."

Quinn fought hard to keep his expression neutral. The Frenchman knew better than to set him up like this without warning. Especially when the third party was former KGB. With remarkable calm, Quinn said, "There seems to be a misunderstanding. I don't take work from individuals."

"Just hear him out," Julien said.

No longer able to contain himself, Quinn stared at his "friend" as if he'd lost his mind.

"I am serious," Julien said. "You will like it."

"Jonathan," Vassily said. "May I call you Jonathan?"

"No."

"Mr. Quinn, then?"

"Quinn."

Vassily gave him a sympathetic smile. "Quinn, I think conversation has taken unnecessary bad turn. Please accept my apologies. I not mean to insult you."

"*You* haven't insulted me. You didn't know any better." Quinn switched his gaze to Julien. "You, on the other hand..."

"Whoa, my friend," Julien said. "This is just a little talk, that is all. It does not hurt to listen. Besides, like I say before, you will like it."

Quinn glared at him, and seriously considered getting up and leaving. The only thing that kept him from doing so was the fact Julien had always been a reliable colleague, excellent resource, and someone who had never done anything to get Quinn into trouble. He could at least hear the Russian out.

"Fine," he said. "I'll listen, but I'm telling you now the answer is no."

Both Julien and Vassily smiled.

"It is very small job I am needing," Vassily said. "One or two days, no more."

"One or two days I won't be giving you," Quinn reminded him.

Vassily laughed. "Good. Very good. I like you, Quinn."

"I *was* starting to like you, too."

This time Vassily laughed so loudly, several diners at the other end of the deck turned to see what the ruckus was all about.

"I appreciate your honesty," the Russian said. "Tell me, how do you feel about child slavery?"

"I fall firmly in the anti- camp."

"*Da, da.* Me, same. Is terrible thing, no? Let me tell you story."

The story Vassily wove concerned a man named Avros Yurlov, who had set up a facility in Burkina Faso in Western Africa, for the manufacturing of ecstasy and amphetamines and whatever else he could get away with. Most of his factory employees were unpaid children, ostensibly working off the debts of their parents. As for the pills, they were distributed throughout southern Europe.

"I am putting together group to remove Yurlov from power," Vassily said.

"I'm not an assassin," Quinn said.

"And I am not asking you to kill anyone. That is job of others. Better, though, I think if no one finds bodies after job is done. This I understand is specialty of yours?"

Julien was lucky he was sitting on the other side of the table, or Quinn would have punched him by now. Revealing what Quinn did for a living to Vassily was an even more egregious breach of trust than bringing Quinn unknowingly to a surprise meeting like this.

Instead, Quinn concentrated on the Russian's words. "Bodies? I thought you said you are only after Yurlov."

"If remove only him, one of his people take over and nothing change. Must eliminate his entire power structure."

"Why do you even care about any of this?"

"Yurlov's business is repulsive, and he gives all Russian expats bad name."

"Is it that? Or is he a competitor?"

For the first time, Vassily's good nature disappeared. He twisted his head and spit on the ground. "I do not deal in narcotics and I would never exploit children. Yurlov is rotting sewage."

Quinn would later learn there had indeed been some overlap between the men's businesses, just not with the drugs or child labor.

"Who would you exploit?"

This brought a smile back to the Russian's face. "If I can help it, no one."

"Okay, so you don't like the guy. And you don't like what he's doing. It still doesn't sound like enough to make you want to take him out."

Vassily shared a quick look with Julien. "If you will excuse me for moment. I need to show face around the restaurant. Makes diners feel special." He stood and walked away.

"Vassily has a hard time talking about this," Julien said. "His—"

"What the hell were you thinking? You told him what I do."

Julien seemed to shrink, not an easy task for someone his size. "I am sorry. I-I should have asked you first."

"Asked? No, Julien, you should have never considered it an option in the first place."

"It was a moment of weakness and too much whiskey. But I guarantee that you can trust Vassily, even if you do not take the job."

"You mean trust him like I thought I could trust you?"

Julien winced. "I deserve that."

"You deserve a lot more than that."

Julien nodded and kept his mouth shut.

Quinn looked away and took a few deep breaths to bring his anger under control. "Why does he hate this Yurlov guy so much?"

"Because Yurlov killed his nephew."

"How?"

"Bad drugs. After his nephew died, Vassily spent a lot of time and money tracing where the drugs had come from. That's how he found Yurlov."

"Vassily didn't know him before?"

"He did, but he didn't know Yurlov was in that particular business."

"So, this is a personal vendetta to avenge his nephew."

"*Oui*, in part. But if it was just the death of his nephew, I am pretty sure he would have found Yurlov and killed him himself. What he wants is Yurlov's *business* destroyed. He doesn't want another family to go through what he did."

"Even if he eliminates the entire operation, someone will fill the void," Quinn said. "Someone always does."

"Perhaps. But that does not mean Yurlov should be allowed to continue."

Quinn mulled that over until Vassily returned a few minutes later, carrying a bottle and three glasses.

"Is nothing like a little port after dinner, *da*?"

The Russian filled the glasses and passed them out.

Leaving his untouched, Quinn said, "Explain to me exactly what your plan is and what my part would be in it. In detail."

Vassily's eye lit up. "You will do it?"

"Let's just say it's not a firm no yet."

Exactly three weeks after the meeting at Vassily's restaurant, the entire power structure of Yurlov's operation had been eliminated. And thanks to Quinn, the bodies of each of the twenty-seven men and four women who had been terminated would never be found.

Not only did the disappearance of Yurlov and his associates send shock waves through the European organized crime world, it also did not escape the attention of the world's intelligence agencies. Peter, head of the original version of the Office, questioned Quinn about what was called the Yurlov Event, all but accusing him of being involved. Quinn played the no-matter-what-I-tell-you-you-won't-believe-me card and neither confirmed nor denied his role.

Over time, Quinn's feelings about the job became mixed. While he was glad it had happened and was satisfied with the results, finding out Vassily had benefited financially from Yurlov's death made Quinn feel used.

He didn't see Vassily again until several years later, when Quinn and Orlando were in Madrid, enjoying a few days off between jobs, and went to a restaurant recommended to them. It turned out the restaurant was owned by Vassily. When the

Russian came to their table to greet them, a terse, one-sided conversation ensued, in which Quinn let Vassily know exactly how he felt about being lied to. And as soon as Quinn had his say, he and Orlando left and ate somewhere else.

Neither had seen Vassily since.

17

Since Quinn's last conversation with Vassily Levkin, the Russian's restaurant empire had expanded considerably, to over forty-two restaurants throughout Spain and southern France. According to sources, he'd also gone legitimate and jettisoned his illegal gambling establishments, high-end escort businesses, and dodgy investment schemes.

More recently, in the wake of the Russian president's hard turn toward what amounted to a dictatorship, Vassily had taken on the role of anti-government agitator, mostly by funding organizations that helped people escape the country after they'd fallen afoul of the president and his cronies.

Another change from the time of Quinn and Vassily's last encounter was that Vassily had relocated his homebase from Barcelona to the port city of Málaga in southern Spain, where a pair of his restaurants were located. Hence the reason Quinn, Orlando, Jar, and Thomas had flown there.

"I count five bodyguards," Jar reported over the comm. She and Thomas were at a table inside the restaurant where Vassily was that evening.

Thomas's voice came over the comm next. "Five? I see only three."

"You are not counting the man eating alone at the table by the window," Jar said. "Or the woman at the front."

A pause, then, "The hostess? She can't be—"

"She is," Jar said.

"How can you possibly know that?"

"Because I do."

"Where's Vassily?" Quinn said. He and Orlando were on the sidewalk across the street, tucked into a dark nook.

"He's talking to some diners at the back," Jar said.

"See anyone there we need to worry about?" Orlando asked.

"Only his bodyguards."

"Okay," Quinn said. "We're coming in."

He and Orlando crossed the street and entered the restaurant.

"Good evening," the hostess/bodyguard greeted them in Spanish. "Two?"

"Yes," Orlando replied in kind.

"This way."

As they entered the dining room, Quinn noted the locations of Vassily and his bodyguards. The former was standing next to a table, laughing at something one of the diners had said. His mane of hair was more gray than brown now, and while he was still a big man, he had lost some weight and looked smaller than Quinn remembered. The guards, with the exception of the hostess, were all still where Jar had reported them to be.

The hostess took him and Orlando to a table with a view of the port through floor-to-ceiling windows. "A waiter will be with you shortly."

Before the hostess could turn away, Quinn nodded across the room and said, "Is that Vassily Levkin?"

The subtle tensing of her shoulders would have been missed by most, but not Quinn. She glanced toward Vassily and back, her smile leaving her eyes but not her lips. "It is. Do you know him?"

"I met him a long time ago at one of his restaurants in Barcelona. I would love to say hello, if he has a moment."

"I will let him know."

The hostess walked over to Vassily and waited a few steps away until there was a break in the conversation. When she whispered in his ear, his gaze flicked to Quinn and Orlando, and his pleasant smile turned surprised and curious. He said something to the hostess, who headed back toward the entrance.

From the slight movement of her lips as she walked, Quinn guessed she and the other bodyguards were wearing their own comm gear, and she was informing them of a potential threat from the diners she'd just seated. Right on cue, he could feel the eyes of her colleagues falling on him and Orlando.

Vassily stopped at one more table before he made his way to Quinn and Orlando's.

"This is a surprise," he said, his words underlined with his trademark laugh. "Long time no see, my friends."

"Hello, Vassily," Orlando said.

"Join us for a drink?" Quinn asked.

"I would love to, but I'm a very busy man these days. I don't—"

"Trust me. You'll need a drink."

Vassily and Quinn locked eyes for several seconds, before the Russian turned and motioned to one of the waiters. "A bottle of Vega Sicilia Unico Gran Reserva and three glasses, please."

After the waiter hurried off, Vassily pulled out a chair and sat. "I am surprised you would come here. I believe your last words to me were, if you ever see me again, you will kill me."

"Untrue," Quinn said. "My last words were if I ever saw you again, I wouldn't stop anyone else from killing you."

"Not quite same, I guess." Vassily touched his chest. "But still hurt."

"Then you'll be happy to know I was wrong."

"About what exactly?"

"That I wouldn't do anything if I found out someone wanted you dead."

The Russian cocked his head. "Are you telling me someone wants to kill me?"

"Eventually, though I believe they have other plans for you first."

Vassily leaned back. "You have my attention."

"This is probably something best discussed in a less public setting," Orlando said.

"Unless you are the ones here to kill me," Vassily said, grinning.

"No one's coming to kill you," Quinn said.

"Not *yet*."

"Right. Not yet. But even if they were, it's not us."

"And I'm to believe you because…?"

"As I told you a long time ago, I'm not an assassin."

Vassily nodded. "You did. But that doesn't mean you haven't killed before."

"Only when I had no choice."

"Okay," Vassily said, chuckling. "Somewhere more private, then. Would my office be acceptable?"

"We have someplace else in mind," Orlando said. "How do you feel about a boat ride?"

The boat was a cabin cruiser that normally took tourists on fishing day trips. That afternoon, a generous fee had secured its use for a no-questions-asked evening cruise.

Getting Vassily to say yes to taking a ride on it was not quite as easy.

"I am not so gullible to let you take me out to sea in the dark where no one will notice when you wrap weights around me and push me over side."

"I have never done that," Quinn said, then added, "to anyone who was alive, that is."

"Shoot me first then push me over."

"Again, not assassins."

They compromised by allowing Vassily to bring three of his

bodyguards, one of which was Silvia, the hostess who, it turned out, oversaw Vassily's security.

After the boat was underway, Quinn, Orlando, Vassily, and Silvia went belowdecks into the main cabin, while the others stayed in the enclosed bridge with the captain.

"So," Vassily said, "who are these people who don't want to kill me right away?"

"Not sure if you are aware of this or not," Quinn said, "but your friends back in Russia are rounding up people they aren't happy with."

Vassily leaned back. "You say that like I have friends there."

"A figure of speech."

"Of course I know this," Vassily said. "I know about everything that those assholes in Moscow do."

"Then I assume you also know Filip Krutov, Andrei Barsukov, and Uri and Anya Sobolevsky weren't the first people they took."

That got Vassily's attention. "Who was?"

"Dimitri Melnikov."

The Russian snorted. "Melnikov? He died last year. You must know about bombing in New York."

"Yeah, I was there."

"You were...what?"

"If I had been a few meters in almost any other direction, I wouldn't be here talking to you."

Vassily studied him for a moment. "You are serious."

"I was part of an operation that was supposed to get Melnikov someplace safe. Let's just say things didn't go the way we planned. Hell, after what happened, even I thought he was dead. But the bomb was a distraction that the Russians used to sneak him out."

"And Dimitri is *still* alive?"

"Our most up-to-date information says yes."

"The others, too?"

"Yep."

Vassily sneered. "Let me guess. You are here to tell me I am next."

"Still sharp as ever," Quinn said.

"And you know this how?"

Together, Quinn and Orlando laid out for him what they had learned.

When they finished, Vassily chuckled. "It is not like I not expect my actions to piss them off. Thank you for telling me." He jutted his chin toward Silvia. "My people will take the appropriate precautions."

"About that," Quinn said. "We're actually hoping they don't do that."

Silvia tensed, as if expecting a Russian snatch team to storm the room.

Vassily, on the other hand, looked amused. "This should be interesting. Tell me, why would I do nothing?"

"Our mission is to rescue those who have been taken."

Vassily looked stunned. "Are you joking?"

"I wish I was."

"That is insane."

"Perhaps, but that's the job. Our problem is that we can't do anything until we know exactly where the abductees are being kept."

"You realize Russia is big country."

"Yeah, we pointed that out."

"They could be anywhere. They could even be thousands of miles apart from each other."

"Your first point is our problem in a nutshell. To your second, though, intelligence indicates they are being held together."

"What intelligence?"

"Nothing I'm at liberty to share. But I trust it."

Silvia leaned over and whispered something into Vassily's ear.

"Yes, that is my thinking, too," he answered in Spanish, not bothering to lower his voice. To Quinn and Orlando, he said in

English, "Silvia believes you want me to be location beacon. She is right, *da*?"

"Spot on."

Silvia stood. "This meeting is over." She looked at Vassily. "I will tell the captain to take us back to the port."

Vassily patted the spot where she had been sitting. "Sit."

She clearly didn't want to, but when he patted the seat again, she reluctantly did as he requested.. This did not stop her from glaring at Quinn and Orlando.

"How would it work?" Vassily asked.

"That's not something we'll discuss unless we know you're in," Quinn said.

"Okay, then tell me this. If I help you, can you promise I will be one of those you rescue?"

"I can promise you will be number two on our list."

"Number two?"

"After Melnikov. He's our priority."

"Because of the bombing."

"Yes. Promises were broken that day. We have an obligation to make it right."

"I see." He chuckled and shrugged. "Okay, I am in."

Silvia swiveled to face him, gawking. "Are you kidding?" When he didn't respond, she said, "My job is to *protect* you. I cannot allow this." She stood up again and looked at Quinn. "Find someone else."

"Silvia," Vassily said, "thank you. You have done your job well. But all I have been doing is funding others to fight the problems back home. I have been in little danger myself."

"The fact that they want to kidnap you says differently. And now that we know they are coming for you, we can—"

"Keep it from happening?" Vassily said. "Yes, you could do that. But you will not." Before she could respond, he held up a hand. "Why? Because you work for me, and I do not want you to stop it. How can I support others taking chances if I do not do so myself?"

"But that does not make sense," she argued. "How will you continue assisting those you've been helping if you are locked away in prison? Or dead?"

"Do you really think I do not already have systems in place to keep things going in my absence?"

His head of security searched for a response but came up empty.

"I am old man," he said. "This is probably my last chance for big adventure."

"What they are proposing is *not* an adventure."

"That all depends on how you look at it. Do not worry. I will be okay." Vassily glanced at Quinn. "Right?"

"You know I can't guarantee that."

"See? Even Quinn says I'll be okay."

"That's not..." Silvia turned away, her face flushing with anger. "Excuse me," she said, and headed up the stairs to the back deck.

After the door closed behind her, Vassily said, "You must excuse her. I do favor for her family when she was teenager. Am like uncle to her."

"That must have been some favor," Orlando said.

"Despite what Quinn might think of me, I have never been one hundred percent evil."

"I never said you were," Quinn said. "My issue was—"

"I know what issue was, and you were not wrong." The Russian hesitated before adding, "And I am sorry."

Quinn had not been expecting an apology, especially one sounding as sincere as that had. "What's past is past."

"Indeed, it is." The Russian's wide smile returned. "Tell me, how do you plan on tracking where I go?"

～

The biggest problem was getting Silvia to sign on to the plan. To do so, Quinn had to promise her a role in Vassily's rescue. Which meant Quinn's already extended team of six would be adding a seventh.

With that problem solved, they returned to port, where calmer waters would be safer while they implant the bug on Vassily.

Jar had expected Orlando to do it, and was surprised when Orlando offered her the opportunity. Of course, Jar jumped at it.

With Orlando's guidance, she made a small incision behind the Russian's left ear, where it would be hidden by his hair. Then she used a pair of thin, sterilized tweezers to insert the bug in the area where Vassily's skull met his neck. To close the cut, she applied state-of-the-art surgical glue over the wound. Not only was the seal as strong as the best stitches, it would leave little to no scar.

Jar ran a finger over the incision and could barely feel it. "Any pain?"

Vassily shook his head. "Still numb."

"Signal's strong," Orlando said, looking at her phone.

The bug was designed to piggyback onto any mobile phone network it could find. If none was available, it could hitch a ride on a Wi-Fi network.

"Please roll your head around," Jar said.

Vassily did.

"Do you feel anything?"

"Not much. A little pull on the skin maybe."

"That's to be expected," Orlando said. "In a day or two, that should go away. The incision might itch a little so try not to scratch."

"What if they cut my hair?"

Jar studied the cut again. "If they do, wince when they touch that area. Like they caught your skin."

"Great idea. I can do this. What next?"

"Next," Quinn said, "we make sure you look like a juicy target."

18

"Here it comes," Quinn said.

He, Orlando, and Thomas were on the roof of an apartment building across the street from Vassily's restaurant. Centered in his binoculars was the van driven by the men sent to snatch Vassily.

"Copy," Nate whispered over the comm. He and Jar were in the restaurant, posing as waitstaff.

Daeng checked in last. He was following the van on a motorcycle, via the tracker they'd placed on the vehicle the night before. This allowed him to hang far enough back to be out of sight of the would-be kidnappers.

The previous morning, Nate and Daeng had followed Felix onto a flight to Málaga. During the chaos of boarding, Nate had slipped a bug into the man's carry-on bag that let them track Felix's movements in Spain and eavesdrop on his conversations.

There had been several.

The most important occurring the night before, during a meeting between Felix and the three-person grab-and-go team, in which they discussed their plan in detail and revealed the kidnapping would take place at the restaurant between nine and ten p.m. the following evening. While Nate listened in, Daeng had placed tracking bugs on all the vehicles present, including the van.

One other tidbit learned was that Felix's team planned on making a dry run in the morning. It was that dry run Quinn and the others were currently monitoring.

The van slowed as it passed the restaurant, but quickly sped up again and proceeded on a route to a small airport just outside Málaga, where a private jet would be waiting that night to whisk Vassily to wherever the Russian abductees were.

Hopefully.

Quinn nodded at the roof-access door. "Shall we?"

He and Orlando descended to ground level, with Thomas trailing them. When they reached the lobby, he said, "You still with us, Agent?"

"Huh?" Thomas glanced up. "Oh. Um, yeah." She had been uncharacteristically quiet since they'd convinced Vassily to be their guinea pig.

Once they were outside, Quinn stopped. "If there's something on your mind, now is the time to share it."

After a moment's hesitation, she grimaced and said, "Am I the only one who thinks what we're doing is wrong?"

"What do you mean?"

"We're using Vassily as bait. If everything goes to plan, we're intentionally letting him be kidnapped, and you can't even promise that you'll be able to get him out." She shook her head. "This is way beyond the guidelines of the assignment."

"I disagree. Our guidelines were to get Melnikov and as many of the others out any way we can. That's it. No restrictions."

"Some things don't have to be said. I mean, how is this even close to ethical?"

"This is the reason I was not in favor of you joining us," Quinn said. Thomas's cheeks reddened but before she could say anything, he went on. "I'm not trying to trigger you, but here's the deal. You are an agent of the FBI. Proper procedures and the rule of law have been drilled into you. Staying ethically aboveboard is second nature. Which is all well and good when you're in your world. But the thing is, we're not in your world now. We're in mine and Orlando's, and here we play by an entirely different set of rules. If we did it your way, my team and I would have been killed years ago."

The red in her cheeks lessened, but the conflict in her eyes didn't.

"Think about it," he said, waving a hand between himself and Orlando. "Our job is to make bodies disappear. I guarantee there's not a country we've worked in where doing what we do isn't against the law. The very US government that pays your salary is our biggest client, which means they clearly think our jobs are important. They hired us for this mission because of our abilities and experience."

"Getting rid of bodies is different than purposely putting someone in harm's way."

"Do you think the FBI doesn't put people in harm's way? Isn't that what happens every time they embed an undercover agent in a drug cartel or crime organization?"

"That's different. Those are law enforcement officers. Levkin hasn't been hired for this job."

"Did we coerce Vassily to do it?"

"I have no idea. I wasn't in the room when you talked to him about it."

"But you saw him right after. Did he look coerced to you?"

"No. But...this just doesn't feel right. I...I think Deputy Director Pierce should know about this."

"Fine. Call him."

"What if he tells me to shut you down?"

"He won't."

"You can't know that."

"He and Deputy Director Suarez came to us because we get things done. No one is pulling the plug. But if you have a viable alternative of finding out where Melnikov is, I'm all ears."

She said nothing.

"Vassily knows the risks," Orlando said. "We would have never let him volunteer if he didn't."

"We also have no intention of leaving him to rot in prison, and will do everything in our power to get him out," Quinn said. "But I would be a fool if I made a blanket promise to him. And even if I did, he wouldn't believe me. He knows how this world operates. Go ahead. Make your phone call. See if I'm right."

Quinn caught Orlando's eye and the two of them headed across the street, leaving Thomas on the sidewalk.

When they entered the restaurant, Orlando said, "Who are you and what did you do with Quinn?"

"What do you mean?"

"I was sure you were going to lay into her. How did you remain so calm?"

He turned his palms up and uncurled his fingers. On each palm were four red crescents from where his fingernails had dug into them. "It's something I used to do when Nate was starting out and kept asking me stupid questions."

Orlando laughed.

Nate, heading their way, said, "What's so funny?"

Orlando shook her head, smiling. "Nothing."

"Where's Vassily?" Quinn asked.

"In back." Nate narrowed his eyes. "You guys were talking about me, weren't you?"

"Spoiler alert," Orlando said. "Not everything we discuss is about you."

Quinn shrugged. "Well, except this time."

"True," she agreed.

"I knew it," Nate said.

∼

By eight thirty p.m., everyone was in place.

Like earlier that day, Nate and Jar were once again acting as servers. Quinn and Orlando, on the other hand, were ensconced at a table, playing the part of a couple out for a nice dinner, and Thomas and Daeng manned the lookout position across the street from the restaurant. Quinn had no idea if Thomas had talked to her boss or not, but she had made no further protests about the plan.

If there was a wild card, it was Vassily's security team. Their participation was crucial. Felix and his hired help would know Vassily employed bodyguards and would expect to meet resistance. Quinn needed Silvia's people to make that resistance seem genuine, without doing such a good job that someone was killed. Silvia said she'd briefed her people and they were all on board, but she still didn't look happy, which, in turn, made Quinn uneasy. Vassily had said she could be trusted, however, so Quinn had no choice but to do just that.

At 8:56 p.m., Daeng's voice came over the comm. "They're on the move."

Orlando opened the tracking app, and she and Quinn watched the dot representing the van move along a map of the city until it stopped two blocks from the restaurant. Per Felix's plan, two of the kidnappers—one of whom was Felix himself—entered the restaurant a few minutes later, posing as diners. Silvia showed them to the preselected table that was close—but not too close—to where Vassily sat.

Nothing unusual happened for the next eight minutes. Menus were perused, orders were taken, and drinks were served.

Thirty seconds after Daeng announced, "Looks like it's showtime," the kidnappers' van screeched to a stop in front of the restaurant, and two men, dressed in all black and wearing masks, rushed into the restaurant.

Several diners screamed at the sight of the assault rifles the new arrivals brandished, and everyone, including Quinn and Orlando, dove for cover. Everyone, that was, except for Felix and the man with him. The moment the restaurant door flew open, they had begun moving and were now standing at Vassily's table,

Felix's colleague pointing a pistol at the closest bodyguard, while Felix pointed his own gun at Vassily.

The colleague barked at the guard in Spanish, "Face the wall, hands above your head."

The guard hesitated, and for a moment Quinn thought the plan was about to fall apart, but then the guard turned to the wall and did what he'd been told.

The two new arrivals had their rifles aimed at Vassily's two other bodyguards in the dining room and issued similar instructions. After another hesitation, those bodyguards also complied.

Quinn was just starting to feel like everything would be fine when Orlando muttered, "Uh-oh."

He followed her gaze.

The intruders had missed the fact Silvia was also a bodyguard, and she was now eyeing the back of the abductor nearest her, looking as if she was ready to rip him apart, joint by joint.

Quinn flicked his comm to channel two and whispered, "Silvia, stand down."

Her gaze remained fixed.

"Silvia."

One of the intruders glanced toward where Quinn and Orlando were huddled on the floor. "No talking!"

This seemed to crack Silvia's focus, and though she was still clearly pissed off, she no longer looked like she was preparing to launch herself at the kidnapper.

"There's no reason for anyone to get hurt," Vassily said. "Just take the money and go."

"We do not want your money," Felix said. "We come for you."

Vassily's shocked expression was a bit over the top for Quinn's tastes, but the kidnappers didn't seem to notice.

Felix bobbled the muzzle of his pistol. "Up."

Vassily didn't move.

"Up or people die."

"Okay, okay," Vassily said as he pushed out of his chair.

"Over here," Felix said.

Vassily stepped around the table.

"That's far enough. Hands behind your back."

After Vassily did as ordered, the man with Felix zip-tied the Russian's wrists together and shoved him toward the restaurant entrance. Felix followed them, while the other two kidnappers covered the room with their rifles. When Vassily reached the front door, all four kidnappers hurried him outside and hustled him into the van.

The vehicle raced off, and for a few moments the restaurant remained dead silent. Then the dam burst, and the diners began speaking and yelling and crying all at once.

Quinn switched back to channel one. "Daeng?"

"We're good. Tracker working. Anyone get hurt?"

"Nope. Will meet you at the vehicles."

Quinn, Orlando, Nate, Jar, and Silvia rushed through the chaos, out the kitchen door, and to the side street where two sedans waited at the curb. Daeng and Thomas had already arrived and were climbing into the vehicle in back, Daeng behind the wheel. Nate and Jar joined them, while Quinn, Orlando, and Silvia ran to the lead car.

Once they were in, Orlando checked the tracker. "Same route as this morning."

Which meant the kidnappers' plan hadn't changed, and they were on their way to the private airstrip.

Quinn clicked on his mic. "Daeng, as planned."

"Copy," Daeng replied.

The cars pulled out and raced south. Quinn's team was also headed to an airport, only the destination was the city's Málaga-Costa del Sol Airport, where a chartered Learjet awaited them.

They arrived twenty-two minutes later and quickly boarded.

Before Quinn had even settled in his seat, Orlando, who'd been tracking Vassily's bug, announced, "They're airborne."

Quinn picked up the phone that connected him to the cockpit. "We're ready. Please get us in the air."

Thanks to an assist from Deputy Director Suarez, they had

priority clearance, and within fifteen minutes were off the ground and nearing cruising altitude.

"They're making a turn," Orlando said, her eyes glued to her screen.

For the next two minutes, no one said a word.

"Okay, they're on a straight course now," Orlando said. "Northeast."

There were many countries northeast of Málaga: France and Italy…

And Russia.

Quinn had zero doubt which of those was the other plane's destination. Unfortunately, following it into Russia would likely either get them shot down or arrested once they landed. Either outcome would mark the end of their mission.

Any chance of succeeding would start by entering Russia without alerting authorities. They had, of course, planned for this exact contingency.

Quinn picked up the cockpit phone again and said, "Itinerary A."

19

Dmitri Melnikov added another mark to the wall. Yes, it might have been cliché, but he had no other way to track the days. It was the two hundred and forty-seventh mark he'd made, though only the sixth in his newest cell.

He'd been in at least fourteen cells so far, some for only a few days, others for months. The reason he didn't know the exact number of cells they'd kept him in was the same reason the two hundred and forty-seven marks were not an accurate total of the days he'd been imprisoned. There had been a period of time following the bombing in New York City when his captors kept him drugged. He had no idea if that had been days or weeks or even months. The two hundred and forty-seven marks represented only the time in captivity when he was lucid.

There *was* one glaring difference between this cell and the others. He was positive this was his last.

No one had told him that directly, of course. That would require someone talking to him. Which had happened only once since he'd started making the marks, the day he made his twenty-third one, to be exact. On that day, a man in the uniform of a Russian army colonel had opened Melnikov's cell door but had not stepped inside.

"Dmitri Alexandrovich Melnikov," the man had said in an arrogant monotone, "you have been deemed a threat to the Russian people."

Melnikov laughed. "By who?"

The colonel ignored him. "For your crimes, you have been sentenced to life in prison."

"Sentenced? I haven't even been tried yet."

The briefest of smiles graced the colonel's face. "Your crimes are self-evident. A trial would be a waste of resources."

"Tell me, Colonel. How much did it take to buy your loyalty? Or does your dear leader have something he can hold over you?"

"Enjoy your solitude," the man said.

As the door closed, Melnikov shouted, "How much?"

There was no answer.

Though no one had talked to Melnikov since, he'd overheard snippets of conversations between the guards, and had pieced together that a special facility was being built to house not only him but others, too. Likely more "troublemakers" like himself. Melnikov had heard more than one of the guards whine about how cold the new facility would be.

All his previous cells had been battered and worn from use. Not so with his new cell. It was too pristine to have ever been used before. Combine that with the fact that when he arrived here almost a week ago, the temperature outside had been magnitudes colder than he'd ever experienced—and as a Russian, he and cold were well acquainted—one could conclude this was the special prison the guards had talked about.

But while the prison might be shiny and new, the routine was the same as it had been everywhere else. Meals were shoved through a slot at the bottom of the door twice a day, and the rest of his waking hours was filled with nothing. The only real difference was the guards were no longer stationed close enough for him to overhear them.

Isolation.

Silence.

Zero human contact.

It was a recipe for madness, which he was sure was his captors' intent. Melnikov had no intention of falling prey to it anytime soon.

To be chess grand master, one had to have an eidetic memory. He was no exception to this rule, and he used his gift to keep his mind fresh. Every day, after he marked the wall, he would stretch out on his cot and replay famous chess matches in his head.

Today, he was in the middle of the 1918 match between José Raúl Capablanca and Frank Marshall when he heard people moving down the corridor outside his cell. He tiptoed to the door and pressed his ear against it.

Four, maybe five people.

They were almost abreast of his cell door when he heard an angry, muffled voice, the words indistinct.

Another voice spoke up, this one clear and authoritative. "Zap him!"

Melnikov heard a sizzle and an electric snap and then a groan, muffled like the earlier voice.

Another prisoner? he wondered. As far as he knew, in the time he'd been here he'd never been as close to anyone else sharing his fate.

"Do it again and we won't be as nice," the zap-him man growled.

The group moved past Melnikov's door and stopped a few meters down. A door slammed open, something thudded on the floor, and the door shut again. The steps retreated the way they'd come and soon faded to nothing.

Melnikov got onto his hands and his knees next to the tray slot, the thinnest part of the door.

"Hello?" he said, his voice tentative. When no response came, he raised his voice. "Can you hear me?"

Still nothing.

Maybe the electric shock had knocked the new arrival unconscious. Or maybe there was too much distance between their cells for Melnikov to be heard.

He started to push himself up.

"H-hello? Is someone there?"

Melnikov dropped back to the floor.

"Yes, I'm here," Melnikov said. "I'm in a cell down the hall from you."

A few seconds passed before the other person said, "Where are we?"

"I wish I knew. I'm not sure it matters anyway."

Melnikov heard what sounded like a snort, and the other man said, "How long have you been here?"

"In this cell? About a week. But they've had me for almost a year, I think. What about you?"

"They took me a few days ago."

This surprised Melnikov. He'd expected the man to be kept at another facility for a while, like he himself had been. "Then you must know what month it is."

"It's January. The twenty-fifth, I think. You didn't know that?"

Melnikov had been a prisoner for ten months. "The calendar was missing from my welcome basket."

The man laughed, deep and ragged. "Maybe you should complain to management."

"If any of them would talk to me, I would."

"What's your name?"

"Dmitri. You?"

"Vassily."

"Nice to meet you, Vassily."

"Under the circumstances, you'll excuse me if I can't say the same."

"Give it a few months."

"I don't plan on being here that long."

"I don't think we have a say in that matter."

"If you say so."

Melnikov cocked his head. "What does that mean?"

Silence.

"Vassily, what does that mean?"

Vassily did not answer.

20

"Anything?" Quinn asked.

"No," Jar said.

Up until ninety-four minutes ago, Vassily's bug had been pinging along nicely, providing continuous data on his location. Then it was like someone had flipped a switch and the signal stopped. No warning, no weakening of the signal first. Just there one second and gone the next. Jar had been trying to reestablish contact ever since.

Up until it vanished, the signal indicated Vassily had been traveling north, along the western edge of the Ural Mountains. Its last position had been less than a hundred kilometers from the Kara Sea, off the Arctic Ocean. Based on the near-constant speed Vassily had been moving in, he must have been on a train. The only problem: there were no tracks in that area on the map.

It took Jar nearly an hour of studying spy satellite images to figure out tracks were indeed there. Whoever had built them had gone to great lengths to hide their existence, because Jar had only been able to identify small stretches, some sections no more than ten meters long. By linking the micro segments, Jar pieced together a route that branched off a known line several hundred kilometers south of where Vassily's tracker had gone silent. The unseen sections of the route were either camouflaged or ran through tunnels.

At the point where the signal was lost, Vassily's train had been traveling north steadily at sixty kilometers per hour. Given the approaching Arctic coastline, that was not something it would have been able to maintain much longer. Either it was nearing its stop or would soon turn east or west.

At the other end of the kitchen table, Orlando let out a triumphant "Ha!"

"Find something?" Quinn asked.

"You tell me," she said.

He moved behind her and examined the satellite image on her screen. It featured a wide expanse of snow-covered ground, broken up by several frozen lakes with similar, roughly oval shapes but, as far as Quinn could tell, nothing unusual. "What am I looking for?"

She pointed at one of the ovals.

"It's a lake," he said.

"Is it?"

His brow creased and he leaned in. It certainly looked like a lake. It was the same gray-white ice color as the other lakes.

"Uh, it's a lake."

She gave him her patented disappointed-mother frown. "Maybe this will help."

She clicked her mouse, and the image was replaced by another satellite picture of the same area, only this one had been taken during the summer when there was no snow.

And no lake.

"Last summer?" he asked.

"No. August, three summers ago."

"Still not getting it. That's plenty of time for a lake to form."

"Perhaps, but…"

As she opened another image of the same area, Nate joined them. The new shot looked very much like the wintery first one, the only real difference being the lake in question was only about a quarter of its current size.

"This is from five months after that previous one."

"Okay," Quinn said. "So we know when the lake was born. What am I missing?"

Orlando rolled her eyes. "You're not using your head. This is above the Arctic Circle. If a new lake forms, it would happen in the late spring or early summer, not after August when everything has started to freeze again."

"I see your point, but it could be an aberration, right?"

She stared at him and said, "Fine. Let's assume that happened." She clicked on another shot. "This is from two summers ago."

The lake was there again, not as large as in the most current image, but larger than the one they'd just looked at.

"Can I get a hint?"

"The lake is twice as large as the last shot."

"Okay. And?"

"*Exactly* twice as large. And it stays this same size *all summer*. It doesn't grow or shrink even a centimeter."

"I think that qualifies as weird," Nate said.

"You think?" Orlando brought up another image. Winter again. "One year ago."

The lake had grown again.

"Don't tell me," Quinn said. "Exactly twice its previous size again."

"Now you're catching on." She brought up another image. "And last summer."

"Is that the same size as it is now?"

"Exactly the same. *And* exactly twice the size as last winter."

"First off, I agree, this is bizarre. But I'm going to ask a question and I don't want you to get annoyed again, okay?"

"Ask."

He looked at her, waiting.

"Okay," she said. "I won't get annoyed. Ask your question."

"Is it possible the Russians have purposely doubled the lake's size every year?"

"I mean, sure, theoretically. But the increases are too precise, and you're forgetting that in between, the size is static."

"Could it be aliens?" Nate said.

"If it is, then we have bigger problems than the Russians to worry about," Orlando said.

"So you're saying they're camouflaging the area to look like a lake but there is no actual lake," Quinn said.

"Correct."

"Are there any images of a fake lake being installed?" Nate asked.

"Nope. That area is largely uninhabited and satellite coverage is not consistent. All they had to do was use a window between satellite flyovers."

"How large are those windows?"

"The longest is a little under twenty hours."

"And that would have been enough time to get the camouflage up, plus setting up and taking down whatever equipment they need?"

"With the right planning, it probably could be done," Orlando said. "And I think it likely they would have left the equipment underneath the camouflage."

"Wow," Nate said. "That's…"

"Impressive?"

"I was going to say insane, but we can go with impressive. But why the doubling? Why not do something more random?"

"My guess—bureaucracy," Orlando said. "Whoever was in charge was given a starting size and an ending size and told to increase it over a two-year period. They just broke it up into equal parts."

"Damn."

"So, you think this is where Vassily is headed?"

"It's directly in line with the path he was on. Unless you're aware of another secret base in the area, I think it's a pretty fair bet."

~

Daeng and Thomas returned to the safe house a few minutes before noon. Quinn waved Daeng over and they moved to a quiet corner of the living room.

"How did it go?" Quinn asked.

"As advertised. It will be cramped, though."

"As long as it gets us where we need to go."

"I'm ninety percent confident."

Quinn raised an eyebrow.

"Kidding," Daeng said, then shrugged. "Mostly."

"Meet time?"

"Midnight."

"How was Thomas?"

"Fine. When you get her alone, she's actually not that bad."

"Are we talking about the same person?"

"She bought me breakfast."

"Then she's a saint."

Daeng nodded his chin toward her. "Do you still plan on…?"

"What choice do I have?"

"She's not going to like it."

~

At nine p.m., after finalizing the plan and getting a little rest, the team gathered once more in the living room of the safe house, packed bags lining the wall next to the entrance.

Focusing on Silvia, Quinn said, "Things are about to get considerably more dangerous. If we get caught, we'll either be thrown into prison or executed. The one thing I can guarantee is that we'll be in situations where it'll be either us or them. Any hesitation and one of us will likely die. If that person is you, I won't be happy. But if it's one of my team, you'll wish it *had* been you."

"If anyone hesitates," Silvia said, "it won't be me."

"Good." He turned his gaze to Thomas. "Agent—"

"I get it," she said. "I might have to kill someone."

"Actually, my comments weren't aimed at you."

"What do you mean?"

"I mean, this is where we part."

Her brow furrowed. "Excuse me?"

"We're about to illegally enter a country that is not a friend of the United States. You are an employee of the US government. It will be bad enough if we get caught without you on the team. If that happens with you, it'll be a major international incident. Given the current political atmosphere, who knows what that could lead to? Trade embargos? Sanctions? Skirmishes? All-out war?"

"All-out war? I doubt that—"

Quinn's stare stopped her.

She took a breath. "Okay, I get it. It wouldn't be great."

"What it would be is something impossible for the US to deny involvement in."

A clash of emotions enveloped her before her expression resolved itself into one of reluctant agreement. "So, what am I supposed to do? Go home?"

"That's one option."

"What's the other?"

"It would be helpful if you were to go back to London and make sure Annabel doesn't back out on helping us."

"I thought you said she could be trusted."

"She can be, but we made a big ask. She's going to run into a lot of flak to make it happen. We can't afford for her to lose focus." He paused. "You and I might not always see eye to eye but believe it or not, I respect you. You are tenacious. Annoyingly so at times, but it's a good quality."

"Um, thanks?"

"You're welcome," he said, meaning it. "What we need is for you to use that tenacity to make sure Annabel follows through. Will you do that for us?"

"I don't even know what *she's* supposed to do. You never told me what Starfish is."

"Unfortunately, I don't have time to do that now, either."

"I can email her a brief," Orlando offered.

Thomas stared at the two of them, then nodded. "If that's what you need, I'll do it."

"Thank you," Quinn said.

Orlando opened her phone and tapped the screen a few times. "I've just emailed you your boarding pass for a flight to London in the morning and information on how to contact Annabel."

Thomas smirked. "That confident I'd say yes?"

"I will also be cancelling a ticket to DC," Orlando said. "We like to be prepared for all contingencies. I'll send you the Starfish info as soon as I have time. I'll also keep you updated on our progress when I can."

"Our lives are in your hands," Quinn said.

"No pressure, huh?" Thomas said.

"Plenty of pressure."

"You can count on me."

The team arrived two hours early for the rendezvous with the smugglers who would take the group into Russia. The location was on the bank of the river Narva, several kilometers south of the Estonian town with the same name. Quinn dispersed his people around the area to keep watch.

At eleven fifty-one p.m., Nate's voice came over the comm. "Movement in the water." He was stationed two hundred meters west, on a slight rise overlooking the river. "Hard to tell if it's them but whatever it is, it's moving against the current."

"Copy," Quinn said. He was in a tree, approximately halfway

between Nate's position and the rickety-looking dock where they were supposed to meet their ride. "Location?"

"One hundred meters west of me."

"Speed?"

"Slow but steady," Nate said.

"Keep us posted."

"Copy."

"Anyone else see anything?" Quinn asked.

"Position one, quiet," Daeng reported from the main road.

"Position two, quiet," Silvia said from her position to the east.

"Position three, quiet," Jar said. She and Orlando were with the equipment by the dock.

"Copy," Quinn said.

Ninety seconds passed before Nate came over the comm again. "It's them. They're passing me now."

"Are they alone?"

"Nothing else on the water." A pause before Nate added, "Far shore is still clear."

"Copy. Everyone else still clear?"

A trio of affirmatives came over the line.

"Nate, hold your position for another minute. If there are no surprises, return to the dock."

"Copy."

"Daeng, Silvia, same goes for you."

"Copy."

Quinn pointed his night vision binoculars downriver, and soon spotted water rippling around a solid oval sitting a few centimeters above the surface.

"Heading back now," Nate said.

When he reached Quinn's position, Quinn climbed down and they returned to the dock together, arriving moments before Daeng and Silvia.

"How's it looking?" Quinn asked Jar. She was watching the river through her binoculars.

"Ninety seconds away," she said.

He turned to Daeng. "It's your show."

Daeng nodded. "Weight distribution is important, which means we'll go out one by one. Nate, you're first. Once inside, move to the front. Quinn, you go next and head to the back. One of the crew members will be there, so stop before you get in his way. I'll go next and join Nate. Silvia after me, to the back. Then Orlando and Jar. You two will stay in the middle. There'll be another crew member there so make sure to give him room."

Nate pulled his bag over his shoulder and toed the dock. "You sure this isn't going to collapse on us?"

"I have no idea," Daeng said. "That's why you're going first."

"You're a real pal, you know that?"

"That's what people tell me."

"What people?"

"Well, for one—"

"Here it comes," Jar said, with more than a bit of you're-both-idiots in her tone.

When the rippling oval reached the end of the dock, it stopped and a hatch lifted into the air.

The silhouette of a head poked through the opening. "Ready?" the shadow asked in heavily accented English.

"All set," Daeng said.

"Send first person."

Nate stepped carefully onto the dock. It swayed a bit but didn't collapse. When he reached the end, he lowered his bag through the opening and followed it in, looking to the others like he was stepping into a hole in the water.

A few seconds later, Quinn slipped through the open hatchway, and found himself in a tube not quite tall enough for him to stand upright. He made his way to the back, where one of the two crew members was perched in front of a rudimentary control panel. One by one, the others followed him into the vessel. Once Jar was inside, the crew member at the middle lowered the hatch and sealed it shut.

"There are holds on both sides," he said. "Use them. Can get…" He mimicked being jostled. "If get hurt, not our fault."

After everyone had grabbed a handle, the guy next to Quinn hit a button and the boat started moving.

Though the total distance they traveled was under a kilometer, the journey took nearly a half hour to complete. This was due to the crew spending most of that time checking feeds from the camera they had positioned along the river to spot potential trouble. Once they'd deemed the Russian side safe, the remaining distance was quickly crossed.

Offloading took only marginally longer than boarding had, and by twelve thirty-seven, the team was standing on Russian soil and the submarine had disappeared back down the river.

Quinn opened his map app. A white dot indicated their position, and a red one the position of the vehicles that were waiting for them.

"Okay, everyone, we've got about a forty-minute hike ahead of us. Strap 'em on and let's get moving."

21

The team reached Moskovsky train station in St. Petersburg shortly after five a.m. They split into three groups, each group taking a different bullet train to Moscow. Quinn and Orlando left first at 5:50 a.m. Daeng and Silvia took the 6:50 a.m. train, and Nate and Jar followed ten minutes later on the seven o'clock.

Nate and Jar were the last to reach the rendezvous point, an apartment on the east side of Moscow. As soon as they entered, a woman Nate had never seen before rushed over and wrapped her arms around him.

"Uh…hello?" he said.

The woman took a step back and put her hands on his cheeks. "Is so good to finally meet you. Last time I hear about you, you in hospital." She tapped his chest. "Bullet."

The only time he'd ever been shot in the chest had been years ago, in….

Holy crap.

"Are you…Petra?" he asked.

"*Da.* Is me." She motioned to the equally unfamiliar man who'd followed her over. "And this is Mikhail."

The man shook Nate's hand and said slowly, "Happy to make your acquaintance. Sorry, not speak English in many years."

"Good to finally meet you."

Petra and Mikhail had been part of a mission years ago that had turned personal for Quinn when his family was targeted. That was also the mission on which Nate had met and fallen for Quinn's late sister, Liz. While Nate had been protecting Liz in Paris, Quinn worked with Petra and Mikhail to catch a former KGB officer known as the Ghost.

"This is Jar," Nate said.

"Happy to meet you," Petra said, her smile as bright for Jar as it had been for Nate. "Welcome to Moscow."

"Petra and Mikhail loaned us this place," Quinn explained.

"Oh," Nate said. "Thank you."

"Not need to thank us," Petra said. "You know we do anything for Quinn. He could have killed us when we first meet but he help instead. We owe him and all of you more than we can ever repay."

"Petra, how many times do I have to tell you that you don't owe us anything?" Quinn said.

"Sweet man, very nice to say, but not true. We do anything for you and friends."

"All right, everyone," Orlando said, "There are three bedrooms in back. Find a mattress and get some rest. Petra and Mikhail have arranged transportation to take us east, and we need to be up and ready to leave by evening."

"Have you heard of Directorate Eleven?" a man named Stepka said over the speaker of Petra's phone.

It was 6:15 p.m., and Quinn, Orlando, Jar, Nate, Petra, and Mikhail were gathered in the living room. Daeng and Silvia were still in the backrooms of the apartment—the former taking his turn in the shower, and the latter having already done so and was now getting dressed. Stepka had been Petra and Mikhail's technical support specialist while they hunted the Ghost, and he'd continued in that role as their organization transformed into one that helped Russian citizens who found themselves at odds with the government.

"That's a new one on me," Quinn said.

"Sounds very Dr. Who," Nate said.

Jar nodded.

Ignoring the comment, Quinn said, "Tell us about this directorate."

"No official information available," Stepka said, "but what we pieced together, Directorate Eleven formed five years ago, as what I think people in intelligence business call special projects organization."

Quinn glanced at Orlando, but she seemed as surprised by this information as he was. SPOs—how they were often referred— were elite groups formed to handle difficult tasks, typically ones in which governments could deny any participation. Kind of like Quinn's team right now, only on a larger scale. More often than not, SPOs were disbanded as soon as a specific task was completed. The existence of a long-term one was rare.

"This Directorate Eleven is responsible for the kidnappings?" Quinn asked.

"Evidence not all there, but enough show they have hand in at least three incidents. If they behind one…"

"Then they're behind them all," Quinn finished.

"*Da.*"

"What do you know about them?"

"Head of directorate named Colonel Stepan Annenkov. Will send bio. Short story, he start in special forces then recruited into military intelligence. Information on him after this not so easy to find. He must have impressed superiors to have such important position.

"The directorate outside the normal chains of military command. From what can tell, it answer directly to either head of army or president. Not know for sure, but because evidence General Churkin may also be involved, probably president."

Both Petra and Mikhail visibly tensed at the mention of the general.

"Who's Churkin?" Quinn asked.

"Blood leech who only cares about keeping president in office," Petra said.

Mikhail muttered something in Russian.

"What?" Quinn asked.

"It is name some of us call him," Petra said. "The Puppet Master."

"He sounds fun," Nate said.

"He is not."

"Sorry," Nate said, cringing. "Bad joke."

"The directorate info is good background," Quinn said, getting the conversation back on track. "But I'm more interested in who has responsibility for the prisoners now."

"Also is Directorate Eleven, I believe," Stepka said.

"Is that normal?"

"After you give us information about secret base, I checking more. In last three years, Colonel Annenkov take seventeen trips to area where expanding-lake-that-not-lake located. Majority of trip happen in last sixteen months. Cannot physically place him at exact spot, but would be foolish to think trips not connected to base construction."

"How big is the directorate?" Quinn asked. "I mean people-wise."

"Exact number I cannot say, but two army companies have been reassigned to Annenkov."

That could be anywhere from three to four hundred soldiers.

"Are the companies stationed at the headquarters or the Arctic base?"

"Not have that information, either. But think it smart to assume split between both."

"Directorate Eleven worry us for some time," Petra said.

"They rise quick in importance. So far, we think activities only outside of Russia, but are sure only matter of time before Annenkov turn attention inward."

"If I were you, I'd be concerned, too," Orlando said.

Petra started to say something but stopped herself.

"What is it?" Quinn asked.

She was silent for a moment before she said, "I know you come to us for help, but have favor to ask. If have chance can damage directorate, please do it. Anything that hurt their operation big help for us."

"We *are* planning on springing all their prisoners," Quinn reminded her. "That won't reflect well on them."

"Is true, but organizations like Directorate Eleven have way of pushing blame on someone else. Better would be something more…"

"Crippling?"

Petra smiled. "Yes."

"This headquarters Stepka mentioned," Quinn said. "I'm guessing it's not in the north with the secret base."

"Correct."

"Then I'm not sure how we can help. Our only chance at accomplishing the rescue is if no one knows we've been in country until after we're gone. Hitting the directorate's Moscow offices before we do that would put our actual reason for being here in jeopardy."

"Offices not in Moscow," Petra said. "Is located a few hours east and is more army base than office."

"Which makes it even less appealing."

"Does it, though?" Orlando asked.

Quinn looked at her, brow furrowed. "What?""

"Will you excuse us for a moment?" she said.

She grabbed Quinn's hand and walked him to the front door, where they grabbed their coats before exiting the apartment.

Neither said a word until they were on the street, walking toward a park at the end of the block.

"You're not seriously thinking we should go after the directorate?" Quinn whispered.

"Hear me out."

"About adding an impossible side quest onto our already impossible main one?"

"If our main task was impossible, you wouldn't have taken the job."

"You know what I mean."

"Can we agree the rescue is only a temporary fix to the problem?"

"Tell that to Dmitri Melnikov."

"What I'm saying is, even if we're able to free everyone the directorate is currently holding, it likely won't stop them from going right back out and kidnapping others, or even the same people again. The only way to stop them is to cut them off at the knees."

"Even if I agree with you, destroying Directorate Eleven isn't our assignment. In fact, I'm pretty sure if we were to ask for approval, the answer would be *hell, no*."

"Maybe."

"No maybe about it."

"These people are responsible for the bomb that nearly killed you, Daeng, Janet, and Steve, and *did* kill several FBI agents."

"You think we should do this for revenge?" he said.

"We have the opportunity to damage them, and hopefully even cripple them enough to stop them from hurting anyone else. Revenge would be a byproduct."

He exhaled a deep breath, sending out a large cloud of frozen vapor. "Okay, let's say we decide to do it. How are we going to destroy an organization that's housed on a military base we know nothing about, without it affecting our primary mission or screwing up the timeline?"

"We turn it into a diversion that will *help* our primary mission."

Quinn eyed her suspiciously. "Elaborate."

"We time our action against their headquarters with our raid on the prison. It'll cause confusion and maybe even tie up resources they could send to stop us. In the process, we give Petra what she wants."

"I'm still waiting for the how."

"I haven't had time to figure everything out, but I do have an idea." She explained what she was thinking.

Quinn had several questions, all of which she answered.

"That's not half bad," he admitted.

"Right?"

He pulled out his phone and texted Petra, asking her to join them.

After she arrived, he said, "This base where the directorate is located—what do your people know about it?"

The corner of Petra's mouth ticked up. "Much, actually."

"Define much."

"We talk to several people who build it. Also steal detailed plans. We even know of potential way in."

"Potential?"

"We not used it yet, so would be misleading if I not use...what is word?"

"Caveat?" Orlando suggested.

"Yes, caveat."

"Question number two," Quinn said. "Is the base on our way?"

"It can be," she said, and quickly added, "With little change to overall route."

Quinn shared a look with Orlando and could tell she wanted to go ahead. He still wasn't ready to say yes, but he also wasn't a firm no now.

"One other thing I think you like," Petra said. "Stepka say secret base is similar design as directorate headquarters."

"Really?" Orlando said.

Petra nodded.

If the two bases were of a similar design, Quinn knew seeing one that was easy to get into could be a big help. He blew out another deep breath. "Okay. *If* we do this, there are things we will need."

"Like what?"

He and Orlando rattled off items.

Petra said, "Not problem."

"How long will it take to pull together?"

"If someone start now, truck arrive before we leave city."

"We have one more condition," he said. "We won't make the decision whether we do this or not until we see the place with our own eyes."

"Also not problem."

22

Night still ruled the winter sky as Quinn hopped down onto a narrow, snow-covered road.

"Over here," Petra called, her voice coming from around the side of the tractor trailer.

He joined her and a man named Alek, both of whom were looking out over the downward slope of the hill.

"How was ride?" she asked.

Quinn tilted his head to the left, releasing an audible crack from his neck. "Cramped."

"But warm enough, yes?"

"Thankfully."

The secret compartment Quinn and his team had been riding in since leaving Russia was inside the trailer, which was being pulled by a semitruck driven by Alek. The compartment was barely large enough for everyone and their gear but at least it had a heater, because outside it must have been several degrees below freezing.

"How close are we?" Quinn asked.

"About eight kilometers," Petra said.

"This is as close as we can get?"

She nodded. "More too risky."

"Does anyone live around here?"

She pointed toward the back of the trailer. "Two houses two kilometers that way. Closest town twenty-seven kilometers past them. Between here and the base, nothing."

"And where *is* the base?"

"Follow me."

She led him fifty meters down the road, beyond the front of the truck, then pointed at several distant pinpricks of light over the trees on the descending slope.

"That's it?" he said.

"*Da.*"

He pointed at the binoculars hanging around her neck. "May I?"

She handed him the glasses and he raised them to his eyes.

The lights resolved into over a dozen separate glows. Half were in a diagonal line along what he could just make out as a wall. The others were farther back, some on a building that was only partially visible, and some lighting areas he couldn't identify.

He handed back the glasses, said, "Thanks," and returned to the open end of the trailer. "Jar, Nate, Daeng, let's go."

The trio joined him on the ground. Jar and Nate had backpacks slung over their shoulders and were carrying snowshoes, while Daeng held two sets of each. He gave a pack and a pair of snowshoes to Quinn.

Orlando appeared at the back of the trailer but didn't climb out. She and Silvia would remain at the truck with Petra. "Don't do anything stupid," she said.

"You mean like coming here in the first place?" Quinn asked.

"Hey, you agreed to do it."

"Don't remind me."

He put on his snowshoes and was adjusting his backpack when Alek joined them, wearing matching gear.

"Ready?" the Russian asked.

"Lead on."

~

By the time the first sign of the coming sunrise leaked over the horizon, they had traveled six and a half kilometers. Their destination was the summit of a small hill, a half kilometer away from the Directorate Eleven base's western perimeter.

To mitigate the possibility of triggering an early warning system, Jar continually scanned for electronic signatures as they hiked. So far, she'd detected nothing.

Another three hundred meters on, they came to the edge of a small clearing. Alek lifted his hand and said, "Wait here," then trudged across the open ground and disappeared into the trees on the other side.

"You know," Nate said, "this would be a great setup for a horror movie. A group of hikers is led into the wilderness, and then their guide tells them to wait somewhere and that he'll be back in a few minutes, but he never returns."

"I'd watch it," Daeng said.

"Don't encourage him," Quinn said.

Taking the opposite tack, Daeng asked, "What would happen next?"

"Naturally, we'd start getting picked off one by one," Nate said. "I'd probably go first, because I'd be the swoon-worthy guy all the girls like."

Daeng raised an eyebrow. "*You'd* be the swoon-worthy guy?"

"Well, yeah, of course. Who else would it be?" Before Daeng could respond, Nate continued, "You'd be next because the last two alive have to be the crusty old man and the smart woman. Quinn would then use Jar as a decoy to save his life but it would backfire, and Jar would be the sole survivor."

"This makes sense to me," Jar said.

"Crusty old man?" Quinn said.

"You *are* the oldest," Jar said.

"Exactly," Nate said. "And in the sequel—"

"There's a sequel?" Daeng said.

"There's always a sequel. In it, a police officer or reporter or someone like that would talk Jar into returning to the woods, and the whole thing would start again."

"A documentary film crew," Daeng suggested. "They're making a movie about the original killing spree."

"Hasn't that already been done?" Nate asked. "What was it? The something something project?"

"Blair Witch?" Daeng said.

"Right. So not a film crew. Anyway, it doesn't matter. In our story, no one really believes Jar's story of what happened."

"Now you are being ridiculous," Jar said. "First, no one would ever be able to talk me into going back, and second, why would no one believe what I tell them if it's true?"

"It's a movie. Believability is not a requirement."

"The movies that don't care about believability are the worst movies," she countered. "Why would you want to make something like that?"

"Duh. Because those are the movies that make a ton of money."

"Do you have statistics to back that up?"

He made a show of padding the pockets of his jacket. "Gee, I seem to have left my Excel spreadsheet in my other superspy outfit."

"You should not make statements without being able to back them up."

"I feel it's necessary to point out that no one is actually making a movie about us," Nate said.

"And I feel like you are saying that to avoid the fact you cannot back up your claim." She turned to Quinn. "Am I correct or not?"

Before Quinn could respond, Nate said, "The crusty old man doesn't get a say in this."

Quinn's eyes narrowed. "In light of new information, I'm siding with Jar on this one."

"Were you not listening?" Nate asked. "The crusty old man—"

Jar hissed out a low *shhhh*, pointed at her ear and then at the woods beyond the clearing.

They all dropped to a crouch, their eyes on the trees. After a moment, Quinn heard the faint crunch of snow. Not long after, two silhouettes stepped into the clearing, both too tall to be Alek.

Quinn carefully retrieved his binoculars and trained them on the shadows. "Soldiers," he whispered.

Each had a rifle slung over his shoulder. But thankfully, they'd entered the clearing a dozen meters west of where Alek had crossed and likely had not seen his tracks.

Nate tapped Quinn's arm and pointed across the clearing at the trees directly opposite them. Quinn moved his binoculars that way and saw Alek hunkering next to a tree. Quinn returned his gaze to the soldiers.

They had stopped in the center of the clearing and one was now lighting a cigarette. They shared a few words too low to pick up and fell silent again. The smoker sucked on his cigarette while his colleague rubbed his own arms to keep warm. A couple of minutes passed before the smoker finally tossed his cigarette butt into the snow. He said something, and he and his partner disappeared into the woods, never knowing they'd been watched the whole time. Once the crunch of snow had faded to nothing, Alek made his way across to Quinn and the others.

"That was close," Quinn said.

"We did not think patrols come out this far," Alek said.

"Are they the only patrol or are there others?"

"Not sure, but very unlikely two in same area."

Not quite the answer Quinn wanted but he didn't disagree. "What are the chances they cross the trail we left getting here?"

"They appeared to head away from our path so we okay, I think."

～

It took another forty minutes to reach the viewpoint.

As soon as Nate had the drone ready, Quinn said, "Send it up."

Nate used to be their main drone pilot, but he had made the mistake of teaching Jar how to fly one, and in typical Jar fashion, she had surpassed his abilities within a month. Which was why she was the one with the controls up on her phone. She tapped the screen and the drone rose from Nate's hand. She flew to a point high above the base and set it to hover.

Nate, relegated to the job of drone camera operator, zoomed the lens in until only the area within the base's walls could be seen.

"Let's get a personnel count," Quinn said. He and Daeng were standing on either side of Nate, watching his screen.

Each man began counting.

When Quinn finished his tally, he said, "Thirty-eight."

"Same," Nate said.

"Same," Daeng said.

"Check the bunkers out front," Quinn said.

Jar moved the drone while Nate swung the camera to the road on the other side of the walled entrance. Though they couldn't see into the guardhouse or the bunkers that lined the road, plenty of soldiers were still visible.

"Seventeen," Quinn said.

"Nineteen," Nate said.

"Seventeen," Daeng said.

Quinn counted again. "Still seventeen."

Nate frowned. "Two of them must have gone inside."

"Sure," Daeng said. "It has nothing to do with your eyesight."

Ignoring them, Quinn said, "Thirty-eight and seventeen is fifty-five. Figure there are another fifteen to thirty inside the bunkers and guardhouse. That brings it to eighty-five. Let's round it up to a hundred to be safe."

Nate said, "The main building must hold another...what? Fifty? Hundred?"

"We'll call it a hundred," Quinn said. "That gives us two hundred, plus or minus. Less the fifty-five we've actually seen, there are up to one hundred fifty unaccounted for."

"That's a lot of soldiers," Nate said.

"They are probably not all soldiers," Jar said.

"A lot of people, then."

This seemed to satisfy her.

Quinn glanced at Alek. "Where's the secret entrance?"

Alek studied Nate's screen. "Can make this..." He spread his hands apart.

Nate zoomed out until the base and a few hundred meters of the surrounding area could be seen.

"More," Alek said.

Nate did as asked.

"Stop."

The zoom halted.

Alek stared at the feed and pointed at a spot northeast of the base, near the edge of the screen. "I think is here. Can move closer?"

Nate increased the magnification, but from the drone's current position, trees blocked the spot.

"Let me reposition," Jar said. She flew the drone over the spot and set it to hover again.

Nate tilted the camera straight down. Below the drone were several mounds not large enough to be called hills.

"Good," Alek said. "Thank you."

To Quinn, the mounds appeared too symmetrical to be natural. "Is this a mining site?"

"Was," Alek said. "Fifty years ago. Now, no." He pointed at the southside of a mound. "Can push in here?"

Nate zoomed in.

"More," Alek said.

Nate increased the magnification again. "That's as far as I can go. Jar could lower the drone, but we're still kind of close to the base so I'm not sure that's a good idea."

"No. This okay." Alek studied the image. "There!" He jabbed a finger at what appeared to be several rocks partially encircled by a small copse of trees at the base of the swell. "Under overhang is old mine entrance. We told mine runs all the way to base."

"But you haven't seen it for yourself," Quinn said.

"No, but we trust source. Am sure they not lie."

"Jar, how far is that overhang from the base?" Quinn asked.

Jar tapped her screen a few times. "One point zero five kilometers."

Quinn frowned.

Jar might not always be able to understand why some people did what they did, but sometimes her ability to read other's thoughts seemed supernatural. "You want me to fly the drone down to it but are still worried the drone may be spotted."

Quinn nodded, not even surprised.

She tapped her screen again. "I could fly it another five hundred meters farther from the base, descend, and come back low to the ground. No one should see."

He considered it for a moment before saying, "Do it."

Twelve minutes later, the drone hovered in front of the rocks that formed the arched opening to the mine. When Jar inched the craft inside, Nate turned on the drone's LED light, illuminating the rocky sides and two rusted rails running along a tunnel floor. Thirty meters in, the tunnel widened into a small cavern. The tracks curved to the left and Jar followed them as far as she could, which turned out to be only an additional five meters.

Alek grinned and slapped Quinn on the shoulder. "See, I tell you. That is way in. We go, *da*?"

On the screen, the rails ran straight under a wide metal door, set in the rock.

Quinn gazed across the top of the forest, toward the distant mine entrance. The safe move would be to put the kibosh on this side mission, return to the truck, and continue following Vassily's trail. But Orlando wasn't wrong in thinking a diversion here could be the difference between success and failure.

Dammit.

He turned to Jar and Nate. "See if you can find us a way to get there without being seen from the base."

23

"Run your scan again," Quinn said.

Jar waved the sensor over the metal door. "Still nothing."

Quinn glanced at Alek. "Why wouldn't they have secured this?"

"People who tell us about mine say base does not know."

"Does not know what?" Quinn asked, incredulous. "That it's here?"

Alek nodded. "People at construction company find when build base. They keep quiet and use tunnel to remove building supplies."

"You mean steal."

"*Da*, steal. They order more than need, charge army, then take what not used. Tunnel make easier for them to move everything without army attention."

"But then why the door? Shouldn't this just be an open tunnel?"

Before Alek could respond, Jar said, "Because it stops airflow and prevents pressure changes that might be noticed." She looked around at the others as if that was obvious. "Shall I open it?"

"Go ahead," Quinn said. "But be careful. It could still be booby-trapped."

The hinges groaned as she turned the lever and pulled the door open. The beams of Nate's and Daeng's flashlights cut into the darkness, revealing a tunnel identical to the one leading to the chamber.

"If we are going in, we should do so quickly and close the hatch again," Jar said.

Quinn nodded. "Nate, you take point." He looked at Alek, who had started moving toward the door. "No, you stay here. We don't know what we'll find and if things go sideways, I don't need you getting in the way."

"I would not get in the—"

"You would." Quinn's tone left no room for debate, a fact Alek acknowledged by taking a step back. "Give us two hours," Quinn told him. "If we haven't returned by then or if Petra and Orlando notice any unusual activity at the base, return to the trucks and get the hell out of here."

Alek nodded.

Quinn followed the others into the tunnel and shut the hatch.

Daeng marked their way with Day-Glo paint so they wouldn't mistakenly take one of the occasional offshoots on their way back. At each branch, Nate and Jar would travel down it far enough to determine it wasn't the way they should be going. Most offshoots dead-ended after several meters, and those that didn't narrowed enough to make it impossible for anyone to move stolen construction materials through.

Twenty-six minutes after leaving Alek, they came to a second door. According to Jar, they had traveled far enough to have reached the base. Flashlights were replaced by night vision goggles and sound suppressors were attached to pistols.

When everyone was ready, Quinn said to Jar, "Okay."

She sprayed lubricant on the door's hinges, the locking rod that held the door in place, and the lever housing, then Quinn pushed down on the lever and pulled the door open. The tunnel on the other side continued for only three meters before opening into what appeared to be another cavern.

After signaling the others to wait, Quinn stepped through. The cavern was twice as large as the one by the first door, and instead of cut rock completely encircling the space, the ceiling was a smooth, gray slab of concrete.

He looked around for another doorway but didn't see one.

He activated his mic. "Clear."

The others joined him.

"Split up and look around," he said. "There has to be another way onward."

Two minutes later, Nate said, "Found it." He was near one of the walls, pointing at the ceiling. "See the seam?" He pointed at another spot, a few centimeters from the first. "And that rectangular outline? I'll bet that's a handle."

"Give me a boost," Jar said.

He cradled his hands and lifted her up.

When she touched the rectangular outline, a handle indeed popped down. She studied it for a moment, then touched something in the space the handle had been tucked into. There was a click and the section of ceiling above her started to swing down.

Nate let go of Jar's foot and caught her as she fell, the moving door barely missing her head. He set her on the ground. "You okay?"

"I'm fine." She looked up at the door. "That is not a good design."

"It is not," Quinn agreed.

"Also, that hatch isn't big enough to move a lot of material through," Nate said. "How did they get stuff out?"

"No clue," Quinn said. He'd been thinking the same thing.

Daeng pointed at the top end of the ceiling flap. "Is that a ladder?"

"Lift me again," Jar said.

Nate raised her high enough for her to pull herself through the hole. She disappeared from sight, then said, "Watch out."

The three men moved back and the end of a ladder extended downward, stopping a hand's width above the floor.

Quinn tested it to make sure it could hold his weight, then he climbed up and through the opening.

The room he found himself in was definitely not part of the tunnel. Its walls and ceiling and floor were concrete. The dust covering the floor told Quinn no one had been there in a long time. Mounted to the ceiling above the hatch was a motorized winch that had clearly not been used for a while.

He had a pretty good idea now why the hatch was the size it was. The floor of this room must have been put in after the thieves had taken all they could, and they'd installed the hatch just in case they ever wanted to come back. It was as good a theory as any.

After Nate and Daeng came up the ladder, they all crowded around Jar's tablet computer. On it were the base blueprints Stepka had uncovered and sent to them.

"We're here," she said, pointing at a room at the bottom of the image. "According to Petra's contacts, this entire floor was only used during construction so there were no security cameras."

"Yeah, but let's not count on that still being the case."

"Obviously not," she said, chiding him.

"Where do we need to go?" Nate asked.

"Here." She pointed at a level that was two above them. "There are two ways to get there. The emergency stairwell." She tapped a spot on the blueprint. "Or the elevators. Both elevator cars and the stairwell have cameras. I don't know about the elevator shaft, but I think that's our best option."

"You heard her," Quinn said.

They entered a corridor and moved carefully down to the elevator lobby. Nate and Daeng leveraged open a set of doors wide enough for Jar to insert a gooseneck-mounted micro camera into the shaft.

"Both cars are three levels above. I do not detect any cameras."

Quinn nodded to Nate and Daeng, and they opened the doors the rest of the way. Quinn jammed the doors in place with a pair of wedges.

"Nate, you're first," he said.

A minute later, Nate had the looped end of their climbing rope hooked over his shoulder and was climbing up the metal girders in the shaft. He stopped at the door embedded in the wall, one level below where the cars sat, and tied the rope off. He extracted a wireless listening device from his bag and pressed it against one of the doors. The device transmitted a signal directly to the team's comms.

Quinn could hear the hum of machinery.

"Give us a visual," he said.

Nate used a short pry bar to part the doors wide enough to slip a gooseneck camera through. A beat later, the feed popped onto Jar's phone. The image was of a lit and empty hallway running straight out from the elevators.

"Pan left," Jar said.

The picture shifted, revealing a second hallway running parallel to the elevators. This section was also empty.

"Right," she said.

The feed swung one hundred and eighty degrees. The right section was also empty.

Quinn gave Daeng a nod and Daeng started up the rope. When he reached Nate, they moved to the opposite sides of the doors.

"Set," Daeng said.

Quinn and Jar scaled the shaft and stopped just below the doors, out of Daeng and Nate's way.

"Final check," Quinn whispered.

With one arm hooked through a metal support, Jar checked her phone. "Corridor still clear."

"Which way first?"

"To the left," she said. "Third door down. Give me one more sweep of the other halls."

Nate had to lean out to reach the gooseneck.

"Wait," Jar said. "Movement."

Quinn leaned in to see her screen. A pair of soldiers was walking toward the camera, down the hallway that led straight out from the elevators. Like the soldiers in the woods, both had rifles slung over their shoulders. Thirty meters from the elevators, the men vanished through a doorway on the right.

For the next three minutes Jar monitored the halls, and when no one else showed up, Quinn said, "Open it up."

Jar and Quinn slipped through the gap first, then held the doors open so Nate and Daeng could follow. After the doors closed again, Jar led them to the target door. On the wall beside it was a small scanner pad.

Quinn tried the handle but as expected, the door was locked.

From her pack, Jar extracted a small disc with a wire dangling from it that she plugged into her phone. She placed the disc on the scanner pad. She tapped her screen a few times, removed the disc, and nodded to Quinn.

He turned the handle, pushed the door inward. He moved inside the room alone and did a quick scan of the space. The only light in the room came from dozens of LED lights on the electronics equipment mounted in the racks lining the walls. It was more than enough illumination to determine no one was present.

"Clear," he said.

As soon as the others entered, Jar made a beeline for the nearest equipment rack, and began tracing connections from one device to another with her finger. After she completed a full circuit of the room, she bounced back and forth between racks before finally stopping in front of one and staring at it.

When a minute passed without her moving a muscle, Daeng whispered to Nate, "I think she needs to be rebooted."

Nate took a step toward her. "Um, Jar, are you—"

Her finger flew up in his path, forcing him to jam to a halt. She continued to study the equipment for another thirty seconds, and then pointed that same finger at the rack she'd been staring at and the one next to it. "We need to pull these two out."

Thankfully, the racks had wheels that were easily engaged via levers. While Nate and Daeng rolled them out, Jar retrieved from her pack a signal relay and one of the incendiary devices Petra had obtained for them. When triggered, the device would melt everything within a ten-meter radius.

She squeezed behind the racks, and when she reappeared three minutes later, the relay and firebomb were no longer in her possession. "Push them back," she said.

As Nate and Daeng returned the racks to their places, Quinn asked, "Any problems?"

Jar glanced at him, confused. "Why would there be problems?"

"Never mind. Where to next?"

They left the room and quietly made their way back to the T-intersection in front of the elevators. Quinn held his hand back to Jar and she placed her phone in his palm, the gooseneck camera once more attached. He eased the lens around the corner and checked the feed. The other corridor was still empty.

He gave the clear sign, and they moved quietly across the intersection to a door on the other side. Jar did her thing again, and in less than thirty seconds, they were in another room filled with racks of equipment. After installing another incendiary device, they returned to the corridor intersection.

Quinn checked the other hall with the camera again. Their final destination was a room about halfway to the one the soldiers had entered earlier. He was about to give the signal to move when Jar touched his shoulder and pointed at several pipes running along the wall near the ceiling.

"Signal booster," she mouthed.

He nodded.

The boosters were both essential to, and the Achilles's heel, of their plan. The boosters would allow them to trigger the bombs remotely when the time came. Jar had already planted over two dozen on their trek through the tunnel and another two in the elevator shaft, creating an invisible antenna to the outside.

Nate and Daeng lifted her, and she placed the booster on the top of the highest pipe and nestled it against the wall out of sight.

When she was back on the ground, Quinn signaled for Nate and Daeng to head back to the elevators, where they could keep constant watch on the corridors. As soon as they were in the shaft and the doors were closed again, Quinn and Jar proceeded to the target room.

Jar disengaged the lock and they slipped inside, dart guns ready. But the only thing present was the expected array of large batteries that stored electricity generated by a massive solar farm topside.

"Your show," Quinn whispered.

Jar hid her four remaining firebombs evenly among the array, then stowed another booster inside the housing of the emergency light above the door.

As soon as she finished, Quinn said into his mic, "We're done. Status?"

"Hold position," Nate responded.

"What's up?"

"Two soldiers heading down the hall toward the elevators."

"Current location?"

"Approximately fifteen meters from your door."

"Copy."

Quinn and Jar retreated to the nearest set of batteries and crouched behind them.

"Ten meters," Nate said.

Quinn could hear the footsteps now.

"Five meters."

In the hall, one of the soldiers said something and the second one chuckled.

"Passing your door in three seconds. Two. One."

Quinn tensed, anticipating the steps stopping and the door opening.

"Zero."

The steps did not stop, and it wasn't long before Quinn couldn't hear them any longer.

"You're clear," Nate said.

24

ST. PETERSBURG

Major Vetrov, deputy administrator of border security, northwestern sector, opened the morning report and scanned it for any surprises. In twenty minutes, he would be meeting with General Olenev, and the last thing he needed was for the general to ask about something for which Vetrov was not prepared.

The report was broken into dozens of short summaries, each topped with a headline.

Vetrov's gaze stopped on one at the top of the second page.

INCURSION: Narva River

That would be along the border with Estonia. It had been a weak point for years, but under Vetrov's leadership, illegal entries via the river had been reduced to only one or two cases a month. In most instances, those who tried entering were quickly apprehended and transferred to prison, and anyone who had helped them rounded up and given a similar fate.

He read the summary, expecting to find the situation had already been handled, but much to his chagrin, it had not.

According to the summary, a group of five to ten individuals had crossed the river and disappeared into the countryside. There was no concrete evidence of how they had entered the country, but local agents believed they had been aided by a group of smugglers that had been plaguing the area for several years.

The most surprising parts of the report were: 1) the crossing had not occurred the night before but at least two or three nights ago, and 2) the group appeared to consist of professional soldiers. Both tidbits had come from an informant in Estonia who had ties to criminal elements in the area. The man apparently did not have direct knowledge of the event or of the group that had crossed, and was only passing on what he had learned from associates. The agent who had passed it on to Vetrov's people noted the informant had an excellent track record, so there was high confidence in the report.

"Lieutenant!" he yelled.

Lieutenant Fedin entered quickly. "Yes, Major?"

"Get me"—he paused as he looked at the report for the name of the person who had forwarded the information— "Gregor Umanov on the phone. From the St. Petersburg office."

The phone call occurred three minutes later. Umanov had no additional info beyond what he'd already sent, leaving Vetrov in a testy mood as he arrived at the meeting with the general.

But they made it to the end of the meeting without Vetrov's boss even mentioning the Narva river incident.

"If there's nothing else..." the general said, as way of dismissal.

As much as Vetrov might have wanted to return to his office, he knew saying nothing now could come back to harm him later. "We haven't discussed the Narva river incursion."

"The what?"

"The Narva river incursion. It was in the morning brief. I talked to the handler who received the—"

Olenev held up a hand, silencing the major, and looked at his computer screen. When he finished reading, he turned back, seeming uninterested. "Do you really think an assault squad is roaming the Russian countryside?"

"Well, sir, the report is—"

"A group this large could not have gone unnoticed for more than a few hours. This report says they have been here at least two days." The general snorted. "Don't waste my time. It is a rumor only."

"It *is* probably nothing. But don't you think it would be wise to send a bulletin to other departments, just in case?"

"And make us look like fools when it proves to be nothing?" Olenev's gaze hardened. "Have you received any other reports that corroborate this? No, you have not. It is a phantom, Major." He looked back at his computer. "Dismissed."

Vetrov nodded and stood. "Thank you, General."

He saluted and left.

What he didn't do was let the matter go.

At lunch, he visited a restaurant several kilometers from work and proceeded to the private phone booth in the back. The general may have forbidden him from issuing a bulletin, but that didn't mean Vetrov couldn't have an off-the-record conversation with his cousin, who just happened to be his counterpart in charge of the north central district.

The line rang once, then, "This is Major Speransky."

"Victor, it's Aleksandr," Vetrov said. "Do you have a moment?"

Major Speransky looked over the latest information from the checkpoints. There were forty-five locations, set up on all the main routes throughout the north central district, under the guise of a training exercise.

What he was really looking for was any sign that a squad of professional soldiers had indeed infiltrated the country. If anyone else had told Speransky of the potential problem, he would have

ignored it. But his cousin Aleksandr was not prone to wild specu-
lations, so Speransky couldn't just dismiss the warning.

The major's district sat between Estonia and Moscow, and
given that most high-profile targets would be in Moscow, the
potential group of mercenaries would likely travel through his
domain.

In the hours since the "training exercise" had commenced,
nothing out of the ordinary had been found. And the latest data
was no different.

Despite his trust in his cousin's instincts, Speransky could tie
up resources for only so long without questions being asked. He
picked up his phone and called Lieutenant Mitkin, the man he'd
put in charge of coordinating the operation.

"Yes, Major?"

"If we don't find anything in the next six hours, end the
exercise."

"Understood, sir."

Speransky hung up and returned to the reports he'd been
reviewing before the latest checkpoint data arrived. But try as he
might, he couldn't focus. His cousin was overly cautious, and one
of the most unlikely people Speransky knew to engage in hyper-
bole. Which was why Speransky couldn't rid himself of the
feeling something was going on.

*What if the intruders had passed through before the checkpoints were
up?* Shit.

He picked up his phone again, intending to call a colleague
high in the administration of the security sector surrounding
Moscow, but before he could finish dialing, he set the receiver
back down.

The last thing he needed was for military intelligence to record
him passing on information about a border incursion that hadn't
been reported to the higher-ups. He didn't know for sure that they
had his phone bugged but it would be foolish to think otherwise.

He would have to send his message the old-fashioned way.

Other than Aleksandr, Speransky trusted only three people in the service without reservations. All were men he had come up with through the ranks, though one had outshined all of them and already attained the rank of colonel.

Speransky wrote three identical letters, sealed them in envelopes marked for recipient's eyes only, addressed each to one of his colleagues, and called in his adjunct.

"I want you to personally deliver these," he said and handed the man the envelopes. "These are time critical. Leave immediately and report back when you are done."

"Yes, sir." The man shuffled through the envelopes, and held out the only one with an address not in Moscow. "Directorate Eleven? I don't know where that is."

Speransky handed him a map he'd printed out, with the location marked on it. "We need to keep this secret, so I can't call them to let them know you are coming. Expect a less than friendly greeting."

"Yes, sir."

"And burn the map once you're finished with it."

The adjunct nodded.

"Dismissed."

Captain Bebchuk tapped on Colonel Annenkov's door and entered. "Ready when you are, sir."

Annenkov finished the email he'd been composing, sent it, and shut down his computer. "My bag?" he asked as he stood.

"Already on board."

They made their way to the elevator and rode it to the surface. On the helipad outside the main facility sat an Mi-8MTV-5 transport helicopter, its rotors already spinning. It had been modified for long distance travel, so it could fly him all the way to the train that would take him to the directorate's new prison.

Before the motor could drown them out, Annenkov said, "Weather update."

"The storm looks like it's going to be bigger than expected. There's also a chance it's going to hit a day earlier."

Not great news, but not a total disaster, either. If the storm kept to that schedule, he should still have enough time before it hit to get in and out of the arctic prison.

He exchanged salutes with Bebchuk and hurried to the helicopter.

Forty-seven minutes after Annenkov departed, a lone military sedan approached the gates of Directorate Eleven headquarters. The unscheduled arrival was met with maximum caution. The driver was ordered to exit his vehicle, and both were subjected to thorough searches. It wasn't until he was deemed not a threat that he was asked why he was there.

"I have a message for Colonel Annenkov," the man said.

A call was made to Captain Bebchuk, and Bebchuk arrived at the gate seven minutes later. He was directed to the small guardhouse interrogation room where the visitor waited.

The man repeated the purpose of his visit.

"Unfortunately, the colonel is not here," Bebchuk said.

"I can wait."

"He won't be back for at least three days."

"I see," the man said, clearly not expecting that.

"If you give the message to me, I'll make sure he gets it."

"Can't do that. I'm supposed to personally deliver it."

"Then I'm not sure how I can help you."

The man thought for a moment, then pulled a phone from his pocket. "If I can have a moment?"

"Of course."

Bebchuk exited the room.

Less than a minute later, the door opened and the man looked out, still holding his phone. "Major Speransky would like to speak to you."

~

"This is Captain Bebchuk," the voice said over the line.

"Captain, this is Major Speransky, north central district," Speransky said.

"How may I help you, Major?"

"My courier tells me Colonel Annenkov will be unavailable for the next few days."

"That is correct."

"The colonel and I are old friends. So be honest with me—is he really not there, or is he just too busy to be bothered?"

"He's really not here, sir," Bebchuk said.

Dammit. Speransky was afraid of that.

"If your courier gives me the message, I can relay it to the colonel," Bebchuk offered.

"The message is eyes only." Speransky paused. "Can you forward it to him?"

"You mean the physical envelope?" Bebchuk sounded surprised.

"Yes, Captain. That's exactly what I mean."

"I'm sorry, Major. He is not someplace easily reached, so I doubt we could get it to him before he heads back."

Speransky silently cursed again. "How long will he be gone?"

"He is scheduled to return on the twenty-ninth."

By then, the threat might have passed. But if it hadn't…

"Captain, it is imperative he receives the message the moment he returns."

"Yes, sir. I understand."

"Please put the courier back on."

The phone was passed again and Speransky's adjunct said, "Yes, Colonel?"

"Please give the message to Captain Bebchuk."

"Yes, sir."

25

Quinn sat up when he realized the trailer was no longer moving and looked around. Orlando was zipping her pack closed, but no one else was in the secret compartment.

"What time is it?" he asked.

"Ah, you're up."

"I wasn't sleeping."

"Then you were snoring out of choice?"

"I wasn't snoring."

"Nate has a recording that says otherwise."

He frowned at her. "The time?"

"The wee hours of the morning."

"That's not helpful."

She shrugged, picked up her bag, and exited the compartment.

He rolled his eyes, then rose, grabbed his bag, and followed.

The back of the trailer was open, revealing a sky awash in stars and a half moon nearing the horizon, providing just enough light to pick out the silhouettes of several people standing outside. Quinn hopped down and joined them.

In the opposite direction of the moon, a mountain range rose like a wall of darkness, extending north and south as far as he could see. What he didn't see in any direction were lights or other hints of civilization.

"The Urals?" he asked, nodding toward the mountains.

"Unless you know of another range in this part of the world," Orlando said.

"Would it be possible to hold the sass down until I've had some coffee?"

"Sorry, no coffee."

"Seriously?"

She shrugged and he groaned.

"I take it this is the end of the line," he said.

"Petra didn't want to drive any closer."

"How much farther?"

She pointed in the direction the truck was facing. "Two kilometers that way."

Quinn nodded before walking over to where Petra, Mikhail, and Alek were standing. "Thank you for all your help. Not sure how we would have gotten this far without you."

"If need anything else, you call, *da*?" Petra said.

"I will. I'd say that we'll give you a heads-up when things are about to go down, but chances are we'll have our hands full."

"Do not even worry about this," Mikhail said.

"Need not tell us anything," Petra said, smirking, "Will know." She wrapped him in a hug. "Be safe."

"You, too."

He turned to the others. "Time to go."

They found the railroad tracks exactly where Petra said they would be, and began following them north. While these were the same tracks that connected to those leading to the hidden base, walking the thousand-plus kilometers was not the plan.

The state-owned section of tracks that were noted on all maps traveled north for another seven hundred kilometers before turning east toward a pass over the mountains. The route was used by both freight and passenger trains. According to the information Orlando had obtained, three trains would be passing through the area within the next fourteen hours. The first two were passenger trains, one heading south to Tyumen, and the other to the north where it would cross the Urals on its way to Yakutsk. The Tyumen train was going in the wrong direction, thus of no help. And though the Yakutsk train initially would be heading in the right direction, it took a more southern pass, three hundred kilometers shy of where they wanted to go.

The third train—or as Nate called it, the momma bear—was exactly what they needed. The freight hauler would travel the entire seven hundred kilometers of public rails before turning east, putting them as close to the base as any scheduled train could. It was supposed to come through the area between five and five thirty p.m., which gave them a little more than half a day until its arrival.

That was a good thing. The tracks closest to where Petra had dropped them off were in the middle of a relatively flat and straight section, upon which the freighter would likely be moving too fast for them to jump on board.

The same could not be said for the section of rails twenty-seven kilometers to the north. There the tracks curved east around a lake before curving north again, just prior to crossing a bridge over a wide, frozen river. To pass through the area, the train would have to slow considerably. And unless its engineers were foolish, they wouldn't increase speed again until after the train cleared the bridge. Which meant the easiest place for the team to catch the train was the point where tracks met bridge.

To get there, Quinn and his friends would need every minute of the time they had to reach it.

Nate handed the binoculars to Jar. "Ten degrees to the right."

Jar looked through them. "I see it. Fifteen minutes."

Nate nodded and tapped his comm. "Bridge in sight. Estimated ETA from here, fifteen minutes."

"Copy. Any sign of the Tyumen train?" Quinn replied.

Jar turned the binoculars the other direction and shook her head.

"Nothing yet," Nate reported.

"Copy."

The southbound passenger train to Tyumen was supposed to have been the first train through the area, seven hours earlier, but the only one they'd seen so far had been the passenger train bound for Yakutsk. It had come through thirty minutes earlier, right on schedule.

Russian passenger trains had a reputation for being on time, so the multiple-hour delay of the Tyumen-bound train was unusual. Though it wasn't the train they wanted, the concern was the delay might also affect the freighter's schedule.

Nate looked south down the tracks from the small hill he and Jar had climbed, and could see the others about a half kilometer back. He was about to turn away when a dark spot beyond them near the horizon caught his eye.

A *moving* dark spot.

He held a hand out to Jar. "Let me see the binoculars."

She handed them over.

He raised them to his eyes and immediately said, "Oh, crap." He clicked on his mic again. "Nate for Quinn. Northbound train, approximately twelve kilometers away."

"What?" Jar said. "There was nothing there."

"Well, there is now." Nate handed her the glasses back.

Jar let out an angry breath. "It wasn't there a moment ago."

"Is it the Tyumen train or the freight train?" Quinn asked.

"Too far away to tell," Nate said. "I think we should assume it's our ride."

Which, if true, meant it was early. It also meant they'd never make it to the bridge in time.

Quinn seemed to be on the same wavelength, asking, "How far are we from the first curve?" From the change in his voice, Nate could tell he was running.

Jar twisted back toward the bridge. "Eight hundred meters from your position."

"Get there," Quinn said. "Now! Don't wait for us."

"Copy," Nate said.

By the time Nate and Jar reached the tracks again, Quinn and the others had closed the gap between them but were still a good two hundred meters back. Ignoring the urge to wait, Nate ran with Jar down the mostly cleared rail bed, and in just over a minute they reached the spot where the tracks began curving.

Nate was about to shout, "We need to find someplace to hide," when Jar veered left off the rail bed into the snow.

He searched for what had caught her attention but didn't spot the slight rise of a snowbank until Jar circled behind it. By the time he joined her, she was on her knees near the midpoint, pushing the snow up to add to the mound's height.

He started doing the same, and they had been able to increase its height by a half meter when a train whistle echoed across the plains.

"Dammit," he said. The blare was a lot closer than he'd expected it to be. He clicked on his mic. "Nate for Quinn."

"Go for Quinn," Quinn huffed.

"Where are you?"

"Just passed the hill you and Jar were on. You?"

"We're fifteen meters west of where the curve starts, building a...um...snow fort."

"Snow fort?"

Jar snapped her mic on. "Not a snow fort. A wall that we can hide behind."

"That sounds better," Quinn said.

Nate stood up and looked toward the tracks. "I see you. In about seventy meters, take a hard left into the snow."

"Or you could just say something when we get there."

"Or I could do that."

Nate clicked off his mic and glanced at Jar. "For the record, snow fort sounds cooler."

He moved around the mound and waved an arm over his head. "Over here!"

Orlando and Quinn were the first to turn from the tracks and race toward him.

"Behind the mound," he said, pointing.

They ran past him without stopping. Daeng and Silvia came next, reaching Nate as the rumble of the approaching train grew louder.

The moment Nate saw the front of the engine poke out from behind the hill, he dove behind the mound. "Here it comes!"

The others were already tucked against the snowbank, as out of sight as they could get.

The roar of the engine soon drowned out all other sound.

Nate peeked around the end of the snowbank. Three engine cars were leading the train, and behind them—

Nate glanced at the others. "It's the freight train!" he yelled to be heard over the noise.

He looked back at the tracks. As they'd hoped, the train was in the process of slowing as it neared the curve. He focused on the windows of the engines' compartments, searching for anyone who might be looking out, but while he saw lights on in the first two engine cars, there was no sign of the crew inside.

He waited until the last of the engine cars took the curve and was blocked from view by the rest of the train before he said, "We're clear."

They hurried around the mound and raced toward the tracks.

According to Orlando, the train was supposed to be one hundred and thirty-seven cars long. By the time the team reached the tracks again, at least fifteen of those had already passed.

Since they couldn't count on finding an unlocked car, the plan was to get onto the train first and then worry about getting into it.

Nate and Jar went first, jogging alongside the train.

Nate looked over his shoulder. "The red car coming up. Front end."

Jar glanced back. "I see it."

They picked up their pace until they were running at nearly the same speed as the train. When the gap at the front of their target car came abreast, Nate slipped into it and jumped onto the connection between it and the car in front. Jar followed and he pulled her up with him.

"We're on," he said into his mic.

Two minutes later, the others were on board, and twelve minutes after that, they were inside a freight car that was half filled with crates and only marginally warmer than outside.

"Settle in, everyone," Quinn said. "We'll be here for another…" He glanced at Orlando.

"Sixteen hours."

Nate said, "I don't suppose there's a diner car we can visit."

26

Wind whistled past the narrow gap between the railcar doors as Orlando studied the screen of her phone. After several seconds, she said, "Clear," and pulled her gooseneck camera back inside. "Looks like that storm's going to hit sooner than predicted."

"Fine by me," Quinn said. Though the storm might increase the difficulty of what they were about to do, it should make it easier for the team to move around unnoticed. "Okay, everyone. Let's try not to break any important bones."

He nodded, and Daeng pulled the door open.

Seven minutes earlier, the train had begun to slow, signaling its upcoming transition to the eastbound tracks that would take it over the Urals toward Siberia. Which meant it was time to get off.

Nate was first up. He'd already removed his prosthetic leg and was holding it as he studied the terrain rushing by. "Here goes nothing," he yelled, then tossed the leg out and jumped right after it, screaming, "Woo-hoo!"

Jar, Silvia, and Orlando followed in less dramatic fashion, leaving Quinn and Daeng.

Instead of jumping, they maneuvered themselves outside and

clung to the exterior of the railcar. Once they'd shoved the door back into place, Quinn engaged the lock.

Daeng gave Quinn a salute and launched himself backward into the snowbank lining the tracks. With a smirk, Quinn followed. By the time he dug himself out of the snow, Daeng was standing in his own divot ten meters away, cloaked in a layer of white powder.

"Can we do that again?" he yelled, grinning.

"Go ahead. I'll watch."

After the last car passed, Quinn and Daeng made their way onto the tracks and waited for the others to reach them.

"Anyone need medical?" Quinn asked.

Orlando, Jar, and Silvia shook their heads, while Nate, who'd already reattached his prosthetic, rubbed his hip and said, "I think I hit a rock."

"You're walking, so I assume you'll be fine," Quinn said.

"Your bedside manner could use a little work."

"So you've told me before."

They followed the rails in the same direction the train had gone, until a group of buildings behind a two meter-high fence came into view. The facility had the romantic name of Rail Maintenance Station 743, and was located between the eastern curving tracks and a northbound spur that supposedly dead-ended after fifty kilometers.

Quinn signaled the others to wait, then he and Nate made their way down the tracks, staying low so that the snowbank hid them from view, until they were fifty meters from the facility. Nate removed a tiny stealth drone from his pack, attached a dark gray shell that matched the storm clouds hanging heavy in the sky, and sent it aloft.

After a couple of taps on his screen, he said, "Camera's all yours," and controls appeared at the bottom of the screen on Quinn's phone.

Quinn pointed the lens at Station 743. Inside the fence were six structures, the grounds around them mostly plowed. Additionally, a four-meter strip around the outside of the fence had also been plowed. There were two wide gates, both open, through which ran tracks connecting to the main rails. One gate was along the eastbound route and the other faced the northbound spur.

The site was so isolated that the only way to reach it was via train or helicopter. There were no roads.

According to what Orlando had dug up, the facility functioned as both switching station and maintenance hub. The switching functions were automated and required only one technician to monitor them. All remaining employees would belong to the maintenance team, their primary task to keep the tracks cleared of snow in the winter and mud in the summer. When necessary, they also handled emergency train repairs. The facility was designed to accommodate up to eight people. Orlando had been unable to learn how many were currently stationed there.

The next closest facilities were either several hundred kilometers to the south or even farther to the east, on the other side of the Urals. There was no station farther north, due to what nearly everyone assumed was the termination of the tracks. But thanks to Jar's efforts, the team knew the tracks ended at the point where Directorate Eleven's secret tracks began.

The rails that connected the two different main tracks to the facility each ran into separate, mirror-image maintenance buildings, the largest structures at the station.

Of the four remaining buildings, three were each approximately half the size of the maintenance buildings. One of them was a garage with two large roll-up doors that were currently open, allowing the drone a clear view of the pair of snowplows parked inside. The other two structures sat side by side and were connected by an enclosed walkway. These were the living quarters and operations center. Just behind them was the final and smallest building. It housed the generators that kept the place running.

"Take it directly above," Quinn said.

After Nate guided the drone into the new position, Quinn scanned every inch of the complex, looking for anyone outside. The grounds were deserted, which was unsurprising given how cold it was. He wouldn't have gone outside, either, if he'd had the choice.

He switched the camera to thermal mode.

The two maintenance buildings and the snowplow garage emitted the least amount of heat. The generator building, on the other hand, glowed like it was on fire. The living quarters and operations center each had uneven heat patterns, indicating only certain sections were currently in use.

He had hoped to pick out the moving shapes of the facility's personnel, but everything was static. Given the size of the signatures, there couldn't have been more than two or three people inside. He said as much to Nate.

"Maybe sleeping?" Nate suggested.

"Could be. But the train just went through so I'd think they'd be awake for that."

"Is it possible no one's here?"

The thought had crossed Quinn's mind, but he doubted he and the others could be that lucky.

"Take it down twenty meters," he said.

The drone descended, and the indistinct heat signatures in the living quarters and operations center began taking on more definition.

"Stop," Quinn said.

Two of the shapes were definitely two people, both in the living quarters, but not in the same room. One was prone and unmoving, probably asleep like Nate had guessed. The other was sitting on something in a room on the other side of the building. In front of the person was a warm rectangle that was probably a television. Quinn hunted for other personnel but the two were it.

"Low pass, security check," Quinn said.

Nate took the drone down until it was at roof level, then flew it slowly around the complex so Quinn could pick out security cameras and any other devices that might alert the people inside to intruders. But there were none. This also wasn't surprising. In most circumstances, the complex's remote location would be more than enough security. The powers that be had probably decided installing additional measures would be a waste of money.

The other thing the drone had confirmed: no other people were at the station.

"I've seen enough," Quinn said. "Let's check it out."

Nate directed the drone to rise thirty meters, set it to hover, and followed Quinn to the nearest open gate.

After a check of the drone's camera confirmed the two people inside the living quarters hadn't moved, Quinn and Nate slipped into the compound and hurried behind the maintenance building that serviced the north-south route.

Quinn motioned for Nate to hold his position, then he eased around the corner and crept toward the nearest entrance. He was only a few steps away when a light above the door flashed to life.

He halted and whispered into his mic, "Did someone inside turn that on?"

Nate said, "Give me a second."

In the quiet that followed, Quinn eased backward, out of the light's halo.

"Heat signatures haven't moved," Nate reported. "It's got to be triggered by a motion detector."

Quinn remained stationary until the light turned off. When he stepped forward again, it came back on. Motion triggered, then.

He approached the door and tried the handle. It had a lock but it wasn't engaged. Again, the remoteness obviously seen as the only deterrent needed.

He stepped inside and scanned the space.

The interior was one giant room. The tracks entered through the wall to the left, the opening currently blocked by large folding doors. Just inside, the tracks split into two sets. Both continued for nearly the entire length of the room, ending at Mini Cooper-sized metal and rubber bumpers three meters from where Quinn stood.

"Clear," he said into his mic.

He could hear Nate entering behind him as he took a couple of steps closer to the tracks. The near set was empty, while resting on the other were two train cars. The car next to the bumpers was a flatbed, on which were several rail ties and a pile of chains. And the second car—

"Well, that's disappointing," Nate said, walking up, his gaze on the same car Quinn was frowning at.

The rail inspection vehicle was exactly what they'd been hoping to find, only this one was half disassembled and wouldn't be going anywhere.

"Let's check the other building," Quinn said.

They sneaked across the grounds, staying out of sight of the living quarters as much as possible, and slipped through another unlocked door into the second maintenance building.

Just like the exterior, the interior was the same as the other building, only a mirror image. An enclosed cargo car like the one in which they'd ridden north sat on the nearest spur. On the far spur were three empty flatbed cars, and sitting in front of them, nearest to the closed track folding doors, was another track inspection car. This one appeared intact.

Quinn and Nate shared a look before they walked over for a closer look.

In the States, inspection cars were often modified pickup trucks with rail wheels that could be lowered onto the tracks. It was possible there were similar hybrid vehicles in Russia. But the one in front of them was not one of those.

It looked like a stubby version of a passenger car, with a door at the midpoint and identical large windows around each end.

Quinn opened the door and they climbed inside. In front of the wraparound windows were identical sets of master controls, allowing the car to be driven from either end. In the area in between were four seats and several large instruments that Quinn figured were part of the inspection process. It would be a cozy fit for the six members of his team, but it'd be a luxury compared to hiking the remaining distance to the prison. Not to mention that doing the latter would probably end with all of them dying from exposure.

Nate pointed at a switch. "I think if we flip this one, the power should come on." The labels were in Russian, a language Nate read better than Quinn.

"Go ahead," Quinn said.

"Me? That's cool. You should do it."

Quinn raised an eyebrow.

"I'm just saying, if something goes wrong, better if it was your fault than mine."

Quinn stared at him, unamused.

"Or I guess maybe I can do it," Nate said.

"An excellent suggestion."

With one eye closed and the other narrowed to a slit, Nate put a finger on the switch and pushed it into the up position.

Something under the floor vibrated, and the control console lit up.

Nate grinned. "See? I was right."

"All right, smart guy. Figure out what this thing runs on and if we need to juice it up."

"On it."

Quinn switched his comm back to the main channel. "Quinn for Orlando."

"Go for Orlando."

"Vehicle secured in building B. We're getting it ready. Take care of the other problem."

"Copy."

Orlando checked the drone feed.

The prone human shape had moved an arm but nothing else since she'd last checked. The one who'd been watching TV had walked into a new room and stopped in front of what she guessed was a refrigerator. The person removed something from inside and headed back to the seat in front of the TV.

She nodded to Jar and Daeng.

They headed left along the back of the building, and Orlando and Silvia went right.

Forty seconds later, two quick clicks came over the comm, signaling Daeng and Jar were in position.

Orlando used her gooseneck camera to check around the corner before replying with two clicks of her own.

She glanced back at Silvia, motioned for her to stay where she was, pulled out her gun, and attached a sound suppressor. When she was set, she clicked her mic once, paused, clicked again, paused, and clicked a third time. She received a single click of acknowledgment from Jar and Daeng.

Orlando leaned around the corner and aimed her pistol at a massive group of icicles hanging from the roof about a third of the way down. From the corner opposite, she could see Daeng doing the same.

She clicked a final time, and they each fired a single shot.

The bullets smashed through the ice with a splintering crunch, sending shards of frozen water raining onto the ground. Unlike she'd hoped, though, the meter-thick sheet of snow on the roof did not budge.

"Dammit," she muttered.

"The TV watcher just stood," Jar said, her voice low in Orlando's ear. "Sleeper unchanged." A pause. "The first one's just standing there. I don't think—"

A loud crack rang out, and a small hunk of the snow began sliding off the roof.

"That did it," Jar said. "He's heading for the door."

Orlando exchanged her pistol for her dart gun. Loaded in its chamber was a dart filled with enough Beta-Somnol to knock someone out for at least two hours.

"At the door," Jar said. "Opening now."

The door swung inward, and a man stepped outside.

He glanced at the new pile of ice and snow and snorted, as if he couldn't believe he wasted time going outside for something so trivial.

Orlando was just about to pull her trigger when another crack sounded and a larger slab of the snow from the roof raced toward the ground. The man didn't even have time to turn back to the door before the mass of white clipped his shoulder and knocked him off his feet. The rest of the snow kept coming, quickly burying all but his feet.

"Oh, crap," Daeng said.

"Jar," Orlando said. "The sleeper?"

"No movement."

Orlando sprinted over to the snow pile. While incapacitating the man had been the plan, doing so by avalanche had not.

She dug the snow away from his face, whipped off one of her gloves, and placed her fingers against his neck to check his pulse. He was still alive, but from the blood oozing from cuts on his face and neck, she was sure he'd be in a lot of pain when he regained consciousness.

She signaled for the others to join her, then said, "Jar and Daeng, take care of the other one. Silvia, you help me here."

Jar and Daeng headed into the building, while Orlando and Silvia started clearing the snow off the downed man.

When he was free, Daeng's voice came over the comm. "Building secured."

Orlando and Silvia carried the injured man inside to a bathroom, where they used the station's first aid kit to patch him up.

Once they'd done all they could, Orlando said, "Bed?"

"This way," Jar said.

They carried the man into a bunk room and put him under the

covers. Orlando administered a dose of Beta-Somnol large enough to keep him under until the next morning. She did the same for the other man in the room before flicking on her comm. "Orlando for Quinn."

"Go for Quinn."

"Station secured."

27

DIRECTORATE 11 SPECIAL HOLDING FACILITY

Colonel Annenkov's escort pressed a button mounted on the wall and said, "Colonel Annenkov and Sergeant Yegorov requesting entrance."

"Proceed with verification," a tinny voice said over the speaker.

The sergeant stared into the security camera. When the light above the lens turned green, he stepped to the side and Annenkov took his place.

After another green light, a motorized whir reverberated from the walls and the door swung open.

"Proceed," the voice said.

They entered the prison control center. In the middle of the large, circular room was a two-person guard station surrounded by monitors. Around the room at equal intervals were eleven security doors. Ten accessed different wings of the prison, and the eleventh the hall from which Annenkov had arrived.

"Colonel Annenkov to see our newest guest," the sergeant told the guards.

One of them pointed at a door. "Wing four."

Annenkov and Yegorov walked to the door. Like the one

they'd just come through, it whirred and swung inward and shut again after they passed through.

They walked down the brightly lit corridor to a barred gate. When the lock buzzed, the sergeant pulled the gate open.

"Thank you, Sergeant," Annenkov said. "Please wait for me in the control center."

"Yes, sir." Yegorov saluted and headed back.

Annenkov stepped through the gate.

Each wing of the prison consisted of five cells, two on each side of the corridor and one at the end. Currently, only two cells were occupied—one by the directorate's oldest guest and the other by its newest.

Annenkov walked to Dmitri Melnikov's cell first and activated the wall-mounted observation screen. Melnikov was sitting on his cot with his eyes closed and his arms resting on his thighs. Every few seconds, one of his fingers would move, more as if reliving a memory than from a mindless twitch.

After months of no conversations, Melnikov should have been showing signs of psychological deterioration, but the prisoner seemed as calm and collected as he had been on the day Annenkov last talked to him, the day Melnikov arrived in Russia ten months ago. The colonel was not concerned, however. Isolation never failed to break a man. If it took another ten months, or even ten years, so be it. Annenkov had all the time in the world to wait.

He walked to the cell of his newest detainee.

Vassily Levkin was a particularly satisfying prize for Annenkov. Given that Levkin was a former Soviet intelligence agent, his actions against the Russian government made him a more heinous traitor than any of the others, as far as the colonel was concerned.

Annenkov activated the observation screen, then laughed. Levkin was doing sit-ups, as if he wanted to keep in shape for the day he would be released. That was a day the vile apostate would soon realize was never coming.

The colonel pressed the button on the screen that connected him to the guard in the control room.

"Yes, sir?"

"Open the viewing port to Levkin's cell."

A small section of the door at eye level slid outward and up, revealing a thick pane of translucent plastic.

Levkin continued his sit-ups, oblivious to the change.

Annenkov watched for several seconds before he turned on the microphone.

"Vassily Levkin, your attention."

As was protocol, Annenkov's voice was the first Levkin had heard since his arrival in Russia, and it would also be his last. The asshole continued exercising, unaware of the importance of the moment.

"I am Colonel Annenkov, and you are a guest of Directorate Eleven."

"And why should I care about this?" Levkin asked without pausing.

"Because this room will be your home until you take your last breath, and this conversation the last you will ever have."

Levkin finished another sit-up. "Conversation is overrated."

"I wonder if you will feel the same in a few years."

Levkin rose to his feet, stretched, and walked to the door, smiling as if this were just another normal day.

Annenkov had to resist the urge to take a step back. He knew Levkin was big from the man's file, but that knowledge hadn't prepared him for coming face to face with the sheer size of the traitor.

Levkin thumped his hands against the door and leaned in until his face was only centimeters from the plastic barrier. "You think you will break me, Colonel Annenkov?"

"I know I will."

Levkin sneered. "I guess we will see, won't we?"

"There is nothing to see. I am the last person you will see or speak to. This is where you will die."

The man's sneer turned into a wide grin. "One of us may die here, but it won't be me."

Levkin stared at Annenkov for a few more seconds before turning away and lowering himself back to the floor, where he began doing pushups.

Annenkov wanted to say something else, a last word to undercut the prisoner's confidence and get under the man's skin, but he could think of nothing.

In truth, it was Levkin who had gotten under Annenkov's skin.

One of us may die here, but it won't be me.

Annenkov released the mic button. He'd prepared a speech for the man but he wasn't going to waste the oxygen. Levkin was a piece of human garbage, and whatever game he was playing, he'd already lost. He just didn't know it yet.

Annenkov would not allow himself to spend another second thinking about the traitor.

He tapped the control room button. "Close view port."

∿

Annenkov slammed shut his office door and paced angrily to his desk. He pulled out his chair and shoved it back in place again. He was too worked up to sit.

Levkin had not been the first prisoner to act defiant. Andrei Barsukov had acted as if Annenkov wasn't even there when the colonel had told him his sentence, while Uri Sobolevsky had stared out the view port of his cell, repeating over and over, "I do not recognize your authority over me." In both instances, Annenkov had felt nothing but anticipation of seeing each man broken and begging for attention.

Why had Levkin's posturing unnerved him?

He tried to tell himself it was because of the man's ties to the KGB, but Annenkov knew that wasn't true.

It was the way Levkin sounded and acted like he wasn't

surprised to be where he was, that he *expected* to be there. With Barsukov and Sobolevsky, there had been hints of fear underlining their actions.

Levkin had not been even the slightest bit afraid.

The colonel closed his eyes and took a deep breath.

It doesn't matter. When Levkin realizes how screwed he really is, fear will find him.

The roiling ball of rage in Annenkov's gut eased. He was overworked, that was all. At any other time, the former KGB officer wouldn't have gotten to him.

He reached for the phone on his desk. It was time to get out of this hellhole.

"Prepare the train," he told the lieutenant who answered. "I want to be heading south within the hour."

"Sir, em, that's not a good idea."

"Excuse me?"

"Conditions aboveground are worsening. Snow and wind are both increasing."

"I thought the storm wasn't due for another half day."

"It appears the forecast was incorrect," the lieutenant said, quickly adding, "sir."

"It doesn't matter. The storm won't affect the train. Get it ready." Most of the tracks were in tunnels, and any snow that fell on those could be easily driven through.

"True, sir. But by the time you reach the helipad, the helicopter will be unable to fly and you would be stuck there."

The helipad was three hundred kilometers to the south, where the Directorate Eleven-dedicated tracks joined the commercial tracks.

Annenkov's grip tightened around the receiver. He did *not* want to be trapped here, but it would be preferable to spending possibly days on the train. "Fine. I want to be notified the moment I can leave." He hung up without waiting for a response.

It was then that he noticed the dull red light glowing at the bottom of the office phone, indicating someone had left him a message. He played it on speaker.

"Colonel, this is Captain Bebchuk. You've received a message from Major Speransky, north central district. It was delivered by courier to directorate headquarters. I got the impression it was urgent, so I wanted to let you know in case it's something you're expecting."

Speransky? Annenkov hadn't talked to his friend in nearly six months and could think of no reason why Speransky would send an official message. Especially to directorate headquarters.

He called Directorate Eleven headquarters and got Bebchuk on the line.

"Speransky's courier, he came to the base?" he asked.

"I met him at the guardhouse. He never set foot past the gate."

"He didn't indicate what the message concerned?"

"No, sir. In fact, he had to call Major Speransky to get permission to leave it with me. The major made me promise to give it to you the moment you returned."

"And you also talked to Speransky?"

"Yes, sir."

"Do you have the message?"

"Hold on...yes, I have it here."

"Read it to me."

"Um, sir, I was told it's for your eyes only."

"For the moment, you *are* my eyes. Read it."

Annenkov could hear Bebchuk open the envelope and extract the contents. The captain read the message to him.

Someone else might have laughed off the warning of an armed group of infiltrators as just a paranoid's overreaction, but not Annenkov. He had been expecting a reaction to the work his organization was doing, not that this potential incursion had anything to do with the directorate. Still, the possibility that it did was something he could not dismiss.

"Captain, go to threat level two," he said.

"Yes, sir. Right away."

Headquarters would now be on heightened alert, which should be more than enough to discourage an attack.

"And Captain, it appears I won't be returning until after this storm passes. I am relying on you to handle any problems that come up."

"Yes, sir. You can count on me."

"I hope you're right."

Annenkov hung up. He considered issuing the same threat level increase at the prison, but quickly dismissed the idea. Just getting to here would be nearly impossible for anyone other than Directorate Eleven personnel, and with the growing storm outside, even nearly would be impossible.

28

The mystery of the missing passenger train bound for Tyumen was solved when the team discovered a white board in the control center connected to the living facilities. On it was a list of ongoing tasks. An item at the bottom noted that the westbound train had experienced mechanical troubles as it tried passing through the mountains and had moved onto a side track to await repairs. A crew of three maintenance technicians had been dispatched from Station 743 to deal with it. This explained why only two crew members were currently at the station. Even better, next to the entry was a notation reading: ONGOING AS OF 1430, giving Quinn and his team more than enough time to get out of there before the absent station personnel returned.

They just needed to move the inspection car from the maintenance building that served the east-west tracks onto the north-south tracks. A simple enough procedure in and of itself, but they couldn't do it immediately due to a small hitch, in the form of another train heading their way. Data in the control room indicated it would be there in twenty minutes.

If they didn't run into any problems, Quinn was confident they could get the inspection car moved within the window. But if something happened to delay them...

One of the top ten rules of working in the secret world: if an *if* can be avoided, avoid it. And this *if* could easily be removed from the equation by waiting until the coming train passed, so he told the others that's what they'd be doing.

"Um," Silvia said, grimacing.

"What?" he asked.

"Do we know if the station and trains have some kind of standard communication when they go by? Because if so…"

She didn't need to finish the thought.

Quinn looked at Orlando. "Do we know?"

"We don't, but it would be a mistake to think there isn't any."

"Well, crap. If anyone has any ideas, I'd love to hear them."

Nate said, "How much time until it passes?"

Jar checked her watch. "Eighteen minutes, forty-five seconds."

"What if we make it look like the station is having communication problems?" Nate said. "There are satellite dishes and antennas on top of the garage beside the east-west tracks. We put a couple people up there and have them act like they're working on the equipment when the train goes by."

Quinn nodded. "I like it."

"We could also knock over an antenna, make it look like there's a big problem. The train crew might report it to officials down the line so no one will raise the alarm when they can't reach this place. That could buy us even more time."

Quinn glanced at Orlando.

"Works for me," she said.

By 3:10 p.m., two satellite dishes and one antenna had been tipped on their sides, the latter hanging partially off the roof toward the tracks.

Quinn and Nate went up to play the part of the repair crew. To make sure the train crew didn't miss seeing them in the dusk of the winter night, powerful work lights were rigged up to flood the area.

Quinn watched the tracks for the train and was rewarded a few minutes later when the lights on the lead engine appeared from around a snowy hill.

"Contact," Quinn said into his mic. "Three minutes out."

He and Nate positioned themselves next to the downed antenna at the edge of the roof and pretended to work on it.

When the engine neared, Quinn waved at it in greeting, and almost immediately received a quick double blast of the train's whistle. And then the engine curved out of sight.

Just in case there was crew watching elsewhere on the train, Quinn and Nate continued their faux repairs until the last car receded into the night.

Nate pressed the start button and the inspection car's engine rumbled to life.

From outside the car, Quinn yelled, "Try moving it forward."

Nate nudged the lever that put the car into motion, intending to move it only a few meters. Instead, the car lurched quickly toward the exit from the building. He yanked the lever back and engaged what he was pretty sure were the brakes.

The car screeched to a stop just shy of outside.

Jar looked up at him. "That did not go the way you said it would."

"No one got hurt," he said. "I call it a win."

Everyone climbed on board save Daeng, who was operating the track switcher controls. Nate eased the train into gear more carefully than before, and this time the forward lurch was not nearly as dramatic. He guided the car out of the building and down the spur to where it linked up with the main line. Daeng had already activated the switch and they merged seamlessly onto the track. Nate continued on for another thirty meters to make sure the car was clear of the transition zone before he hit the brakes again.

"Nate for Daeng."

"Go for Daeng."

"We're clear. Switch it back."

"Copy." The line went silent for a moment, then, "Switch complete."

Nate squeezed past everyone to get to the identical set of controls at the other end of the car, and started them moving in the direction from which they had come. As expected, instead of transitioning back onto the spur, they continued along the curve of the main line to just past where it met up with the north-south route.

Daeng electronically switched the junction, allowing Nate to transition the car onto the northbound tracks, then Daeng switched it back so that the train due to pass through the area early the next morning wouldn't accidentally find itself heading north.

Nate slowed as the car came abreast of the maintenance building serving the north side. Daeng jogged out from the station and jumped on.

"Next stop, the North Pole!" Nate declared as he increased the speed.

"That is impossible," Jar said.

"It isn't if you *believe*."

"Jar," Orlando said, "if you'd like to move to San Francisco with Quinn and me, you are more than welcome."

They traveled for fifty kilometers before stopping again.

A dozen meters in front of them, the single line they were on split into ten separate tracks, like a railroad candelabra. Each new track traveled parallel to the others for approximately two hundred meters before terminating at another of the Mini Cooper-sized barriers. Three of the spurs had train cars stored on them, while the remaining seven were empty.

"Orlando, Daeng, Jar, with me," Quinn said.

The quartet filed out of the car and walked down the center spur to the barriers.

Quinn scanned the area. "Split up and look around. There has to be a way past this point."

He headed to the left and began looking for hidden tracks that led beyond the barriers, while the others spread out and did the same.

Not long after, Daeng shouted, "Quinn! Something you should see."

He was standing in a flat area several meters beyond the tracks at the far left end, kicking at the snow.

Quinn jogged over and saw Daeng had unearthed a section of flat concrete. Daeng pointed at another cleared spot several meters away, where more concrete peeked through. "It's a big slab. And look at this. It's what drew my attention in the first place."

He walked over to what Quinn had thought was just a bump in the snow, but turned out to be a gray box sitting next to the concrete. A large metal pipe ran from the box into the slab, but Quinn saw no obvious way to open the box.

"Helipad?" Daeng said, looking back at the concrete.

"Gotta be," Quinn said.

He'd seen setups like this before. The metal box was probably a remote-controlled heating unit that melted the snow when the pad was needed. A helipad in the middle of nowhere, next to the end of a rail line with no civilization around would be weird, if you didn't factor in that this must be where the secret prison rail system started.

"Tracks!" Orlando called out, waving from several meters beyond the end of a spur that had an unused passenger car on it.

By the time everyone had converged on her position, she'd brushed away enough snow to reveal that the rails continued beyond the barrier for at least another ten meters. None of the other spurs they'd checked did so.

"Daeng, check the passenger car out," Quinn said. "I'm betting there's an easy way to move it."

Daeng nodded and jogged off.

Quinn turned back to the barrier to find Jar crouching next to it, studying it.

"Find something?" he asked.

She pointed at one of the clamps that secured the barrier to the rails. "This is different than the other barriers I checked."

She stared at it a moment longer, then sprung to her feet, grabbed a metal support bar on the east side, and pushed down. The bar lowered like a giant switch, and something clunked beneath the barrier.

The corner of her mouth ticked up. She circled behind the barrier and pushed. The whole thing began sliding down the tracks.

"Okay, good," Quinn said. "But pushing it all the way off the spur? I would think they'd have come up with an easier way to move it."

"They did."

She motioned for Quinn to follow her and circled around to the front of the barrier. Apparently, when she pushed down the bar, it had not only released the clamps holding the barrier in place, but it'd also extended a previously hidden train car connector.

Jar nodded toward the parked passenger car. "This attaches to the back of that, and both move out of the way together."

They pushed the barrier to the car and locked the connectors together.

Daeng hopped out of the car a moment later and eyed the barrier. "That's nifty. Jar figure it out?"

Quinn's eyebrow shot up. "Are you implying that I couldn't?"

"No, not at all. But you'd probably still be working it out."

"He's right," Jar said.

Quinn stared open-mouthed at them.

"Hey, if it's any consolation, you'd definitely figure it out before I could," Daeng said.

"He is also right about that," Jar said.

Now it was Daeng's turn to look offended.

"Did you find a way to move the car?" Jar asked. "Or do I need to deal with that, too?"

Daeng huffed, doubling down on his mock indignation. "As a matter of fact, I did. It's set up like the inspection car, only not as many bells and whistles. Just start, stop, and throttle. Nate just needs to move the inspection car back to give me some room, then I can park this on one of the other—"

"Nate doesn't need to move," Orlando said, walking toward them.

They all turned to her.

"There's another spur just long enough to fit the cars and the barrier, about fifteen meters past the end of the line. We move them there, Nate drives by, we move them back in place, and no one will know we were here."

They ran dark to cut down on the possibility of someone seeing them, even going as far as to cover the inspection car's control panel lights. To cut down on the chances of unexpected collisions, they took turns watching the tracks ahead through night vision goggles. The storm had finally started in earnest and was growing stronger by the hour, and the last thing they needed was to smash into a fallen tree or slam into a landslide. For that reason, Quinn had made the decision to keep their speed to a steady thirty-five kilometers an hour.

By ten p.m., approximately halfway into their journey, the snow and wind had intensified so much that it blew past them in thick sheets, cutting visibility down to a couple dozen meters, even less at times. Quinn was forced to order another speed reduction and told anyone who wasn't on watch or driving to get some sleep. He, Nate, and Jar took the first watch shift.

By midnight, it was impossible to discern where the ground ended and the sky began. But if they slowed again, they wouldn't reach the area of the secret base until after the sun rose. Granted, the storm would make the day murky, but any increase of light would be suboptimal.

Quinn was about to give the order to lower the speed anyway when the storm vanished, like someone had flipped a switch.

"Stop," he said.

Nate disengaged the engine and applied the brakes. Metal wheels squealed on metal rails until all movement halted.

Someone bumped into Quinn's back. "What's going on?" Orlando asked, voice sleepy.

"Not sure," he said.

He lowered a window and could still hear the storm. Only now instead of surrounding them, it was coming from somewhere behind them, low and distant. He turned on his phone's flashlight and aimed it outside.

Approximately three meters from the inspection car was a wall of curving rock that went up and over them. "Looks like we've found one of the hidden passages."

That was good for avoiding the storm but potentially dangerous, as the possibility was high that tunnels along the secret tracks were being monitored. This potential was something they'd discussed and come up with a plan to mitigate any issues.

Hopefully.

"Who wants to drive this thing?" Nate asked.

"I'll do it," Orlando volunteered.

Nate gave her the driver's seat and retrieved one of his drones. He prepped it and flew it out the window to a position in front of the train.

"You have camera," he said to Jar.

Quinn had positioned himself behind her, and had eyes on her screen when the video feed and control overlay appeared on her phone. She quickly tested the pan, tilt, and zoom, then nodded.

"Good to go."

When Orlando started them moving again, Nate kept the drone at a constant forty meters in front of the car.

Four minutes in, Jar said, "Stop."

Orlando eased back on the accelerator and applied the brakes.

Jar had superimposed the output of the electronics scanner—another feature of the drone—over the feed. On the screen, a white line ran along the top of the tunnel and disappeared into the distance.

"Conduit?" he asked.

"I believe so," she said, and instructed Nate to fly the drone forward four meters.

As he did, the line grew more prominent.

"Hold there," she said, and typed on her phone When she finished, a new screen appeared, filled entirely with what looked to Quinn like unreadable text.

She studied it and nodded. "It's an electric line connected to a series of cameras."

"Where?" Quinn asked.

She pointed at the nearest end of the white line. "That's the first one. It is motion triggered and currently in standby mode."

"Do your thing," Quinn said.

With Daeng's assistance, Jar sent a second drone up. Its main feature was a device Jar had put together to disable motion detectors.

When it reached the first drone, she turned on the disrupter. After a beat, a block of text scrolled down one side of her screen. She scanned it and said, "Blocking successful."

With a nod from Quinn, Orlando began moving the inspection car again. Nate moved the first drone forward, searching for additional cameras, while Jar piloted the second drone several meters behind it.

For the next fifteen minutes, they played leapfrog with the

drones. The first identifying cameras and the second temporarily killing their motion detection abilities so the inspection car could pass. After finding the sixth camera, they entered a kilometer-long section of the tunnel that wasn't monitored.

When the drone finally detected a camera again, it was pointed in the direction they were headed, instead of the other way like the others had been. Five more cameras followed, all facing the same direction. The reason for the change became clear soon after they passed the last one and the end of the tunnel came into view. No need to monitor the middle of a passage when both entrances were being watched.

Over the next several hours, the route alternated between stretches of near blizzard conditions and the eerie calm of more tunnels with more cameras to be deactivated.

During one of the tunnel passages, Quinn reluctantly allowed himself to lie down to rest his eyes.

Turned out the rest of his body wanted in.

29

S lava Kramnik glanced out the triple-paned window at the blowing snow and felt the urge to shiver.

According to the latest weather reports, the storm was turning into the biggest one to hit this part of the country in over forty years. Already it stretched from the Urals to Moscow, and from the Arctic Circle to the Kazakhstan border, and was not expected to stop for another four days.

A dozen trains were behind schedule, and those that weren't underway were likely to be delayed until the storm ended. It would take weeks for Slava and his colleagues to untangle the mess.

And delayed trains weren't the only issue. Communication problems with several remote facilities had been cropping up since the snow started falling.

Case in point, Slava had just received a report from a Moscow-bound train that had crossed the Urals that afternoon. When passing Maintenance Station 743, located on the western flank of the mountains, the train's crew had seen workers trying to fix the station's antenna. Slava checked the records and saw that communication with the station had ceased an hour before the train passed.

He noted the observations of the train crew into the system and attached a copy of the report. What he didn't need to add—because anyone who checked it would realize—was that even if Station 743 was able to get its communication gear back in working order, it was unlikely to reestablish communications until the storm subsided.

Slava submitted the report and turned to the next item on his far too long list of problems.

30

"Rise and shine," Orlando whispered in Quinn's ear. He cracked open his eyes. The only thing he could see in the dimness was her, hovering above him. He reached up to caress her cheek.

"Go ahead," she said. "I dare you."

He blinked, suddenly remembering where they were, and that they were most definitely not alone.

Screw it, he thought, and cupped her face.

Orlando's eyes widened in surprise but she didn't pull away, so he rose on an elbow and kissed her.

"Good morning," he said.

"Good morning," she replied.

"What time is it?"

"Four fifteen."

"And we're stopped because...?"

"It's the end of the line."

From somewhere behind her, Nate said, "Um, do you guys want us to go outside and give you some privacy?"

Orlando kissed Quinn again, then grabbed his hand and pulled him up. "Come on, sleepy head. We're burning daylight."

From near the front of the inspection car, Jar said, "Incorrect.

The sun will not be up for another three hours and twenty-five minutes."

Orlando looked like she was going to respond, but then she just smiled and shook her head.

Quinn looked out the window but could see nothing. "Where *are* we?"

"In a tunnel," Orlando asked.

"Yeah. That much I could tell. But if this is the end of the line, where's the exit? I can't even hear the wind."

"We're on a dead-end spur off the main line. We think they use it when there are two trains here, so one can get out of the way of the other." She shrugged. "Or I could give you the GPS coordinates, if you'd prefer that."

"Your sarcasm is touching."

"I'm glad you're awake enough to notice." She tossed him a set of comm gear. "I sent Daeng and Silvia to scout ahead. The rest of us are ready to head out when you are."

Quinn zipped up his jacket and donned his radio. "After you."

They hiked back to the main tunnel and headed down to the exit, where Daeng and Silvia were waiting a few meters from the end of the tunnel. Outside, the storm continued to churn.

"The base should be approximately a hundred and eighty meters that way," Daeng said, pointing a few degrees left of exit. "I went a couple dozen meters outside but there was too much snow to see it from here."

The storm seemed even worse than predicted. That would make getting to the base more difficult, but the camouflaging benefits from the near blizzard conditions outweighed the negatives.

"Orlando, Jar, you're with me," Quinn said. "The rest of you wait here."

They put on their snowshoes and tied themselves to one another—Quinn in the lead and Orlando at the back—before setting out into the storm.

Quinn kept his binoculars handy, set on thermal vision, and

every few minutes checked for heat signatures in the direction of the base. Even with the snowshoes, the going was slow, and it was nearly fifteen minutes before he spotted a faint glow of orange.

He passed Orlando the glasses and she scanned the area, then handed the binoculars to Jar.

"Could be a pipe," Orlando said.

"Or an air shaft," Jar said.

As they resumed walking, a new noise began fighting for attention with the wind. A whir or maybe a hum, there one moment, and washed away the next by the storm. After another few dozen meters, not only did the hum become too strong for the wind to mask, but the storm seemed to suddenly lessen.

"Hold," Quinn said.

The view ahead was now much clearer and he could see the side of a building. He checked behind them and realized that just a few steps back, the storm was whirling as strong as it had been since they left the tunnel.

He glanced up. Even in the darkness, he could make out a flat black surface about ten meters above. The underside of the fake lake, he realized.

He turned his attention back to the building and scanned it with his binoculars. It was large enough to disappear from view to both the right and left and up to a few meters below the canvas, or whatever material the lake was printed on.

Along the wall, he picked out more than twenty distinct points of heat. The three highest must have been vents, as heat radiated from them and dissipated into the night. Below these ran several pipes of varying sizes. The remaining shapes were squares and rectangles, all but one no bigger than a large fuse box. The exception was a rectangle about the size of the windshield on a small car, standing on its end.

To Jar, he said, "Do a sweep."

She attached the security detection sensor to her phone, aimed it toward the wall, and slowly moved it left and right.

"I can tell there are electronics ahead, but too much interference to know anything specific."

They proceeded with caution toward the wall, Jar continuing to scan.

When they were approximately fifteen meters away, she said, "Stop," then pointed ahead and to the right. "One camera." She consulted her screen again. "Appears to be in standby mode. If you give me a moment, I should be able to hack into it from here."

"Do it."

For the next several seconds, her thumbs flew over her phone, and then she said, "I'm in. And…I have control. It won't come on again unless I tell it to."

"Anything else in the area we need to be worried about?" Quinn asked.

"Nothing."

They walked to the wall.

The large rectangle of heat Quinn had seen turned out to be a steel panel set in the concrete wall, with no bolts or brackets on the outside holding it in place.

Jar ran her sensor over it. "No electronics connected to it."

Orlando attached an audio amplifier to the surface and linked the feed to the comm. They heard the distant rumble of machinery, but that was it.

Orlando tapped once on the surface. An echo, not the dull thud of something solid on the other side.

She removed a drill from her pack, inserted a 6mm bit, and drilled a hole in the lower right corner of the panel. As soon as she punched through, she reversed out, and Jar slipped a gooseneck camera inside.

On normal light mode, all they saw was black. When Jar switched to thermal vision, several areas of heat appeared—pipes mostly, outlining the walls of a small, unoccupied room.

On the far wall, the pipes moved around a rectangle of darkness that had to be a door.

Quinn turned his mic back on. "Quinn for Nate."

"Go for Nate."

"We're ready for you."

～

Nate fired up the acetylene torch and cut a flap in the metal rectangle, then he and Daeng pushed it inward.

"Hold on," Jar said before anyone could enter. She was standing a few meters away, looking at the top of the wall. "I need to leave the booster. Up there would be best."

"I got you," Quinn said.

He made a cradle with his gloved hands and lifted her into the air.

"A little higher," she said.

Nate, who was a couple of inches taller than Quinn, came over and pushed up on her other foot, enough for her to grab the lip and climb onto the roof.

She disappeared for nearly a minute, before popping her head over the edge. "Check the connection."

Quinn pulled out the sat phone. "It's not full strength but should be enough."

"I cannot control the weather," she said.

"And here I was thinking you could."

The look she gave him was not amused.

While most sat phones had serious problems in stormy conditions, theirs was a specialized model, not available to the public and designed to work in harsh conditions. Still, this was no regular storm, and a booster would help guarantee their call getting through when it needed to.

Once Jar was back on the ground, the whole team climbed through the opening. Nate and Daeng then bent the flap back into place and held it there so Silvia could spray foam sealant around the edges. This would keep the storm from leaking through the gap and creating a draft that could be noticed. Nate placed a relay on the inside of the now resealed flap and confirmed it was connected to the booster on the roof.

While all that was going on, Quinn and Orlando checked the door on the other side of the room. It was metal and had just enough space underneath for Orlando to slip a camera through. On the other side was a deserted hallway lined with more pipes.

"We're clear here," Quinn said. "Jar?"

Jar was sitting on the floor, back to a wall, her computer propped on her lap. "Working on it."

While waiting for her to gain access to the base's security system and computer network, the rest of them geared up, slipping pistols and dart guns into holsters, knives into sheaths, and flash-bangs, smoke grenades, and other incendiary devices into pockets. As Quinn pulled his pack back on, Jar said, "Done."

"Base map?" Orlando asked.

"Just sent to you."

Orlando pulled the map up on her phone and studied it. "Just like we were told, the design is similar to their headquarters but not an exact copy. This level's the only one aboveground. Lots of storage rooms, and the train platform where the tracks end." She paused, her gaze not leaving her screen. "They apparently have four central elevators here instead of three, and there's a guard station next to them." She dragged her finger over her phone, moving the map. "Below us are five more levels. Level two— that's the one right below us—appears to be administration offices, a medical facility, and training rooms. Level three is housing, cafeteria, and rec area. And let's see…level four is facility operations."

"Let me guess," Nate said. "The prison's at the very bottom."

"Yep." She studied her screen for a moment longer and blew out a breath. "I count fifty cells, broken up into groups of five."

"*Fifty?*" Daeng said.

"That's not the worst part."

"Of course it's not," Nate said.

"The only way in and out of each cell group is through a

central hub. Think tree trunk and branches."

"And there's only one way into the central hub, I bet," Nate said.

"Gold star. And the only way to get to level five is via the elevator."

"No stairs?" Quinn asked.

"The stairs stop at level four. I'm guessing they don't want anyone sneaking up or down them."

"Rude," Nate said.

"Show me," Quinn said.

Orlando held her screen so he could see it and scrolled through the maps of the different levels.

"What about air shafts to the prison level?" he asked.

"Systems aren't detailed on this map, but given that they've restricted access to only the elevators, I think it's a safe bet that they use ducts too narrow for a person to crawl through. We could try to find out, but that would probably be a waste of time."

"True. Forget vents for now. Can you show me our location?"

Orlando returned to the map of level one and pointed at a small room along the outside wall, labeled ELECTRICAL NO. 7. The hallway outside the door was part of a corridor that encircled the entire level, except where the train tracks entered the building. Four spokes connected to the ring, each hallway leading to the center of the structure. The closest was about thirty meters down the corridor to the left.

"Six," Jar said.

Everyone turned to her.

"Six what?" Quinn asked.

"Only six cells are being used."

"Melnikov, the two Sobolevskys, Krutov, Barsukov, and Vassily. That's six," Orlando said. "Maybe they haven't taken anyone else yet."

"Six will be a lot easier to get out than fifty," Silvia said.

"Not as easy as you think," Jar said. She turned her screen for everyone to see the map of the prison level. "One is here." She pointed at one of the cell groups, then moved to a different one. "One here." She did this three more times. When she touched the last, she increased magnification so the individual cells could be seen. "Two prisoners in this wing." She pointed at one of the cells. "Melnikov." She moved her finger to one a couple of doors away. "Vassily."

Silvia leaned in for a closer look. "Then that branch is our priority, yes?"

Quinn nodded. While he was determined to free everyone, if push came to shove, he'd settle for Melnikov and Vassily. The fact they were being held near each other was a welcome break.

"Go with a modified Plan C?" Orlando suggested.

"That would be my recommendation," Jar said.

They had sketched out several plans over the last few days, each dependent on what they found at the prison. None was a perfect fit, but plan C came closest.

"Modified how?" Quinn asked.

They spent a few minutes refining the plan. When everyone seemed satisfied, Quinn pulled out the sat phone and tapped a prestored number.

The ringing line was littered with digital noise.

"Hello?" The voice was tinny but immediately recognizable.

"Good morning, Agent Thomas."

A beat of silence, then, "So you're still alive."

"You say that like you're surprised."

"A little." She laughed. "But not as much as you might think."

"Has Annabel played nice?"

"She has."

"And everything is ready for us?"

"It is."

"Great. If you don't hear from us in the next three hours, tell her to recall Starfish."

"Wait. Are you already at the—"

"Gotta run." Quinn hung up, turned to the others, and nodded at the door.

31

Annenkov cursed as he hung up the phone.

Communications had been crap since the storm hit. Though he'd managed to reach Directorate Eleven headquarters, the connection had been so bad, he could only understand every third or fourth word Captain Bebchuk said. If he'd understood the gist of it correctly, things were quiet there.

Did that mean the infiltrators had already been caught? Or just that they were targeting somewhere else? Or had there been no infiltrators in the first place?

Whatever the case, it seemed his organization had nothing to worry about.

He woke his computer and navigated to the security camera feeds, and selected the option that would cycle through the cameras in each of his prisoner's cells. With little else to do, this had quickly become his favorite pastime. There were few things more satisfying than spying on enemies of the state, ones he'd been personally responsible for silencing.

He leaned back in his chair and smiled.

I wonder if the cafeteria has popcorn..

32

Quinn clicked his mic once, paused, and clicked twice.

A second later, the same pattern came back to him, telling him Nate and Jar were in place. After a beat, Daeng and Silvia chimed in with the same response.

Orlando held her phone for Quinn to see it as the two of them stepped noiselessly around the corner and moved up to the nearby closed door. On the screen was the feed from the base's own security camera, inside the room on the other side.

There were three guards: one sitting in front of a window that provided a view of the elevator lobby; another standing at a counter, pouring a cup of coffee; and the last sitting at a desk in front of a wall of monitors displaying live feeds from cameras throughout level one. Or rather, what the guards believed to be live feeds. Unbeknownst to the men in the room, the feeds were actually playing video loops of unoccupied rooms and hallways created by Jar and Orlando.

Quinn gave the three-click go signal over the comm, and turned the door handle until the latch retracted. He gave Orlando a quick nod, shoved the door open, and they rushed inside, dart guns raised.

As soon as his dart was zooming toward the guard sitting at

the window, Quinn twisted to the left and sent another flying at the standing man. The former was blissfully ignorant of any danger until the dart struck him. The latter had been slightly more on the ball and looked over his shoulder at the sound of the opening door. In his confusion, however, he failed to dodge the dart speeding toward his thigh. It pierced him with a muffled *thwap.*

Quinn turned to the third guard in case Orlando'd had any problems with him. She hadn't.

He checked his watch. All three guards had been dispatched in under seven seconds.

He clicked his mic twice, signaling the guard station was secured, and received double clicks from both Nate and Daeng.

Nate and Jar had dealt with the pair of soldiers guarding the train platform, while Daeng and Silvia had handled another pair in a break room. That made seven guards down, the exact number they counted while checking level one via the security cameras.

There was one location the camera system did not cover, however.

Quinn gave the signal to commence the next step.

Keeping to the shadows, Nate and Jar stepped around the two unconscious guards they'd taken down, and crept across the train platform to the tracks. The train was only five cars long: an engine, two passenger cars, and two enclosed freight cars. They could hear the low hum of a generator resonating from one of them.

Nate climbed onto the side of the engine car and peeked into the dark window of the driver's compartment. No one was inside and the controls were all dark.

He moved to the rear end of the car and opened the crew door. The engine's interior passageway was also dark and silent. He motioned for Jar to stay outside, then entered the passage and crept toward the front end, scanning every space. The engine car was deserted.

He and Jar moved to the near door of the first passenger car. Jar sprayed the hinges with lubricant and Nate eased it open. After waiting several seconds to see if anyone responded, they climbed inside.

The air in the car was artificially warm and the generator hum was louder. There was also another noise, low and rhythmic and easily identifiable. Someone was snoring.

They snuck past a bathroom and entered the main cabin. Half of the dozen seating areas had been converted into sleeping berths, each closed off by a curtain. The snore was coming from the closest berth on the right side.

Nate moved down the aisle and peeked behind each curtain. Given that it was barely six a.m. and, with the raging storm, the train wouldn't be needed anytime soon, it wasn't surprising all six occupants were fast asleep. He continued to the end of the car to make sure he accounted for everyone.

By the time he returned to Jar, she'd already attached the triangular plastic mask to a metal bottle containing a gaseous anesthetic.

Starting with the person in the berth below the snorer, Nate pulled the curtain back and Jar poised the mask right above his mouth and nose, without letting it touch him. She twisted the valve open just long enough to give him a dose of gas to ensure he wouldn't wake anytime soon. They continued in this manner with the rest of the train crew, saving the snorer for last.

Once they were done with him, Jar administered shots of Beta-Somnol that would keep the train crew unconscious well into the following day. She and Nate then moved to the second passenger car. Unlike the first car, it was locked. Jar checked for alarms. After detecting none, Nate picked the lock.

The car was far fancier than the one the crew had been in, boasting a private bedroom, a swanky passenger area, and a bathroom with a shower and tub. The car was obviously intended for someone important, but whoever that might be, she or he was not staying in the car.

Nate and Jar hopped down to the platform and approached the first freight car. Its door was wide open and there was nothing inside. The door of the second was closed but unlocked. Nate pushed it open far enough to get a look inside. It, too, was empty.

He clicked on his mic. "Train clear."

Uniforms were liberated from the unconscious soldiers for Quinn, Nate, Daeng, and Silvia. Unsurprisingly, none of the guards wore clothes small enough for Orlando or Jar, so they remained in their all-black outfits. When everyone was ready, the team proceeded to the elevator lobby.

Though the doors to each of the four elevators had a security feature meant to prevent them from being opened unless an elevator car was present, the designer of the system hadn't anticipated that those breaking in would have gained access to the base's security network.

It took Jar less than a minute to disarm the safeguards, and Nate and Daeng another few seconds to open the doors of the elevator at the left end.

Quinn leaned into the shaft. The space was shared by all four elevators, separated only by the framework needed to guide each car. All four cars were stopped at level three, which was likely their default position.

He twisted to look at the top of the shaft. It stopped a meter and a half above the height of the door and was crisscrossed with more structural supports.

"Plenty to work with," he said, and moved out of the way.

Daeng removed a collapsible rod from his pack and extended it to its full three-meter length. Nate attached a connector to the end, into which he secured a heavy-duty metal ring welded to a palm-sized square metal plate. He tied the end of a climbing rope to the ring and left the rest coiled on the lobby floor near the shaft opening. He then connected a double strand of wire to the back of the metal plate, the other end of which was attached to a fob in his hand.

"Ready," he said.

Daeng swung the pole into the shaft and guided the anchor up to one of the elevator supports at the top of the shaft. When the back end of the plate was pressed firmly against it, he said, "Let 'er rip."

Nate pushed the button on the fob, and the darkness at the top of the shaft vanished in a blaze of white hot light. Within ten seconds, the glow and its accompanying sizzle stopped.

To Jar, Quinn said, "Anything?"

She was toggling through security cameras covering the areas outside the elevator doors on each of the levels below them, where it was most likely for someone to have heard the noise. After a few seconds, she shook her head. "No reaction. We're clear."

Quinn glanced at Nate. "How long?"

"Forty seconds," Nate said.

Beside Nate, Daeng still held the pole in place.

"You good?" Quinn asked him.

"Peachy."

Nate kept his eyes on his watch until the time ran out, then said, "Done."

Daeng released the clamp and retracted the pole. Nate gave the rope a yank. The anchor held steady. Nate fed the rope into the shaft, until it was within a meter of the elevator car waiting at level three.

"Jar, Orlando, you're up," Quinn said.

The two women had already donned climbing harnesses. Orlando approached the doorway first, hooked onto the line, and swung gently into the shaft. Fast and quiet, she slid down to the car and landed softly on its roof.

Jar went next, followed by Nate, then Silvia.

As Quinn attached his harness to the line, he said to Daeng, "We shouldn't be too long."

"Famous last words," Daeng said. He'd drawn the short straw and would be staying at the top to keep the way clear for their escape.

"Hopefully not last. But if they are, you know what to do."

"Yes, Dad. I remember."

With the storm, the diversion they'd planned was no longer necessary, but that didn't mean they'd let their prep work go to waste. They would just wait until they were on their way out to make the call that would turn the guts of Directorate Eleven's headquarters into slag. Quinn planned on making that call, but if things did not go as planned in the prison, it would be up to Daeng to set the explosives off before getting the hell out of there.

"Don't get too bored," Quinn said as he swung into the shaft.

"No promises."

Quinn slid down to the roof of the elevator car. Orlando and Jar were still there, while Nate and Silvia had moved on to the roof of the next car over.

Quinn disconnected from the line and gave it a yank. Daeng began pulling it up.

"Ready when you are," Quinn whispered to Orlando.

"Fasten your seat belts," she said, and touched her phone's screen.

Their car and the one Nate and Silvia were on began descending. Jar had rigged the base's monitoring system so that anyone checking would think the elevators were still waiting at level three.

The cars slowed as they neared level four, but instead of bringing them to a stop in the normal positions, Orlando kept them moving until the roof of each car lined up with the bottom of the respective level four door.

Quinn's eyes were on Jar's phone, which showed the feed from the security camera directly on the other side of the doors. The area was more the end of a wide corridor that stretched away from the doors than a dedicated elevator lobby like back on level one. The corridor ran approximately twenty-five meters to a T intersection with another hallway. Currently, the corridor was unoccupied.

Jar switched to the camera positioned at the intersection and panned it to check the other hall in both directions. It was also empty. She cycled through feeds that covered the five rooms where she had previously seen facility personnel. There had been a total of sixteen people.

Quinn counted the soldiers and technicians in each feed. When the cycle finished, he said, "Sixteen."

"Same," Jar said.

"Any new faces?"

"No."

Quinn nodded. "Phase two."

He joined Nate and Silvia, then he and Nate pried the level four door open and passed through. Silently, they proceeded to a security monitoring room occupied by two soldiers.

Upon reaching the door, they paused to check the feed from inside. The men were sitting in front of a wall of monitors, their backs to the door. Most monitors played feeds from the cameras spread around that level, most of which featuring loops created by Jar. The exception was the center monitor, playing a TV show or movie of some kind.

Quinn eased the door open, and he and Nate crept in.

The soldiers didn't know they were there until syringes were plunged into the base of the men's necks, by which point it was too late for them to do anything.

"Room one neutralized," Quinn said into his comm.

"Yeah, we saw," Orlando said. "Kind of easy when they're not paying attention."

Quinn and Nate moved to the next room on the list. Inside were two men and a woman, all wearing the dark blue coveralls of base technicians. The room itself was a good ten times larger than the security room they'd just left, its walls lined with office-type cubicles. The three occupants sat at separate desks—the woman in one against the far wall, and the two men in adjacent cubes close to the door.

Quinn and Nate set their backpacks on the corridor floor and retrieved their dart guns. When Nate indicated he was ready, Quinn opened the door and they strode in, like soldiers on routine patrol.

The two men glanced at them before returning to whatever they were doing. The woman didn't even look up.

Quinn and Nate walked down the center of the room until they were equidistant between the men and the woman.

Finally sensing their presence, the woman looked at Quinn, who was projecting the image of a bored soldier just going through the motions. Seeing nothing to be concerned about, she swiveled back to her computer.

Quinn gave Nate the signal, then sent a dart flying toward the woman. She yelped when it pierced her shoulder and she tried to stand, but wobbled before she could get her feet under her. She collapsed to the floor, one of her arms slapping her keyboard on her way down and dragging it down with her.

Across the room, both of Nate's targets were slumped over their desks.

Quinn and Nate laid the techs on the floor beside one another and administered doses of Beta-Somnol.

"Room two neutralized," Quinn reported.

"Copy," Orlando said.

The next room was a break room where two soldiers were having cups of coffee and another blue coveralled tech was eating some kind of soup. Once again, Quinn and Nate walked in like they belonged there. They took out the soldiers first, giving the technician just enough time to widen his eyes in terror before he, too, was subdued.

The final two rooms had four people each in them. The first was the digital heart of the base, where the servers and other computing assets were housed. Everyone present wore blue coveralls. The last room was the giant air/water systems room, where two more techs and two soldiers were working.

Quinn and Nate headed to the server room first. Unlike the other doors on this level, the door was locked, with a touch pad on the wall beside it.

Quinn whispered into his mic, "Door to server room is restricted access."

"Hold," Jar said.

When thirty seconds passed without any further response, Quinn said, "Jar?"

"I said hold." Her tone was as flat and unemotional as before. Another half minute of silence, then, "Got it. Ready when you are."

Quinn checked the server room feed playing on his phone to confirm the occupants' locations. "Ready."

The electronic lock clicked open.

33

Annenkov frowned.

Something was wrong with the camera in Filip Krutov's cell. Every few seconds the image would stop moving and pixelate into squares of dancing colors before reverting to normal.

Krutov was asleep on his bunk, so it wasn't as if he was doing anything interesting, but Annenkov had a low tolerance for problems that could be easily fixed. He wouldn't be surprised if the camera had been glitching for days. That was the problem with people working at an isolated base such as this. They became sloppy.

Well, if they needed a little motivation, he was more than happy to give them some.

He snatched up his phone.

34

Four rows of equipment racks ran the length of the computer room, filling most the space.

Quinn glanced down the aisle nearest the door and confirmed no one had moved into it since they'd checked the feed. The same was true of the middle aisle.

He and Nate moved to the last aisle. All four techs were still there, hovering in front of a rack at the far end.

Quinn was about to signal which two Nate should take when a phone rang. One of the men broke from his colleagues and disappeared behind the far end of the rack. Quinn motioned for Nate to deal with the remaining men, then went in search of the wayward tech.

He found him clear back in the first aisle, reaching for a phone mounted to one of the racks. Even if Quinn pulled his trigger right away, his dart wouldn't hit the man before the tech picked up the receiver and likely alert the caller that something was wrong.

"Hey!" Quinn shouted.

The tech's hand stopped centimeters from the receiver. As he turned, Quinn pulled his trigger twice. The guy's eyes widened at the darts streaking toward him, but he kept his head enough to jerk out of the path of the first dart. Unfortunately for him, doing so moved him directly into the path of the second. The dart punctured his stomach and sent him staggering backward. By grabbing the nearest rack, he was able to remain on his feet for a few more seconds before crumpling to the floor.

Which was also the moment the phone stopped ringing.

"Dammit," Nate muttered.

Quinn whirled around as Nate fired his dart gun again. Quinn hurried over, ready to join the fight. Only all three techs were already down.

"What happened?"

"One of them moved as I pulled the trigger," Nate said. "I hate it when they don't stand still."

Back in the first aisle, the phone started ringing again.

"Should we answer that?" Nate said.

"I'm going to assume you're joking," Quinn said.

Nate flashed him a toothy smile.

When the ringing stopped, Quinn turned on his mic. "Room four cleared. But someone just called here so they might get curious why no one answered."

"Copy," Orlando said. "We'll keep an eye out."

35

Annenkov brought up the video feed of the computer center. He'd called twice but neither call had been answered, so he expected to see that the room was unoccupied. Instead, the feed showed four techs huddled at one of the racks.

What the hell?

One of them should have answered his call.

Keeping the feed on his monitor, he called again. As the line rang, he expected one of the men to look up at the very least, but none even twitched.

He hung up. He knew tech types had the tendency to get absorbed in whatever they were doing, but he refused to believe all four would do so at the same time. No, it had to be a problem with the phone itself. Maybe the ringer was off. Or perhaps there was a problem with the line.

"Sergeant Yegorov!" he yelled.

The sergeant entered the office. "Yes, sir?"

"There's something wrong with the phone in the computer center. Go down there and tell them I need to talk to them."

"Yes, Colonel. Right away."

36

Quinn and Nate stood outside the door to the facility systems, studying the room's security feed on Quinn's phone. The space was more than twice as large as the previous rooms they'd visited—combined. About a third of it was occupied by machinery dedicated to air conditioning, heating, and air recycling. The remaining two thirds were a jumble of the pipes and tanks and pumps that made up the water system.

A tech sat at the air systems control station, and another at the one dedicated to the water system. Neither position had a view of the main door. The same couldn't be said about the table seven meters from the entrance. Two soldiers were sitting there, playing cards.

"Ready?" Quinn whispered.

When Nate nodded, Quinn grabbed the door handle.

The moment they stepped into the room, both soldiers looked up. The one on the near side of the table immediately turned back to his cards, but his buddy's gaze remained on Quinn and Nate, his brow creasing. He clearly realized they didn't belong there. Before he could decide whether or not to raise an alarm, Quinn and Nate brought up their dart guns and fired.

The concerned soldier jumped to his feet and made a valiant

effort to get out of the way, but Nate's dart was already too close and the effort was futile.

As the other guard startled at his colleague's sudden movements, Quinn's dart buried itself in his shoulder.

The first man flopped onto the floor, unconscious, while the second ended up sprawled across the table.

Syringes were prepared and shots administered, then Quinn headed quietly toward the tech at the air recycling station, and Nate toward the one manning the water controls.

As Orlando watched Quinn and Nate move away from the two unconscious soldiers toward their next targets, on her phone Jar whispered, "We have a problem."

"What?"

Before Jar could respond, one of the two elevators still at level three began moving. Orlando glanced up at it.

"It's heading to the second floor," Jar said.

"How many people in it?"

"No one yet. A soldier is waiting for it at level two."

"Which call button did he hit?"

"Down."

Orlando blew out a breath. "Fingers crossed he's heading back to three."

"Crossing fingers does not affect anything."

"Humor me."

Jar frowned.

"It could be the person who was calling the computer room," Silvia suggested.

The thought had also crossed Orlando's mind.

Above them, the elevator stopped at level two. A moment later, Orlando heard its doors open, and the creak of weight as the soldier stepped inside.

"He pushed the button for level four," Jar said. "I told you crossed fingers don't work."

The car descended.

Orlando leaned toward Jar to get a better view of her screen. The insignia on the soldier's uniform identified him as a sergeant, and the only visible weapon he carried was a holstered pistol at his waist. All the patrols they'd seen so far had consisted of two soldiers, none above the rank of corporal.

To Silvia, Orlando said, "Up for a little action?"

"It is why I'm here."

"Okay, you and I will deal with him. Jar, see if you can figure out why he's coming down here."

Silvia and Orlando opened the doors and quickly moved into the level four lobby. By the time the door whooshed open and the sergeant stepped out, they were pressed against the wall to either side of his elevator, dart guns loaded and ready. He made it two steps before he seemed to realize he wasn't alone and turned in Orlando's direction.

"*Dobroye utro*," she greeted him and pulled her trigger.

The dart smacked into his gut and snapped him out of his confusion. He twisted back to the elevator, but Silvia had moved between him and the door.

"Sorry," she said. "This elevator is out of order."

He tried to go around her but instead staggered sideways and tripped over his own feet. He crashed hard onto the floor, made an attempt to get back on his feet, and finally lost consciousness.

Orlando administered a shot, then she and Silvia pried open the doors Jar was behind.

"Find out anything?" Orlando asked.

"Yes." Jar showed them a video of the sergeant talking to an officer in a colonel's uniform. She then brought up another clip. "This was two minutes previous to that clip."

The shot was of the same room, though now the colonel was alone and on the phone. He wasn't talking, though, and within seconds, he hung up and dialed a number and waited again.

When it became clear no one would answer, he slammed down the receiver.

Jar stopped the playback. "Silvia was correct. His calls correspond to when the phone rang in the computer center. I believe he sent the sergeant to check on why no one was answering."

"Well, that's not great."

"It is not," Jar agreed. "There's something else."

"Of course there is."

"It's not necessarily bad news. The colonel is Colonel Annenkov, head of Directorate Eleven."

Orlando raised an eyebrow. "Is that so?"

Jar brought up an image with the photo they had of Annenkov on the left, and a screen grab of the colonel in the office on the right. There was no question they were a match.

Over the comm, Quinn said, "Facility systems cleared. That's everyone. You can join us now."

Orlando shared a look with Jar and Silvia and turned on her mic. "On our way."

"Can you do it?" Quinn asked.

He, Orlando, Silvia, and Nate were standing behind Jar, who was sitting at the air recycling station and had spent the last few minutes investigating the computer that controlled the system.

After a beat, she nodded and said, "Yes, I believe so, but I would like to run a test first."

"What kind of test?"

"The system is set up so that it can control air flow to individual rooms. We pick a room."

"How long will it take?"

"Five minutes should be enough."

Orlando had filled Quinn in on the soldier she'd taken down in the lobby—that he'd been sent by Colonel Annenkov—so

Quinn knew they didn't have a lot of time to play with. "Half that time would be better."

Jar stared at him, expressionless.

"If you can," he added.

She turned back to the computer. "I cannot promise that but I will try." She glanced at Nate. "Assist Orlando with the canisters."

"Yes, ma'am."

37

Annenkov glanced at his door, annoyed. It had been over ten minutes since Sergeant Yegorov left. He should have reported back by now.

Annenkov brought up the server room camera again and frowned. The techs were still gathered around the same rack, with no sign of Yegorov.

Annenkov flipped through a few of the other cameras on level four, looking for the sergeant, but the hallways were empty and Yegorov was in none of the rooms. The colonel pulled up the list of cameras covering level two and flipped through them, expecting to find Yegorov on his way to Annenkov's office, but the sergeant wasn't on any of those feeds, either.

Annenkov briefly considered ordering someone to conduct a search, but decided he would do it himself. And when he found the sergeant, Yegorov had better have a damn good reason for disappearing.

38

"I think you're going to have to do this by yourself," Nate said.

He and Orlando were standing near a gap between a large air recycling unit and a wall. Mounted horizontally along the wall and running the length of the gap were four air ducts, turning the already narrow space into a gap Nate would never be able to squeeze into.

Orlando clicked on her mic. "We're here. Which duct do we want?"

"The top one," Jar said. "There should be another duct connecting it to the air recycler machine, about a meter and a half from your position."

Orlando scanned the gap. "I see it."

"Good. You'll find an access valve just past where they meet. You'll tap into that."

"Copy."

Orlando slipped off her backpack, extracted a thermos-sized gas cylinder and a pouch containing several lightweight valve adapters, then slid sideways into the gap down to the junction of the ducts. She crouched to move under it and scanned the area beyond.

"Found it," she said. The valve was on the underside of the

top duct, putting it a good half meter above Orlando's head. "Give me a sec to get into position."

"Copy."

With her back against the air recycler and her feet against the wall, Orlando shimmied her way up until she could reach the valve. She placed the gas canister on top of the duct and turned on her penlight. Holding it with her mouth, she examined the valve and hunted through the pouch until she found the correct adapter. Twenty seconds later, the canister was connected to the duct.

She pulled the penlight out of her mouth and said, "Ready."

"Copy," Jar said. "Open the canister for ten seconds on my mark."

"Copy."

"Three. Two. One. Mark."

Orlando opened the canister's valve and began counting. When she hit ten, she closed the valve. "Okay, it's done."

"Copy."

Quinn and Silvia hovered behind Jar, watching on her phone the security feed from a room on level three. The room contained two sets of bunk beds. Two soldiers sat facing each other on the bottom beds. Between them sat a trunk they were using as a card table. The top bunks were empty.

Quinn frowned. "Are you sure ten seconds was—"

"I am," Jar said without looking at him.

As if on cue, one of the soldiers put a hand to his forehead and fell forward, his face bouncing off the trunk on his way to the floor. The other soldier jumped up to help him and immediately staggered back against the bunk before joining his friend on the ground.

"Oh, okay," Quinn said. "I guess we can call that a success."

Jar glanced at him. "You guess?"

"Is that…is that sarcasm?"

"I have been practicing." She looked back at her phone.

Silvia snorted.

"Don't encourage her," Quinn said.

Silvia shrugged innocently. "Me? I say nothing."

"May I proceed?" Jar asked.

"By all means."

Jar turned on her mic. "On my mark, full dispersal."

"Copy," Orlando said.

Jar adjusted the vent settings. "Three. Two. One. Mark."

39

Annenkov strode angrily to the elevators and pushed the down call button.

His quick search through level two for Sergeant Yegorov had come up empty. If Yegorov wasn't there or on level four, then the only other places he could be were level three or five. Since there had been no reason for the sergeant to go down to the prison, Annenkov assumed Yegorov was on level three, the residential level. Why? He had no idea. Whatever the reason was, it wouldn't be good enough to excuse Yegorov from checking in with Annenkov first.

The colonel stepped into the car and punched the button for level three.

The ride took less than half a minute.. When the doors opened, he stepped into the doorway and froze.

The elevators on level three let out directly into a large community room, filled with seats and tables. As usual, off-duty soldiers and technicians were spread throughout the space, but instead of playing games or watching TV or talking, all were motionless—some draped across tables, others slumped in chairs, and still more sprawled on the floor.

The elevator doors hit Annenkov's shoulders, jolting him from his daze. As they opened again, he suddenly started to feel lightheaded.

He had not risen to his current position as fast as he had without being smart. And even as his head swam, he recognized the danger in front of him.

He stumbled back into the elevator and rapidly tapped the close button until the doors began sliding shut. He then reached up and slapped the button for level two. He pressed against the wall, sure he was about to pass out. It wasn't until the doors opened on level two that the feeling finally ebbed.

He staggered out and hurried to his office. He flopped into his chair, turned on his phone's speaker function, and hit the preset button for base security. As the line rang, he accessed the security cameras for the level three community room.

"What the hell?"

Instead of seeing people lying everywhere, the room was filled with the type of actions Annenkov had expected to find when he went searching for Yegorov.

"Security," a male voice said over the speaker. "How may I help you, Colonel?"

Someone's manipulated the feed, Annenkov thought.

"Colonel?" the voice said.

Annenkov blinked and looked at his phone. "Someone has tampered with the air on level three. Everyone there is either dead or unconscious."

"Uh, sir. I'm looking at level three right now and everything looks—"

"The feeds have been altered! I was just there! I saw it with my own eyes. Go to alert status five."

"Five, sir?" Five was reserved for the base being under attack.

"If you question me one more time, I will have you shot where you sit."

"Level five. Yes, sir."

The alarm began blaring.

"Patch me through the intercom!" Annenkov yelled to be heard over the siren.

"One moment." After a short pause, the man said, "Go ahead."

"This is Colonel Annenkov. The air system has been compromised. All personnel need to don air masks immediately, then assemble by the elevators on level two." Air masks equipped with a ten-minute emergency bottle of air were issued to all personnel as part of the base's safety features. "There are intruders inside the base. This is not—"

Annenkov's brain slipped sideways, and he had to grab his desk to avoid falling out of his chair.

The toxin from level three must be on level two now.

Holding his breath, he yanked open the bottom desk drawer, where his mask was stored. As the fog in his head thickened, he fumbled the mask out and pulled it over his face, then connected the small cylinder of air also stored in the drawer and opened the oxygen valve.

Soon, the tunnel that had been closing around his vision reversed direction, and after another minute, he felt strong enough to stand.

The base had a strict firearms protocol: any weapon not in the possession of soldiers on guard duty must be stored in a vault on level two. The only exception to this rule was the pistol Annenkov kept in a safe behind his desk.

He opened the safe, grabbed the gun and three spare magazines, then raced out of his office into the main corridor.

He jerked to a stop. Half a dozen people were strewn across the floor, unmoving.

Whether they were alive or not, they would be no help to him, so it was not worth his time to check on them. He stepped over the two closest bodies and sprinted down the hall. Halfway to the elevator waiting area where he'd ordered personnel to meet, he caught sight of a door marked OXYGEN and skidded to a halt.

The locked door opened with a swipe of his badge. Inside,

racks of air tanks filled the room. Each held enough breathable air to last three and a half hours and was mounted in a backpack-type harness.

Annenkov grabbed the nearest one and pulled the straps over his shoulders. After taking a deep breath, he disconnected the ten-minute bottle, snapped the feeder tube to the larger tank, and twisted the valve to the open position.

He grabbed two more of the bulky tanks and rushed the remaining distance to the elevator lobby.

Instead of the room full of soldiers he'd hoped to find, he saw four.

Four!

"Please tell me this isn't all of you," he said.

The soldiers looked at one another before the highest ranking among them—a corporal—stepped forward. "I'm sorry, sir. We haven't seen anyone else."

Annenkov swallowed a curse, then shoved the two spare tanks at the corporal and one of the privates. To the other pair, he said, "The oxygen room's unlocked. Get tanks and come right back."

They left.

"Colonel," the corporal said, "do we know how many we're facing?"

"I have no idea."

"What about their current locations?"

"It doesn't matter. I know where they're going."

"Where, sir?" the private asked.

"Level five." The only reason anyone would break into the base would be to free one or more of the prisoners.

"How are we supposed to stop them from getting there?"

"We don't. We make sure they never leave."

40

Though the gas had neutralized all one hundred and seven people on level three, the dispersal on level two had not been quite as successful, thanks to the alarm raised by Colonel Annenkov. Of the fifty-three people present, eight had been able to don gas masks before the gas could knock them out.

Annenkov—one of the eight—had rendezvoused with four of the others near the elevators on level two. The five now sported large air tanks strapped to their backs. The other three men were hiding elsewhere on the level—two in separate closets, and one inside a bathroom. All three were still relying only on their emergency oxygen bottles, and as soon as those ran dry, they would join the ranks of the unconscious.

Unfortunately, the alarm had gone off before Jar had the chance to release gas on the prison level, so all the guards there were able to don their masks. But either there were no larger tanks on that level or the soldiers didn't know about them, because all were sucking air from the smaller bottles.

"Based on size, those can hold up to ten minutes of air," Jar said, checking her watch. "Which means at most, they have seven minutes left. I suggest we disperse the gas thirty seconds prior to that."

"Agreed," Quinn said, then headed out of the room with Nate. He clicked on his mic. "Quinn for Daeng."

"Go for Daeng."

"There are five soldiers wearing air masks and large air tanks on level two," Quinn said. "If they have an ounce of intelligence, they'll assume some of us are on level four messing with their air system, and some topside guarding the way out. They'll also assume we've come for the prisoners. Given how few of them there are, they'll probably try to prevent us from returning to the surface. I doubt they'll head your way but be ready just in case."

"Copy," Daeng said.

"Were you able to deal with the stairwell?"

"Done. No one's getting out that way without my help."

"Excellent," Quinn said.

"And if any of them pokes a head into the elevator shaft, I'll make them realize that's a bad idea."

"I'll leave it in your capable hands," Quinn said.

He and Nate quietly made their way to the stairwell.

Nate eased open the door and scanned inside. "Clear."

They slipped inside and headed up.

Melnikov cocked his head. Something was buzzing, low and distant.

"Do you hear that?" Vassily asked.

Melnikov almost jumped at the sound of the man's voice. They had restricted their conversations to what they assumed were the late hours of night, when the frequency of patrols dropped from one every ten minutes to one every thirty. To Melnikov, it was daytime now, and their hallway was due for the next patrol pass at any moment.

In fact, he was pretty sure the guards were overdue.

Melnikov listened for footsteps. When he didn't hear any, he whispered through the tray slot, "I did."

"Is that an alarm?"

"Maybe, but I've never heard one here before."

For the next several seconds, neither spoke. The buzz rose and fell and rose again.

"That's definitely an alarm," Vassily said. "You should get ready."

"Ready? Ready for what?"

"Just...get ready."

Vassily had been saying cryptic things like this since he arrived. Whenever Melnikov had pushed him to explain what he meant, Vassily would either change the subject or stop talking completely. Before Melnikov could prod him for more this time, the door down the hallway opened and one set of running steps raced in Melnikov and Vassily's direction.

Whoever it was went all the way to Vassily's cell. Melnikov heard a cell door being rattled, then the steps came back his way and stopped at his cell. The person rattled his door but didn't open it.

A sudden, short blast of radio static filled the air. In a voice clearly out of breath, the person in the corridor said, "This is Private Aslanov. Doors in cell block eight secured. No sign of trouble."

A male voice came over a radio speaker. "Acknowledged. Return to control center."

"Yes, sir."

The guard left in the same fashion he'd arrived, and a few seconds later the distant door closed again, and only the low buzz remained.

Melnikov leaned down to the tray slot. "Vassily, what's going on?"

No response.

"Vassily?"

Still nothing.

"Vassily?"

~

Orlando's voice came over the comm. "New bottle in place, ready to go."

"Copy," Jar said.

A grid displaying eight camera feeds filled Jar's computer screen. One was from the security camera in the level two elevator waiting area, where the five still conscious Russians were gathered. Two of the other feeds were from corridors leading away from the area. Another pair displayed views from cameras she and Daeng had placed in the elevator shaft—the one she'd placed near the level four door, pointing upward; and the other at the top, pointing down, courtesy of Daeng. The final three feeds were from security cams at different locations on the prison level.

Unlike with levels two and three, she could not simply gas the entire prison level, as that would mean knocking the prisoners out, too. If that happened, the team might as well pack it up and leave now. For the rescue to have the best chance at success, they would need the prisoners to move under their own power.

Which meant the release of gas on level five needed to be more surgical. Another complicating factor was that of the thirty-eight soldiers on the prison level, seven were in areas she couldn't gas without affecting one or more prisoners. They would have to be dealt with by other means.

For now, she would focus on their thirty-one colleagues, starting with the nine in the control center.

In the top corner of Jar's screen was the countdown clock she'd started when the prison level guards had donned their masks. When it reached thirty-five seconds, she said, "Twenty-second full flow on my mark. Three. Two. One. Mark."

"Valve open," Orlando said.

When the allotted time had passed, Jar said, "That's twenty."

"Copy. Valve closed."

While the masks the Russians wore were designed to work with or without an oxygen feed, their filtering abilities were limited and minus the fresh flow of air, they would heat up quickly. So it wasn't surprising that on the control room camera feed, one guard had already pushed his mask up onto his forehead, his oxygen tank empty. A moment later, two more did the same. Then, just as another reached for her mask, the first soldier staggered and dropped to the floor.

Chaos broke out as those who'd pulled off their masks hurried to yank them back down. The effort was futile, of course, and one by one, everyone in the room lost consciousness.

Nine down. Twenty-two to go.

Jar switched to the break room feed, showing five soldiers watching a movie on a TV, unaware of what was going on elsewhere.

She realigned the air flow to the relevant vents and said, "Ten-second full flow on my mark. Three. Two. One. Mark."

Wearing gas masks with filters specifically designed to handle the gas Jar had released, Nate and Quinn moved up the stairs to the level two access door. Nate placed another booster next to it to link up with the ones he'd left below, and said, "Radio check."

"Read you five by five," Daeng said.

"Copy."

"Level two status?" Quinn asked.

"The group by the elevators has split up," Jar said. "Two men heading your way. The other three are moving down the eastside hallway."

"What's in that direction?"

"Training room and weapons storage room."

"Oh, yay," Nate mumbled.

"Copy," Quinn said. "Keep us posted on second group's movements."

"I'm a little tied up," Jar said. "Daeng, you'll need to handle that."

"Can do," Daeng said.

Nate and Quinn pulled out their dart guns, and Quinn placed his ear to the door.

He mouthed, *They're coming*.

They moved against the wall on the hinge side of the door.

Ten seconds later, the stairwell door swung open, and two soldiers rushed inside and went straight to the descending stairs, never realizing they weren't alone.

Nate and Quinn waited until the men were halfway down the flight before firing their guns. The darts impacted with maximum effect, sending both men tumbling to the landing below. Neither man made any effort to stand again.

"Two guards neutralized," Quinn said. "Daeng, what's going on with the other three?"

Before Daeng could answer, Nate said, "Can I guess? They're in the weapons storage room, aren't they?"

"Bingo," Daeng said. "Why do you even need me?"

"Just watch our backs," Quinn said and pulled the door open.

"Copy."

41

When all of this was over, Annenkov would conduct a comprehensive review of every aspect of the base. He had no doubt that at least one of the supply officers involved in outfitting the prison was now sitting on a pile of cash from money skimmed off the budget. Annenkov had personally approved gas masks with built-in radios, but did the mask he was wearing now have one? No. Nor did any of the masks worn by the soldiers with him.

And then there was the matter of how an unknown number of intruders had circumvented the base's security system and infiltrated the facility. Annenkov had been guaranteed the system was impenetrable.

Corners had clearly been cut, and whatever asshole—or assholes—had thought doing so was a good idea would soon learn the error of his ways. Because when Annenkov got ahold of them, the blood spilled wouldn't be just metaphorical.

Because of the mask fiasco, he was forced to use a walkie-talkie. The problem with that was in order to be properly heard he would need to raise his mask, an action that would put him on the floor with the rest of the fools who hadn't heeded his warning.

Seething, he brought his radio up beside his mask and said as clearly as possible, "Private Kazakov, report." Kazakov had gone with another private to check the stairwell.

Dead air.

"Kazakov! Report!"

The radio remained silent.

Annenkov and the two men who'd stayed with him had just exited the weapons storage room, and each of them was now armed with a rifle, a pistol, and extra ammunition. "Corporal Slivestrov," Annenkov said to the higher-ranking man. "I need you to find out what we're up against."

"Yes, sir. There's a monitoring room not far from here. I can check the—"

"The cameras have been compromised! The intruders have control of—" Annenkov stopped himself and spun around, searching for the camera that covered the area.

The infiltrators had probably been watching their every move, Annenkov realized. He should have thought of that sooner.

When he spotted the camera, he sent a bullet through its lens, blowing the camera apart.

Slivestrov jerked in surprise, while the private stumbled backward and banged his air tank into the wall.

Annenkov refocused on the corporal. "We need to know how many intruders we're dealing with. Find Kazakov and report back immediately."

"Yes, sir."

Slivestrov turned to head off in the direction the others had gone.

"Wait," Annenkov said, and jutted his chin at the private. "Take him with you. Kill anyone who tries to stop you."

"Yes, sir," they said in unison, and took off running.

"And destroy every camera you see!" Annenkov yelled after them.

He took a deep breath.

As far as he knew, the defense of the entire facility was up to him, three privates, and a corporal. The Americans had a word for situations like this: clusterfuck.

The one piece of good news was that it appeared the gas had only rendered his people unconscious instead of killing them like he'd first feared, and at some point they would wake again. If his tiny squad could pin down the intruders until that happened, then he would have the numbers to foil their plans. And if that didn't work, he had one last trick he could use. It was extreme, but if it was the only thing between allowing even one of the prisoners to escape and stopping them all, then he would not hesitate.

Task number one: eliminate routes to the surface, of which there were two—the elevators and the emergency staircase.

Annenkov didn't need to wait for Slivestrov and the others to return. He could handle disabling the elevators himself. Once the others were back, he'd have them fill the stairwell with desks and chairs and whatever else they could find.

After that, they would simply need to—

A gunshot echoed down the hall. At first, he thought it was Slivestrov taking out a camera, but then a second shot rang out, followed rapidly by a third, and a fourth.

When the hallway fell silent, he brought up his radio. "Slivestrov?"

Nothing.

"Slivestrov?"

Nothing.

Annenkov turned in the opposite direction his men had gone, shot a camera that was twenty meters away, and ran.

42

Quinn and Nate had barely entered the second level when Daeng's voice came over the comm. "Two more soldiers heading your way. Coming fast."

They sprinted to the intersection ahead.

"Which way?" Quinn asked.

"Hall to the right," Daeng said. "Seventy meters and closing."

"I'll take the other side," Quinn whispered to Nate and crossed to the other side of the intersection.

They pressed themselves against the wall, where they would be out of sight.

The pounding of boots on cement drifted toward them, growing louder and louder. The soldiers slowed as they neared the intersection, then burst from the other hall, turning into the section of corridor where Nate waited.

The one in the lead pulled up short at the sight of him, forcing his buddy to stumble sideways to keep from barreling into him.

"Hi," Nate said in English and sent two darts flying.

He would have sworn his targets were too close to react in time, but while that was true for the lead guy—a dart stuck solidly in his shoulder—it was not for the guy's buddy.

In a display of exceptional reflexes, the second guard pulled the first man in front of himself, just in time for the lead guy to absorb the second shot, too. The soldier then used his double-drugged colleague as a shield and started backing around the corner. As he did, he tried to pull his rifle off his shoulder, but the front man was quickly becoming deadweight and the second soldier lost his grip on the weapon. In a desperate effort to grab it, his finger caught the trigger and the rifle fired. The bullet ricocheted off the ceiling and streaked down the hall, and the rifle clattered to the floor.

Nate let off another dart, but the slice of shoulder he could see was narrow and the dart missed by a few centimeters.

The man jerked his pistol out of its holster and fired three wild shots toward them. When the third bullet left the barrel, the first guard drooped forward, exposing the other man's upper torso. Both Nate and Quinn fired.

This time neither of them missed.

The second guard took a staggering step backward, inadvertently shifting the weight of his shield onto him, and they fell, the pistol dropping beside them. Before the still conscious guard could reach it, Nate ran over and kicked it down the hall.

"Sorry," Nate said to Quinn. "That guy was quick."

Quinn cocked an eyebrow and frowned. "This won't look good on your performance review."

Nate stared at him. "Did you…did you just joke in the middle of an operation?"

"So not joking," Quinn said with a grin. He turned on his comm. "Two more down. Where's Annenkov?"

"I think he's still near the weapons storage room."

"You *think*?"

Before Daeng could reply, a radio attached to one of the downed soldiers crackled to life. "Slivestrov?"

"I'm guessing that's him," Quinn said.

"Probably, but can't confirm," Daeng said. "He shot out the camera in front of the weapons area."

Annenkov's voice came over the radio again. "Slivestrov?"

Another gunshot sounded in the distance.

"There goes another camera," Daeng said.

"Someone doesn't like their picture taken," Nate said.

"I'm betting he's on the move."

"Does he not realize we can track which way he's going by the cameras he's destroying?" Nate said.

"That will be true right up to the moment he decides to double back," Daeng said.

"Good point."

"And there's another camera down."

This time, Quinn hadn't heard the shot. "Daeng, hold on for a moment." He switched channels. "Quinn for Orlando."

"Go for Orlando."

"Level five update."

"Thirty-one guards incapacitated. We can't get to the remaining seven without affecting some of the prisoners. We're going to have to go down."

"Copy." Quinn turned to Nate. "You think you can find Annenkov on your own?"

"I'm offended you would even ask that," Nate said, clutching his chest.

Quinn clapped him on the arm. "Good. Try not to get hit." He started jogging back toward the stairwell. "Orlando, on my way to you."

~

"Stop," Daeng said over the comm. "The blackout zone begins two meters past the next intersection."

"Got it." Nate shucked off his backpack and withdrew his drone. After clipping on a fresh battery, he powered up the craft and said, "You have control."

The drone lifted into the air and moved toward the intersection. When it turned down the new corridor, it swung wide and grazed the wall. The craft wobbled for a few seconds before righting itself.

"Dude," Nate said. "Do *not* damage my drone."

"Hey, you're the expert, not me," Daeng said.

"You said you knew how to fly it."

"Yeah. Outside where it's harder to run into something."

"I swear to God…"

"If you're interested, the corridor's clear."

Scowling, Nate unholstered both his dart gun and pistol. With a weapon in each hand, he followed the drone around the corner.

Thirty meters down the corridor, he said, "I haven't heard a gunshot in a while. He should have taken out another camera by now, right?" Up to that point, Annenkov had been destroying cameras at the approximate rate of one every thirty seconds.

"Hold your position and I'll check it out."

The drone sped forward and disappeared around a bend in the hall.

Two minutes later, Daeng said, "Huh."

"Huh, what?"

"I'm at the end of the blackout zone but the hallway's clear. He couldn't have gone past here without me knowing."

"Check the cameras in the nearby rooms. He must be in one of them. If there's a camera not working, that's probably where he is."

"Scrolling through them now." Several seconds passed before Daeng said, "All cameras working. There are a few supply and maintenance closets that don't appear to have surveillance, though."

"How many between me and the drone?"

"Five."

"Fly the drone to the one nearest me and I'll check that—"

"Oh, crap!" Daeng said at the same moment a distant gunshot reverberated down the corridor.

"Another camera?"

"Um, no."

"Then what?"

"So, that thing you said about not breaking your drone? I would like to point out that, technically, it's not my fault."

"Do not tell me that asshole shot down my drone."

"Well...."

Nate gritted his teeth. "Where is he?"

"He *was* about five meters behind the drone when I saw him. Now, who knows?"

Nate started moving again.

"You realize I don't have eyes on you now," Daeng said, "so you're going in blind."

"Yeah."

"*And* he knows you're coming."

"Good."

Annenkov toed the downed drone to see if it was still operating and saw he needn't worry. His bullet had destroyed both the camera and the craft's control unit.

He took no joy in the small victory. If anything, it meant his situation was more dire than he'd thought. If the intruders were able to freely fly drones through level two, then he had to assume Corporal Slivestrov and the others had been neutralized.

Annenkov was on his own.

With no one else to help him, his plan to trap the intruders until his people regained consciousness was no longer viable, leaving him with only two options: give up or trigger the fail-safe he'd had included in the base's construction. A just-in-case option he had hoped to never need.

Buried under the floor of the prison level was a small, low-yield tactical nuke, strong enough to collapse the base in on itself and wreak havoc up to a kilometer of the area surrounding the base. Annenkov had overseen its installation himself, and knew for sure no corners had been cut.

The problem was that the activation panel was in his office, and the quickest route there was in the direction from where the drone had come. He'd have to take the long way around and hope he didn't run into any of the invaders. And he'd have to do it fast, which meant not wasting extra seconds disabling cameras on the way.

He glanced one last time in the direction the drone had come from, then sprinted in the opposite direction.

"He's running!" Daeng said.

"I thought you couldn't see him," Nate said.

"He's stopped shooting at the cameras."

Whatever the reason, Nate was sure it wasn't good. "Which way is he going?"

"Away from you."

Nate started running. "Maybe he's trying to reach the stairs."

"Maybe."

Following the trail of destroyed cameras, Nate skidded around a corner into a new corridor, and cursed as he sped past the scattered remains of his drone.

A few seconds later, Daeng said, "I have eyes on you now. You're about forty meters behind him."

Because of the curve in the corridor, Nate couldn't see Annenkov, but he could hear the distant clomp of the man's boots.

"He's coming up on the stairwell door," Daeng said. "And… he just blew past it without slowing."

"Could there be another way up?"

"The elevators and emergency stairwell are the only things on the plans."

"Something not on the plans?"

"Possible, but—" Daeng paused. "Wait, he's slowing."

"Location?"

Daeng was silent for a moment before saying, "He just went inside an office."

The foreboding that had been tingling at the base of Nate's neck intensified.

∼

Quinn exited the stairs on level four and hurried to the elevator lobby, where Orlando, Jar, and Silvia waited. The doors to the two elevators they'd been using were open, the cars waiting on the other side.

"Level five status?" he asked.

"Six guards still active," Jar said.

He raised an eyebrow. "I thought there were seven you couldn't get to."

"One of them was wondering why no one was responding on his radio," Orlando said. "He went to the control station to check and..." She mimed falling asleep.

"I appreciate his willingness to help us out," he said. "Any way we can coax the others to do the same?"

"We could, but the direct route will be faster."

"Where are they?"

"All six in the cell wings," Jar said.

"So, no one conscious by the elevators?"

"No one."

They donned gas masks and entered one of the elevators. Jar tapped her tablet, and both elevators began descending. When they reached the bottom level, Jar opened the doors to the other elevator and flew out the drone she had stationed there. She hovered it in the lobby and spun it slowly around to scan the entire area. Three soldiers lay on the floor, the rise and fall of their chests the only movements.

She opened the door to their elevator and they stepped out. After Orlando administered Beta-Somnol to the soldiers, the team moved down the corridor toward the central hub, and stopped when they reached the security door that sectioned off the rest of the prison. Mounted to the wall next to it were a camera and a square pad about the size of a standard tablet computer.

"One moment," Jar said.

She sped through several screens on her phone and tapped instructions on a digital keyboard. A new screen appeared on which she made a few selections. A green light above the camera came on, and a motor hummed from inside the wall. After a moment, the door swung open, and they stepped into the prison control center. Over a dozen guards were strewn throughout the room, either sprawled across counters or crumpled on the floor. This was where the majority of soldiers on this level had been when Jar released the gas.

They administered Beta-Somnol shots all around, then gathered at the monitoring station in the middle of the room.

"So, which ones do we want?" Quinn asked, referring to the doors encircling the room that led to the cell wings.

Jar took a moment to orient herself before she said, "There, there, there, and there," pointing at the four doors to the wings currently occupied.

"Which one for Señor Levkin?" Silvia said.

Jar pointed at the second door she'd indicated. "He and Melnikov are through there."

"Any conscious guards that way?" Quinn asked

"One." Jar consulted her phone. "He's currently standing by the final gate before the cells."

"Can you tell if Señor—if the prisoners are okay?" Silvia asked.

Jar tapped at her tablet a few times and brought up a feed from Vassily's cell to show Silvia. The Russian was sitting on his cot, looking at the door.

"He looks like he lost some weight," Silvia said, though it was clear seeing him eased some of her tension.

"Show me Melnikov," Quinn said.

Jar switched to a view of the grand master.

Melnikov was pacing, his gaze locked on the door. He had lost weight since his abduction and gained a beard, but showed no visible signs of injury or illness.

"What's the gas status here in the control room?" Quinn asked.

Jar connected a sensor to the end of her tablet and studied her screen. "Enough to still cause disorientation but not enough to knock anyone out. In a few minutes, it will be completely ineffective."

He nodded. "Hold down the fort. We won't be long."

He motioned for Orlando and Silvia to follow him, and headed toward the door to Melnikov and Vassily's wing.

43

Via the feed from inside Annenkov's office, Daeng watched the colonel prop a chair under the door handle and take a step back, breathing heavily. He glanced up at the camera as if just remembering it was there, making Daeng sure the man was about to shoot it. Instead, Annenkov moved quickly behind his desk and swept everything off a credenza onto the floor.

"Which way?" Nate asked.

Daeng switched feeds to see where his friend was. "There's a small hallway coming up on your right that leads to the waiting area outside his office. His door is in the back corner. He's got it jammed so you're not going to be able to just waltz in."

"I was never that good of a dancer anyway."

Daeng activated the two-window option to keep an eye on both feeds, and grimaced.

Annenkov was now standing on top of the credenza, reaching for something near the ceiling. Daeng was still trying to puzzle out what it might be, when a rectangular section of the wall about the size of an American license plate popped out and fell to the floor.

"Oh, shit," he said.

"What?" Nate asked.

"There's a safe in the wall. He's trying to get into it."

"Safe?"

Daeng explained where it was and what the Russian was doing to get to it.

"That does not sound good," Nate said.

"I know, right?"

On the hallway feed, Nate entered the waiting room and skidded to a stop in front of the office door. He whipped off his pack, removed a spool of incendiary cord, then cut off a chunk and pressed the sticky side against the door around the door handle.

Annenkov pressed in the code that unlocked the control panel and brought up the timer menu. The default setting was thirty minutes, meant to allow enough time for whoever activated it to get out of the bomb's range. As much as he would love to take advantage of that, he had little chance of sneaking out of the base even if it was set for an hour.

No, his life was forfeit.

As he reached in to tap the control to change the setting to zero, a loud pop went off behind him, causing him to pull his hand back and duck his head reflexively.

He peeked over his shoulder and swore under his breath.

There was a hole in his office door, and the handle and the chair he'd jammed under it now lay on the floor. As the door started pushing inward, Annenkov turned back to the control panel.

Instead of using time he didn't have to reset the delay, he switched to the activation screen and was presented with a row of ten empty boxes and a digital keyboard to type in the activation code.

He heard someone rush into his office as he entered the first character, but he didn't look back and kept punching in the code.

He was down to the final four characters when something slammed into his back above one of his kidneys. He winced in pain, thinking he'd been shot. But a bullet would have gone all the way through, ripping a hole in his stomach and splattering his guts on the wall. That hadn't happened.

He entered the seventh character and the eighth. Then, as he aimed his finger at the key for the ninth, the world suddenly felt like it was tipping on its end. He grabbed the bottom of the safe with his other hand to steady himself and touched the ninth character.

The room started to go white all around him, as if color was being drained out of everything. He clenched his teeth and focused everything he had on the keyboard. He only had to input the number two, but it kept dancing away from him.

A hand grabbed his leg and yanked him away from the panel. He thrust a finger forward, hoping his aim was true. Its tip grazed the screen a split second before he tumbled backward.

Nate caught Annenkov under the arms, preventing what would have been a nasty collision with the desk, and laid him on the floor. At some point between when Nate had jerked him off the credenza and when he'd caught Annenkov, the colonel had passed out from the dart protruding from his back.

Nate climbed onto the cabinet to see what the pain in the ass had been up to.

Inside the safe was a touch screen. On it was a message in Russian that translated to *activation complete*. Under this were the numbers 29:51.

No, 29:50.

29:49.

"Uhhhhh."

"What's wrong?" Daeng asked.

"I think we need Jar."

~

Quinn, Orlando, and Silvia paused just before the turn to the final gate.

From the security feed, they knew the guard was pressed against the wall near the gate, pointing his rifle right at the spot Quinn would appear if he stepped out.

Quinn whispered into his mic. "Jar, kill the lights."

A beat later, the passageway plunged into darkness.

The guard gasped loudly enough for them to hear him.

Quinn let him stew in his fear for another couple of seconds, then tossed a flash-bang grenade around the corner. He and the others slapped their hands over their ears and closed their eyes. The grenade exploded in a series of lightning flashes and deafening booms.

Once the chaos had stilled, Quinn leaned around the corner and clicked his mic.

Instantly the lights popped back on. The guard was on the floor in the fetal position, his arms wrapped over his head.

When Quinn's dart hit him, the soldier didn't even seem to notice.

~

Melnikov was halfway across his cell when the lights went out.

He looked at the ceiling fixture. Though he'd been in this new cell for only a short time, the lights had never even dimmed during waking hours.

Before he could wonder about the cause, a series of rapid-fire booms echoed down the corridor. He stumbled backward, knocked into his cot, and fell onto his mattress. As the noise continued, bright light strobed through the thin gap between the floor and the flap covering the tray slot.

And then the flashes and the cacophony ceased.

Darkness held for a few seconds before the lights flicked back on as if nothing had happened.

Melnikov stood up, confused.

He became even more so at the sound of someone laughing.

He moved to the door and knelt next to the tray slot.

"Vassily?" Melnikov said.

The laughter quieted. "Remember, I did say be ready," Vassily said.

"What's going on? What was that?"

But Vassily either hadn't heard Melnikov or was ignoring him, because he'd started laughing again.

At the far end of the corridor a door opened, and steps headed in Melnikov and Vassily's direction.

Melnikov scrambled back onto the cot, positive the soldiers were coming to punish both of them for Vassily's laughter.

The steps stopped on the other side of Melnikov's cell door and a male voice said, "I'm here. Unlock it."

Melnikov blinked. The person had spoken in English, not Russian.

The lock disengaged and his door slid out of the way. A man and two women stood on the other side. The man was in a guard uniform, while the women were dressed in all black. Each wore a gas mask.

The man stepped inside. "Hello, Dmitri. Good to see you again."

Dmitri's brow furrowed. "Do I know you?"

"Right, sorry," the man said, then removed his mask.

Melnikov stared at him. He knew that face. Had seen it… where? Not here. Back in—

His eyes widened. "Quinn?"

∽

"Let's get you out of here," Quinn said.

Melnikov didn't move. "But-but you're dead."

"Not quite yet. But we can catch up later. Come on."

He guided a stunned Melnikov into the corridor.

A few doors down, Vassily's voice came through a slot near the floor. "Don't forget about me!"

Silvia hurried to the door. "Señor Levkin?"

"Silvia! You made it!"

"Jar," Quinn said, "please open Vassily's cell."

Nothing happened.

"Jar?"

Another beat of silence, then, "Sorry. I'm here. We…have a problem."

"What kind of problem?"

"You need to come back."

"Can you open Vassily's door first?"

"Oh, right."

"I'll go see what's going on," Orlando said, and raced back toward the hub.

As soon as his cell door opened, Vassily stepped out and wrapped Silvia in a bear hug.

"See, I told you it would be all right," he said.

"If you do something like this again, I quit," she said, smiling.

He let her go and turned to Quinn, spreading his arms wide.

"I'll take a rain check," Quinn said. "We're in a bit of a hurry."

"I will hold you to that," Vassily said.

Melnikov said, "How did…I don't understand."

Ignoring the implied question, Quinn said, "Are you hurt? Any injuries?"

"What? Um, no. No injuries."

"Great. I promise I'll explain everything later. For now, follow us and do everything we tell you."

"Are you *rescuing* me?"

"That's the general idea. Now, come on."

Quinn grabbed Melnikov's arm and pulled him down the corridor, with Vassily and Silvia right behind them.

When they reached the control center, Jar was sitting at the main control station, both her tablet and her laptop open. Orlando was behind her, watching.

"What's going on?" Quinn said.

Orlando looked up, concern in her eyes. "You're not going to like it."

"Just tell me."

"This place has a fail-safe."

"What kind of fail-safe?"

"The exploding kind."

Quinn stilled. "Please tell me it's not—"

"A nuke?" she finished for him, grimacing. "I told you that you weren't going to like it."

He could feel his mouth go dry. "I don't remember seeing that on the plans."

"Because it wasn't on them. At least not on the official ones."

"There are unofficial plans?"

"Jar found them buried on one of the servers."

"Ooookay. Do…do we know how large a nuke?"

"If the notes with the plans are correct, it's a low-yield tactical nuke designed for surgical strikes. Effective range up to maybe a kilometer or so. Since it's at the bottom of a deep hole, it'll be less."

"Wait. Do you mean it's—"

"Under our feet? Surprise."

"Directly under this room," Jar clarified without looking up.

"Oh, I left out the best part," Orlando said. "Annenkov just activated it."

"He…but… didn't Nate take care of him?"

"He did, but not before Annenkov flipped the switch."

"Not a switch," Jar said, her fingers still flying over her keyboard. "Buttons on a touchscreen."

"Figure of speech," Orlando said.

"Ah," Jar said. "Then I guess that's okay."

Quinn looked around at the others. Vassily's grin had vanished, and the blood seemed to have drained from Silvia's face. The only one who appeared unaffected by the news was Melnikov, and Quinn was pretty sure that was because the grand master was still trying to wrap his head around being rescued.

"Hold on, correct me if I'm wrong," Quinn said, "but we're all still here. Shouldn't it have gone off already?"

"It's on a timer," Orlando said.

"Then we should get the hell out of here now," he said, turning toward the elevators.

"It's set for thirty-minutes."

"Less two minutes and twenty-five seconds," Jar said.

"Less two minutes and twenty-five seconds, or thereabouts," Orlando said. "We would have to get at least two kilometers away to be safe. And in case you forgot, there's a storm up top, with several feet of snow on the ground already. Even if it was just us, we'd be lucky to make it a kilometer in time." She inclined her head toward Melnikov and Vassily. "But it's not just us."

"Are you trying to say there's nothing we can do? Because I can't accept that."

"I never said there was nothing we could do. Jar's attempting to hack in. Once she does, she'll disable it."

"You mean if."

"Now who's being negative?" Orlando asked.

"Sorry." Quinn blew out a breath. "Is there anything we can do to help?"

"If there was, I'd be doing it."

"Then I guess for now we stick to the plan."

Orlando nodded, but the fear was back in her eyes.

Quinn pulled her into a hug and whispered in her ear, "It's going to be fine."

"I know," she whispered back.

He took her face in his hands and pressed his lips against hers. The kiss lasted only a few seconds, but it was packed with everything they would have said to each other if time had been on their side.

Orlando put a hand on his chest and pushed them apart. "Go," she said. "I'll unlock the doors."

Quinn held her gaze a moment longer, then turned to the others. "Vassily, please keep an eye on Dmitri. Silvia, how about you help me free some more prisoners?"

The remaining conscious guards were spread among the four wings where the other prisoners were being held. The flash-bang grenade trick worked so well that by the time Quinn utilized it on the last wing, he and Silvia were able to disable the lone guard and get to the final cell in less than thirty seconds.

Instead of asking what was going on, like Krutov and Barsukov had, Uri Sobolevsky said, "Where's my wife?"

The journalist was covered in bruises yellowed with age, and had several cuts on his face at various stages of healing. Either he had done something to infuriate the directorate, or some of the guards had decided to use him as a punching bag to pass the time.

Sobolevsky had spoken in Russian, but Quinn answered in English. "She's waiting for you."

The man stilled. "Who are you?"

"A friend."

He and Silvia led the journalist back to the hub.

The moment they stepped into the circular room, Anya Sobolevsky shouted, "Uri!" and rushed over, her arms flying out to wrap around him, but upon seeing his injuries, she pulled up short.

"Oh, my God." She tentatively touched the side of his face. "What did they do to you?"

"This is nothing." He looked her up and down. "Are you okay? Did they hurt you?"

"They didn't touch me. But…but you…"

Uri pulled her into a hug as tears streamed down both of their cheeks.

Quinn left them to their reunion and jogged over to Jar and Orlando. "That's all of them. How are we doing here?"

Orlando shot him a worried look but said, "Getting there."

Jar, on the other hand, looked as calm and cool as ever.

"We have just under, what…twenty minutes?" he said.

"Eighteen minutes, forty-one seconds," Jar said.

Quinn turned on his mic. "Quinn for Daeng."

"Go for Daeng."

"There's got to be winter gear up there somewhere. We need five sets."

"Yeah, there's a storeroom full of stuff," Daeng said.

"What are you thinking?" Orlando asked Quinn.

"Maybe we can't make it two kilometers, but the farther we can get, the better the chance we have of surviving. Hey, Daeng, we'll need five sets of snowshoes, too."

"Question," Daeng said.

"Yes?"

"Why do we need snowshoes?"

Quinn looked at Orlando. "Didn't anyone tell you about the nuke?"

"Orlando told me," Daeng said.

"We need the shoes so we can get as far from the base as possible."

"You want to *hike* out?" Daeng's tone made it sound like he thought it was the dumbest idea he'd ever heard.

Quinn and Orlando shared a confused look before Quinn said, "Unless there's some way I'm not thinking about?"

"You mean like the train?"

Quinn frowned. They'd left the inspection car back in the tunnel. "Sure, but it's over a kilometer away."

"That's not what I'm talking about."

"Oh, my God," Orlando said, her eyes widening.

The realization of what Daeng meant hit Quinn a second later. Not the inspection car, but the train upstairs at the platform.

"Can you get it started?" Quinn asked.

"I don't see why not."

"Do it."

"Copy."

To Jar, Quinn said, "Do you have to be here to disarm this thing? Or can we set up some relays and you do it remotely?"

"I can do it from anywhere."

"What about Nate?"

Nate had remained in Annenkov's office, in case he had to input anything in the controls inside the safe.

Jar's eyes hardened with an intensity Quinn had never seen before. "We are not leaving him behind."

"Then I'll stay if you need someone there."

"The hell you will," Orlando said.

"Jar, do you need someone there or not?"

A tense silence filled the space between them before Jar said, "Probably not."

"Probably?" Quinn asked.

"Probably is good enough for me," Orlando said, and shot Quinn a look. "Right?"

He took a second before nodding. "Right."

"All right, everyone," Orlando yelled, "on to the elevators! We're leaving!"

The engine was rumbling when the group reached the train platform, and Daeng's head was sticking out of the window.

Over the comm, Quinn said, "You need help up there?"

"Nah, I'm good," Daeng replied. "It's pretty straightforward. Just let me know when you're ready to go."

Jar hurried on first so she could continue working, and was followed by the former prisoners and Silvia and Nate.

"Here," Orlando said, tossing a relay to Quinn. "We need one by the doors." She pulled out another one and headed to a nearby pillar.

Quinn sprinted toward the large outside doors. They'd been closed the last time he was here but were folded open now, the storm whipping by on the other side.

"Where exactly should I put it?" he asked as he neared.

"Just outside would be best," Orlando said.

"I was afraid you'd say that," he mumbled.

"What was that?"

"Put it just outside. Copy."

A gust of wind swept through the opening, strong enough to nearly knock Quinn from his feet. He grabbed the side of the massive folding door and glanced back at the platform. Orlando was standing near the entrance to one of the passenger cars, watching him.

"Just get on," he said over the comm. "Daeng, get the train going. I'll jump on as you pass."

Orlando didn't move.

"Go," he said more forcefully.

She hesitated then climbed on, but stayed in the doorway. Slowly, the train started to move.

Quinn hopped off the platform and onto the tracks. The wind tried to push him off his feet the moment he stepped outside, and the swirl of snow was so dense, he had to hold an arm above his eyes to see anything.

The door folded against the wall like a collapsed accordion and appeared to be made of some kind of polymer framed by metal. He placed the magnetized bottom against the frame and gave the device a tug to make sure it wouldn't go anywhere.

When he turned back, the train was almost to him. He let the engine car pass, then hopped into the doorway where Orlando was waiting.

She hugged him tight and they kissed again, the storm blowing by the passenger car.

"I was starting to think we weren't going to get out of this one," she said.

"Hold that thought until we hit the two-kilometer mark."

She sneered and then shivered.

"How about we go inside?" he said.

They entered the front of the car.

Melnikov, Vassily, and the other former prisoners were sitting at the back. Silvia was with them, standing in the aisle next to Vassily, as if prepared to fend off another threat. Jar and Nate were at the front, Jar focused on her laptop.

Quinn caught Nate's eye. "How much time left?"

"Seven and a half minutes."

That was more than enough time for them to reach the tunnel and hopefully get far enough that the explosion wouldn't collapse the hill on top of them.

Orlando slipped into the seat next to Jar and picked up the tablet computer. "Anything I can do?"

"Actually, yes," Jar said.

The two began talking in a shorthand Quinn couldn't follow. Knowing he could contribute nothing to their efforts, he motioned for Nate to follow him and headed to the rear of the car.

As they neared the former prisoners, Vassily pushed to his feet, a broad smile plastered on his face. "Is okay now to give you hug?"

"We're not out of danger yet."

"Yes, but we *are* out of prison, and that is good enough reason for me."

Before Quinn could react, he was engulfed in a bear hug.

"Vassily, you're suffocating me."

Vassily laughed and pulled him tighter for a moment before releasing him. The Russian turned to the others. "Everyone, this is Quinn. He is big boss."

"How can we ever thank you?" Barsukov asked.

"You should probably hold off saying anything until we get you out of the country."

Before any of them could question him on how he planned to do that, Quinn slid into the empty seat next to Dmitri Melnikov. The grand master hadn't moved since Quinn entered the car.

"I owe you an apology," Quinn said. "I told you we were taking you someplace safe, and we didn't."

Eyes downcast, Melnikov said, "The explosion…did…did any of your people die?"

"No. A few injuries. One pretty bad, but she's mostly recovered now."

"She? You mean Janet?" Janet Major was the only female team member Melnikov had met. The blast had fractured her femur, and it had taken most of the previous year for her to heal properly.

"Yes."

"What about the other FBI agents?"

"All except the one who took you didn't make it."

"Oh." Melnikov's mouth twitched uncomfortably. "I…I didn't know for sure. What about the agent who took me?"

"No one knows where he is. But US Intelligence will find him, and when they do…"

"He is the one who should be apologizing," Melnikov said, anger threaded through each word. "Not you."

Daeng's voice came over the comm. "Entering the tunnel."

Beyond the windows, the blizzard vanished.

Melnikov did not seem to notice the change. He took a deep breath and finally looked at Quinn. "Thank you for not forgetting about me."

"I just wish we could have come sooner."

"But you did come. That's all that's important."

Quinn checked his watch and saw the end of the countdown was looming. "If you'll excuse me. Still have some work to do."

He returned to the front of the car. In the upper corner of Jar's screen, the countdown clock showed one minute thirty-five seconds left.

Into his comm, Quinn said, "Daeng, what's our speed?"

"When we hit the tunnel, I upped it to eighty kilometers. I could probably go faster if you want."

Quinn was tempted to tell him to crank the speed as high as he could, but a derailment could be as deadly as getting caught by the explosion. "Eighty's fine."

"I'm in," Jar said.

Quinn leaned next to her. "You have control of the fail-safe?"

"That's what I said."

The countdown clock on her computer was still going and currently showed fifty-one seconds.

"Should I still disable the bomb?" Jar asked.

"What? Yes! Why would you even ask that?"

"Because I now know its precise size, and we are more than far enough away to survive. I'm just pointing out that letting it go off is an option."

"We are *not* going to be responsible for setting off a nuke."

"Actually, we would not be the ones responsible."

"Jar! Shut it down!"

She hit a couple of keys. "Done."

The countdown, currently at twenty-one seconds, continued decreasing.

"Why hasn't the clock stopped?"

"Oh, that's only for monitoring purposes." Jar clicked another button, and the clock stopped at seventeen seconds.

Quinn stumbled into the seat across the aisle, relief flooding his body. "For God's sake, were you trying to give me a heart attack?"

She looked at him, perplexed. "Why would I want to do that?"

He closed his eyes, then said in as calm a voice as he could muster, "Let's make a rule. Anytime we're in a similar situation, you disarm the bomb without waiting for my say-so."

"Is that a rule for only nuclear devices? Or all explosives?"

"Anything that goes boom."

She was silent for a moment, then nodded. "Understood."

44

Daeng brought the train to a stop and reversed direction to return to the base, as it was the closest to the ocean they could get without hiking through the storm and the meters of snow already on the ground.

As soon as they exited the tunnel, Quinn punched into the satellite phone the code Annabel had given them. A series of electronic buzzes and clicks came through the receiver before the line started ringing. After the fifth ring, there was a click and a mid-pitched tone, and then—

"I was beginning to wonder if I'd ever hear from you."

"Annabel?" Quinn said. He had not expected her to be the one who answered.

"You sound disappointed."

"Not disappointed. Just concerned you're about to tell me Starfish isn't in position."

Annabel laughed. "Like your agent Thomas would let me forget."

"Not trying to be rude, but that's not really an answer."

"Relax, body snatcher. We're ready and waiting."

"You're *on* Starfish?"

"I guess that depends. Was the rescue successful?"

"Yes."

"How many did you get out?"

"All six of them."

"Huh," she said in genuine surprise. "All six. Then, yes, I am very much on Starfish."

"And if I'd said we hadn't been able to free anyone?"

"As far as anyone will ever know, I am in my office at Wright Bains and nowhere near your failed mission."

Quinn snorted.

"Can I assume you're calling because you need a ride?" she asked.

"You can."

"Total number?"

"Twelve."

Orlando whispered something in his ear, causing him to miss what Annabel said next.

When Orlando finished, he arched an eyebrow and smirked. "Good idea." Into the phone, he said, "Sorry, Annabel. My mistake. There are thirteen for pickup."

Starfish was an ultra top secret British Intelligence submarine, designed for the stealth insertion and extraction of personnel into and from hostile territories. The sub came equipped with a drone that could be used to covertly transport said personnel to land. The craft could carry up to three people at a time and was engineered to work in a multitude of conditions, including blizzards. According to Annabel, each round trip would take just under an hour, including loading and unloading. With thirteen people, that meant a minimum of five hours.

When the team was back at the secret base, Quinn and Nate placed a beacon right outside the train doors that the drone would lock on to, then they entered the base and took the elevator down to level two.

As expected, Colonel Annenkov was still lying on the floor of his office, deep in his drug-induced slumber.

"I'll help get him on your shoulder," Quinn said.

"*My* shoulder?" Nate said.

"You're younger."

Nate spun around and pointed at the desk chair. "Why don't we use that?"

The chair had wheels.

"Sure, if you feel like you can't do it."

Nate sneered at him. "Nice try, Obi-Wan, but your Jedi guilt tricks won't work on me."

While Nate rolled the chair over, Quinn picked up a briefcase sitting next to the desk. He attempted to open it but the latch held firm. From the small glass panel next to one of the latches, he guessed the lock was biometric.

After he and Nate deposited Annenkov onto the chair, Quinn placed the colonel's right index finger against the glass reader. When that didn't work, he shuffled through the rest of Annenkov's fingers. The left ring finger turned out to be the winner.

Inside the case were a laptop computer, Annenkov's military ID badge, and several folders filled with documents.

"This is definitely coming with us," Quinn said. "Check around and make sure there's nothing else we should snag."

There were a few more documents inside the credenza and several thumb drives in the top desk drawer, all of which went into the briefcase. Satisfied there was nothing else, they wheeled Annenkov to the elevators, returned to ground level, and joined Orlando and a few of the others on the train platform.

"Everything going all right?" Quinn asked.

Orlando nodded. "The drone's eleven minutes out."

"Good." He looked around. "Where's Jar?"

"Still on the train. Why?"

"We have some unfinished business."

Orlando looked confused, and then her eyes widened. "Right."

"Right what?" Nate asked.

"The promise we made to Petra."

"Oh," he said, finally making the connection. "Right."

They headed into the passenger car and found Jar sitting in the same spot she'd been in on their flee from the base, her laptop still open.

She looked up. "Now?"

"If you don't mind," Quinn said.

She hit a single key on her keyboard. "Done. Would you like to watch?"

"Absolutely."

They crowded around her. On her laptop's screen were several feeds from Directorate Eleven headquarters. Three were from the facility systems level the team had infiltrated, an operation that felt like it had happened weeks ago, and the additional feeds were from the other levels. On the latter, directorate personnel moved around like it was just another day at the office, everyone blissfully unaware of what was about to happen. On the first set of feeds, all seemed normal, too. At least at first. It wasn't long before tendrils of black smoke appeared in each of the three feeds from the facility systems level, caused by the smoke bombs Jar had put in place near the incendiary devices.

It took nearly a minute before the tech at the water systems control looked up from his computer and spotted the smoke billowing toward the ceiling. She jumped up, shouted a warning, and sprinted toward the exit. The four others in the room looked up, saw the smoke, and rushed after her, only one having the presence of mind to trigger the fire alarm before fleeing.

The alarm caused the techs and soldiers in the other rooms on the systems level to stop what they were doing and look around.

When they realized smoke was in their rooms, they too made hasty exits.

That was when the fire repression system kicked in, raining down on everyone as they escaped. A few people stopped at the elevators and pushed the call buttons, but most ran straight to the stairwell door and headed up that way. It took only a handful of seconds before the ones at the elevators also decided the stairs were the better option.

When the last person headed up, Jar said, "Facility systems level clear."

"Let's let them get up a few flights," Quinn said.

Clearing the level was the exact purpose of the smoke bombs, as Quinn's team had no desire to harm personnel who were just doing their jobs.

A feed from the stairwell at level two appeared on Jar's screen, and soon the terrified techs and soldiers rushed past.

"Now," he said, after the final person passed by.

Jar tapped another key.

There were brief flashes on the feeds from the lower level and then the cameras winked out. The incendiary devices Jar had planted were now frying everything in range. Seconds later, the other cameras in the base began shutting down, signaling to Quinn and the others that the base's power system had been destroyed.

While they could no longer see what was going on, it wasn't hard to imagine the entire base plunging into darkness and everyone struggling to get to the surface, while deep below, the guts of the operation were being turned into slag.

Maybe the base could be repaired, but it would take a lot of time and a ton of work to make that happen. And given that the head of the directorate would be missing, along with all of the prisoners from their not-so-secret secret prison, the chances of Directorate Eleven surviving the fallout were minimal at best.

The alarm on Orlando's phone rang. "Drone in two minutes," she said.

∾

It took Starfish nearly thirty-six hours to rendezvous with a CIA ship disguised as a scientific research vessel off the coast of Norway.

Quinn was the last to leave the submarine.

"Thanks again," he told Annabel.

"Just remember to mention me several times in your report," she said, then added, "as helping, not hindering."

"I'll see what I can do." He grabbed the ladder and began climbing.

"Next time you're in town, please forget my number."

He glanced back and she smiled and waved.

Agent Thomas was waiting for him when he crossed over to the ship. She was grinning and shaking her head at the same time. Annabel had not allowed the agent to join her in the sub.

"Is that your way of apologizing?" he asked.

"For what?"

"Not believing we could do it?"

"When did I ever say that?"

"When didn't you?"

Thomas laughed. "I'm sorry," she said sincerely. "And congratulations. I am impressed."

"I accept your apology."

Her expression turning uncomfortable, she said, "I was, um, wrong about New York, too."

He blinked. That he had not been expecting. "We all make mistakes."

She nodded, tight-lipped, like she was considering adding something. But instead, she took a step back and motioned at a door a few meters away. "Your friends are in there."

He held out his hand, and after a moment, she shook it.

MELBOURNE, AUSTRALIA

Daeng knocked on the door for the third time. When no one answered, he pulled out his phone. Just as he was about to open his Uber app, the door swung open and a startled Ian looked out.

"Daeng. We didn't realize you were back."

"Just," Daeng said. "Came straight from the airport."

Ian grinned knowingly. "Couldn't wait, huh?"

"Do you blame me?"

"Not at all. We were about to have dinner. Come join us."

"Thanks."

Daeng stepped inside, carrying his duffel bag in one hand and a large, fancy shopping bag in the other. He left the duffel in the entryway, took off his shoes, and followed Ian through the house.

"Looks like I missed a party," he said, eyeing a menagerie of toys on the living room floor.

"A wedding, actually," Ian said. "Princess Isabella and Mr. Fishy."

"Isn't the princess already married to Thomas the Train?"

"From what I understand, it didn't work out."

"Poor Thomas."

Ian stepped out onto the patio behind the house and said, "Charlie, you have a guest."

The second Charlie saw Daeng as he exited the house, her eyes lit up and she shouted, "Daengdy! Daengdy!" It was her mash-up of Daeng and daddy.

He squatted down next to her high chair. "Hey, Charlie. How's my favorite girl?"

As way of answer, she held out her arms for him to pick her up, a request Daeng was not about to deny. He lifted her out of her chair and stood up, hugging her tight. Over her shoulder, he could see Alison looking at him, an amused eyebrow raised.

"Sorry," he said. "I should have called first."

"He just landed," Ian said as way of explanation.

"It's fine," Alison said. "She missed you."

"And I missed her."

Charlie put her hands on Daeng's chest and pushed back far enough for her to look him in the eyes. "Don't ever go away again," she said, stringing together the longest sentence he'd ever heard her speak.

"Your wish is my command," he said.

Alison's smile slipped into a frown. In a quiet but firm voice, she said, "You shouldn't make promises you can't keep."

"Who said I wouldn't keep it?"

Now she looked confused. "But your work?"

"Is not something we need to worry about anymore."

"What do you mean, not worry about it?" Alison asked. "Did you quit?"

"Retired," he said.

Not only had working with Quinn and the others been the most exciting job he'd ever had, it had also been the most lucrative. Between what he'd been paid and several good investments, he wouldn't have to worry about money for a long while. Maybe never.

His last conversation with Quinn and Orlando before he headed home had gone like this:

"I can't tell you how much I appreciate what you've done for me. Being part of your team has been…incredible. Thank you."

"Why do I feel like you're leading up to something I don't want to hear?" Quinn had said.

Daeng smiled. "Life is different for me now. Before, the only one I had to worry about was me. But not anymore."

"So you're saying this is it?"

Daeng nodded. "This is it."

There were hugs and promises to stay in touch, and then a very long plane ride back to Australia. To his new life. To Charlie.

"What's retired?" his daughter asked.

"It means whenever you need me, I'll be here."

Charlie beamed and hugged him again, and if he had even the slightest doubt about leaving the team, it disappeared in that moment.

REDONDO BEACH, CALIFORNIA

Clint stared at the parking lot, hoping for a miracle.

Since Nate and Jar had left on a work trip after the match with the Kealy Street Wanderers, the Redondo Grave Diggers had played the final two matches of the regular season without them, losing both. If it hadn't been obvious before that Nate and Jar were the heart of the team, those beatings had made it clear to everyone.

The losses had dropped the Grave Diggers into third place. Thankfully, there was a four-team playoff, so they still had a chance to come out on top. The first match was with the second-place team, the very same Wanderers who represented the Diggers' last victory. And the match was set to take place in ten minutes.

"I don't think they're going to make it," Bailey said.

Both she and J. J. were standing with Clint halfway between the sand court and the parking lot. Kole and Weldon, the two subs the team had been using, were by the net, volleying the ball back and forth.

"They promised they'd be back," Clint said.

Bailey grimaced. "They said they'd *try* to be back."

"Same thing."

"Not the same thing," Bailey said.

"Come on," J. J. said. "We should warm up."

As he and Bailey started walking toward the court, Clint sighed, turned, and followed. He paid no attention to the rumble of a motorcycle in the distance. But the noise grew louder and louder, until he couldn't help but look back.

A Yamaha MT-07 pulled into the area designated for motor-bikes. At first it appeared only one person was on it, but that was because the passenger was small enough to be hidden behind the driver.

"Clint!" someone shouted. "Ball!"

A second later, a volleyball smacked Clint in the hip.

But he didn't even notice.

Over at the motorcycle, the passenger reached up, discon-nected the chin strap, and pulled off her helmet.

Clint grinned like a child on his birthday as Jar gathered her dark hair into a ponytail.

Nate took off his helmet and waved at Clint. "We're not too late, are we?"

SAN FRANCISCO, CALIFORNIA

The kids were finally asleep and Quinn and Orlando were sitting at the kitchen table, glasses of wine in hand.

Quinn stared at his, not seeing it.

Orlando took a sip from hers, eyes on him.

After taking another drink, she set down her glass. "It's Daeng, isn't it?"

It took Quinn a moment to register she'd said something. "What?"

"The job went off better than we hoped, but you're sitting there moodier than normal. So I'm thinking it's Daeng's fault."

"Nothing's his fault."

"Not Daeng himself. I mean what he said." She tilted her head a little. "Do you want to retire, too?"

"What? I never said that."

"Do you?"

"No, of course not. It's just..." He fell silent for a moment. "What if...what if Jar hadn't been able to disable the bomb, and we couldn't get far enough away? Garrett and Claire would be orphans now."

Orlando huffed and picked up her glass again. "You think that doesn't go through my mind every time we go out on a job?"

"You've never said anything."

"Why do you think I agreed to help run the Office?"

Her role as co-boss of the Office had limited the number of missions in which she was able to participate. They'd never talked about it before, but as much as Quinn missed her expertise when she wasn't in the field with him, he was glad at least one of them was spending more time at home.

"I...I thought..." he trailed off, not sure how to finish the thought.

"Partly because I could be around more for the kids," she said. "And partly because it put me in a position where I could influence the types of jobs you were offered."

His brow furrowed. "You cherry-pick jobs for us?"

"Hell, yes, I do. Do you think I'd send you on a mission that has a high chance of going sideways?" She snorted. "You have no idea some of the crap clients have wanted you to do."

"You *did* send us on the Melnikov mission in New York."

"In my defense, the job profiled as low risk."

He couldn't help but laugh.

Orlando smiled, took a drink, and said, "So, answer the question. Are you telling me that you want to retire, too?"

He stared at the table and then back at her. "I think I'm just exhausted." He finished off his glass and pushed out of his chair. "Come on. Let's get some sleep."

He started to turn but she grabbed his arm, stopping him. She stood, wrapped her arms around him, and whispered into his ear, "Whatever you want to do, I'll support you."

"Even if I want to open a coffee shop and make lattes all day?"

"Especially if you want to open a coffee shop."

He pressed his cheek against the top of her head. Her hair

smelled of cherries and pine and everything that was her. "Right now, the only thing I want is you and me upstairs in our bed."

She leaned away to look up at him. "I thought you said you were tired."

"I'm not *that* tired."

45

The information was found on Colonel Annenkov's laptop computer.

A discussion of options ensued, and a course of action was decided. Since the FBI did not have the same resources the CIA did, the choice of operatives was made by Deputy Director Suarez.

His selection declined the offer at first, stating she was no longer in the assassination business. Suarez took the unusual step of flying to Maine to pay her a personal visit. He laid out everything, omitting no details. He did not need to explain why this particular course of action had been chosen to deal with the matter. She understood, and as he'd anticipated, was just as outraged by what had happened as everyone else who knew about it.

"If you tell me no, you won't hear from us again," he said.

"And if I say yes?"

"After you complete the mission, you also will not hear from us again. Either way, we will respect your decision to be out of the game."

Two days later, the operative arrived in Budapest, Hungary.

It took her an additional four days to secure a barista job at the café the target frequented, and then for two weeks, she did nothing but observe the target when he came in, something she soon determined occurred every morning between ten and ten fifteen a.m.

On the day she had chosen to act, the target arrived at 10:05 and ordered his customary cappuccino and pastry. Once the coffee was ready, the operative delivered it and a *pain au chocolat* to his table.

He grunted what might have been thanks but didn't even look at her. For twenty minutes, life at the café went on as usual.

And then the target coughed.

Only the operative noticed at first.

A louder and more desperate cough a few moments later caused other customers to turn toward him. The operative, who had been clearing dishes from a nearby table, stopped what she was doing and hurried over to him.

In Hungarian, she said, "Sir, are you okay?"

The man was clearly struggling to breathe. He squeaked out, "Something…in my…throat." Unlike her, he spoke in English with an American accent.

She called in Hungarian to the barista at the counter. "Bring some water!"

The target pushed his chair back and tried to stand, but his legs wouldn't hold him.

She wrapped her arms around him to keep him from falling, and lowered him to the floor.

As she did, she whispered in his ear in English, "Your windpipe is closing. Soon you will take your last breath. The coroner will determine you suffered an allergic reaction." His terror-filled eyes shot sideways at her as he tried to suck in more air. "That's right, Agent Landry, you are about to die. Though I guess I shouldn't refer to you as agent anymore, since you stopped working for the FBI the moment you decided it would be okay to let several of your fellow agents die for a little cash."

The other barista hurried over with a glass of water and gave it to the operative.

Displaying the appropriate amount of concern, the operative said, "Call an ambulance."

The barista nodded and rushed back to the counter. Around the room, customers watched the target with varying degrees of horror, a few recording everything on their phones.

The operative lifted the glass toward the man's lips. "Don't worry," she whispered. "I won't pour any in. It wouldn't go down anyway."

"W-w-who…" the word was barely audible.

"Me? I'm the person your former colleagues hired to get rid of a traitor."

Landry's body seized, and she let him roll out of her grasp onto the floor.

"Oh, my God," she said, playing her part as she dropped next to him. "Sir? Sir?"

By the time the ambulance arrived, the former FBI agent was dead.

Four hours later, Ananke, the once-again former assassin, was sitting in first class on a plane bound for the States.